A WINTER BABY FOR GIN BARREL LANE

LINDSEY HUTCHINSON

Boldwood

First published in Great Britain in 2021 by Boldwood Books Ltd.

Copyright © Lindsey Hutchinson, 2021

Cover Design by Head Design Ltd

Cover Photography: Shutterstock

A CIP catalogue record for this book is available from the British Library.

Paperback ISBN: 978-1-83889-401-6

Large Print ISBN: 978-1-80280-434-8

Hardback ISBN: 978-1-80280-203-0

Ebook ISBN: 978-1-83889-403-0

Kindle ISBN: 978-1-83889-402-3

Audio CD ISBN: 978-1-83889-399-6

MP3 CD ISBN: 978-1-80280-269-6

Digital audio download ISBN: 978-1-83889-400-9

Boldwood Books Ltd
23 Bowerdean Street
London SW6 3TN
www.boldwoodbooks.com

For my agent, Judith Murdoch, who set me on the road to further happiness.

1

'You call the coppers and this little lady is dead!' the man said as he held a knife to Dolly Perkins' throat. He had grabbed her as she'd limped into the bar of Daydream Palace to light the gas lamps. The young woman had dropped her walking cane and was now trying to balance her weight on her good leg.

'Steady now, don't do anything rash,' Billy Bickley said. He was a doorman at the Palace, along with his brother Bobby, but because he was big and lumbering he had not been quick enough and Dolly had been taken hostage. Billy edged forward as he tried to placate the knifeman. 'Just tell us what you want.'

The gin palace was packed to the gunnels with revellers but silence had descended and folk moved away from the scene unfolding before them. The owner of their favourite drinking den was at risk of death and everyone held their breath as Billy inched his way through the crowd.

'What I want,' the man said, 'is some gin for my old mother!'

'Well, that can be arranged,' Billy said in a calm voice.

Dolly felt the cold steel on her skin and she clenched her buttocks and prayed her bladder would not give way and embarrass her in front of her customers. She dared not move for fear of being cut and bleeding to death on the sawdust-scattered floor.

'How? I ain't got any money!' The man's eyes flicked from Billy to the knife and back again.

'That don't matter, mate. You let the boss go and she'll give you a quart for your mum.'

'If I let her go, you'll jump me.'

Dolly could smell the stale sweat emanating from her assailant's body. He was standing behind her, his one arm around her, the other hand holding the weapon at her neck. She could feel him trembling and she was terrified the shaking might increase and cause the knife to prick her skin.

'Nobody is going to jump you, pal, just let the lady go. Come and get your gin and go home to your old mum.'

Bobby Bickley was threading his way around the room very slowly, trying to go unnoticed, but the man saw him.

'You stop right there! Stop or I'll gut your boss lady!'

Bobby halted, holding up his hands in surrender.

Dolly closed her eyes tight for a second as the man dragged her back a step.

'My leg...' she said quietly.

The man nodded to a woman so drunk she could barely stand. 'Pick up that cane and give it to her.'

The woman bent over and grasped the cane and as she straightened up she began to sway.

'Hand it over!' the man demanded.

'All right, hold yer horshes,' the woman slurred. Taking a step forward, she lifted the cane as if to pass it to Dolly and the man's eyes moved to Billy who simultaneously took a step. That was the man's mistake.

In an instant, the woman hefted the stick and swung it in an arc, catching the man sharply on the elbow. The sudden pain of the blow forced his arm down and away from Dolly's neck, the knife falling from his fingers to clatter on the floor. He let out a howl and instinctively brought his other arm round to cradle the injury.

In that same moment, Dolly lunged forward, dragging her crippled leg behind her. In her peripheral vision she saw Billy and Bobby dash to the man and retrieve the knife.

The man's assailant gave Dolly her cane and helped her back to her place behind the bar.

Dragging the man along, Billy called out, 'What shall we do with him?'

Shouts and catcalls sounded as the crowd told Billy exactly what he could do with the man.

'Bring him to the kitchen,' Dolly said, then to Juliet, the barmaid, 'and please fill that lady's glass on the house.'

'Ooh, ta!' the woman said with a grin that showed her blackened teeth.

'Thank you for your help,' Dolly said before going through to the back room, her hands still shaking.

The Bickley brothers pulled the knifeman through to the kitchen where they unceremoniously dumped him onto a chair.

'Now then,' Dolly began, trying to bring her emotions under control, 'what the hell was all that about?'

'I told you! I just wanted some gin for my old mother. She's on her deathbed and it was all she wanted.'

'You could have come and asked me for it, rather than...' Dolly rubbed a hand across her neck where the sharp steel had rested.

'Oh yes, and I suppose you would have given it free of charge, eh?' the man asked sarcastically.

'Actually, if you had explained properly, then I would have.' Dolly watched the man's eyes widen in disbelief and she nodded.

'Look, I was never gonna hurt you – honest! I just wanted...'

'Some gin,' Dolly finished for him. 'Tell me about yourself, Mr...?'

'Whitehouse. Danny Whitehouse.'

'Well, Danny, where do you live?'

'Over in Lawrence Street.'

'And what do you do for work?'

Danny gave a tight laugh. 'I ain't working. I don't know if you've noticed but there's no jobs going out there!'

Billy smacked him across the back of the head, saying, 'Have some respect for the lady!'

Danny rubbed his head and glanced up at the big man.

'So, I take it you are living with and taking care of your mother?' Dolly asked.

'Yes.'

'Is she very ill?'

'Yes. She's seventy-five and is bedridden. She's eaten nothing for two days.'

'Do you have food for her?'

'Yes, but she won't eat. She's ready to die but just wanted a sip of mother's ruin before she goes.'

'I'm sorry to hear it.'

Danny was again surprised at being treated so kindly after what he'd done.

'Bobby, would you please fetch me a quart of the best gin – White Satin I think will do nicely.'

The fellow nodded and lumbered away.

'You gonna hand me over to the bobbies?'

'No.'

'What then?'

'I'm going to give you some gin to take to your mother, then I'm going to offer you a job.'

'You what?' Danny could hardly believe his ears.

'It appears I need more security in the bar so if you're interested...'

'Yes! Erm, yes please, miss,' he corrected himself, with a glance at Billy.

'Good. You can start whenever you wish. Ah, here's your gin. Thanks, Bobby.' Dolly took the bottle and passed it to Danny. 'Boys, Danny will be starting work with you so I'd be pleased if you would show him the ropes.'

'I know what ropes I'd like to show him,' Billy grumbled.

'Thanks, miss.'

'Dolly's the name. I hope that drop helps your mum.'

'Me too,' Danny replied before leaving sharpish via the back door.

'You'm too soft,' Billy said.

'I know.'

'He'll bugger off and you won't see hide nor hair of him again,' Billy said.

'You could have died out there!' Bobby intervened.

Dolly nodded. 'I can't deny I was scared out of my wits.'

'Then you go and give him a job – the man who tried to hurt you!' Bobby said indignantly.

'I know he wanted to frighten me, which he did, but I don't imagine for a minute he would have killed me.'

'You had a lucky escape. One slip and you'd be in the morgue by now,' Billy said.

'His mum is dying, boys, so we have to show a little compassion. Now, back to work before that lot tear the place apart. Oh, and thank you both.'

The two brothers shuffled back to the bar and Dolly finally sighed with relief.

Were the Bickley brothers correct? Had she been too quick to offer her attacker a job? Something inside told her she had made the right choice, however. She had looked into Danny's eyes and it was there she had seen utter desperation. She *had* been frightened for her life, but in the safety of the kitchen moments later, Dolly's heart went out to the man who was trying to fulfil his mother's dying wish. Would she have done the same for her own mother? Probably, yes, but certainly not in the same way.

Holding out her hands, she saw they were still shaking. Rubbing them together she stood, picking up her trusty cane before she too went to the bar.

Despite the large plate glass windows, the gas chandelier and wall lamps were lit in order to bounce the light off the huge mirrors behind the counter. Small casks stood in front of these mirrors, depicting the names of the different gins on offer. This was a ruse as all the alcohol was the same; it was only how much it was watered down that differed. The floor was covered with fresh sawdust to soak up the spills, not that there were many – gin was too precious to lose even one drop. The long counter was highly polished, beneath which sat the bottles within easy reach.

As she glanced around the room, she smiled at the cheer which greeted her, and she hoped she'd done the right thing where Danny Whitehouse was concerned.

She had been lucky these past years running the gin palace, but this incident had been a warning. There were bad people out there and now was the time to ensure she had some protectors in place. Knowing her friend Nellie Larkin would advise her, Dolly determined to seek that advice the following day.

It was then that Aggie walked in. Well known by everyone in the town, Aggie was always dressed in tattered clothes, her grey hair piled untidily on her head. Her pink gums had long since lost their teeth but this did not impede her speech. She was quick-witted and outspoken to the point of rudeness at times, and she was the town gossip. Nothing happened in this part of Birmingham without Aggie knowing about it first. The information she gathered was then exchanged for a free tot in the gin houses so she rarely paid for a drink. The place erupted as the old woman lifted her skirts and began to dance. Aggie laughed loudly as she bent over, showing her bare bottom to everyone.

Dolly sighed. Roll on tomorrow.

2

Dolly Perkins threw open the doors of Daydream Palace early to allow the fresh air to flush away the stink of unwashed bodies and the stale air of the previous night's drinking. She stood outside on the street with a cup of tea in hand and soaked up the rays of sunshine. Nodding to people passing by, Dolly pondered her life.

At thirteen years old she had taken refuge in the yard of the Crown Saloon across the road from where she now stood. Found by Jack Larkin, she had been taken in by his mother Nellie, who owned the Crown. She had run away from home after the death of her mother; her stepfather wanted her to fill her mother's shoes in more ways than one. He had later been found dead by the railway line, suspected of being hit by a steam train whilst drunk.

Nellie Larkin and Dolly had worked together to buy an old public house and transform it into the glittering gin palace she now co-owned. Already her mortgage to the bank was almost paid off since the business had done remarkably well.

During the last seven years, Jack, who was now eighteen and still her best friend, had come to see her every day, despite living at the Crown Saloon. It had been thought for a long time that the two might marry, but Dolly saw Jack as a friend, not a husband.

Grabbing her walking cane, which she'd leaned against the wall, Dolly limped back inside to help with the cleaning. Born with a withered leg, Dolly had never allowed it to hold her back and consequently she achieved everything she set out to do.

Inside, Juliet Jenkins was already well into sweeping up the sawdust so it could be replaced by a fresh supply.

Dolly smiled her thanks and took her cup back to the kitchen. Before long, she heard the voice of Janice, Juliet's sister.

Janice had married Matt Dempster, who worked the bar for Nellie and they had twin boys who were now three years old and quite a handful.

Pouring tea, Dolly took it into the bar for Janice.

'You're looking flustered this morning. Here, sit down and drink this.'

'Thanks, Dolly. The twins had me run ragged. As fast as I dressed Ben, Ethan was stripping his clothes off! It was all I could do to get them to the child-minder and get here on time.'

'Couldn't Matt help?' Juliet asked.

Janice laughed. 'You must be joking. He just encourages them, they can do no wrong where he's concerned. I do love them all, but my God they frustrate me!'

Dolly grinned but deep inside she was envious. She was twenty-one now and had never had a sweetheart. She longed to be wed and have kiddies of her own, but the gin palace took up all of her time. Besides, she felt her gammy leg would put young men off wanting to court her. No man in his right mind would want a cripple for a wife, no matter how much she was worth. Dolly had long since resigned herself to the fact she would never be married or have a family, but sometimes the thought saddened her.

Just then, a man stumbled in through the open doorway.

'We're not open yet, Stanley, give us an hour and come back then,' Juliet said.

'Bloody hell! What am I to do for an hour while I wait for you to finish cleaning up?'

'Go home and sleep it off,' Janice answered, aware he was still drunk from the night before.

'Bugger it, I'm going to the Crown. Nellie will serve me!' With that, Stanley staggered away, doing the *tipple two-step*. Given the nickname by the serving staff, the walk of two steps forward and one back looked like it ought to be a dance.

'I'm going over to see Nellie too, but I won't be long,' Dolly said.

'We'll stock the bar and have the place all clean and tidy for when you get back,' Juliet said.

Stepping out into the sunshine again, Dolly counted her blessings as she watched horse-drawn carts roll by.

Birmingham in 1864 was an industrial town, its dirty streets spreading out like a spider's web. It boasted a railway station, a huge market with over six hundred stalls, a town council, Bingley exhibition hall, a lunatic asylum at Winson Green, a prison, and a public bathhouse. It also boasted the imposing St Chad's, which was named a cathedral by Pope Pius IX. It had a park, a workhouse and the Birmingham mint was the first metal-working company to be contracted to produce coins of one pound sterling. It was a very busy place with people milling about at all times of the day and night, most of whom were out of work. The level of poverty was incredibly high and families were living on the heath under tarpaulins. They were starving and only when they could bear it no longer would they accept a ticket into the workhouse, knowing they would never be able to sign themselves out – a sad life with an even sadder ending.

Dolly knew that could have been her fate and thanked her lucky stars that she had escaped the worst Birmingham had to offer.

She heard the noise before she walked in through the back door. Nellie Larkin and her long-time friend Nancy were exchanging un-pleasantries at full volume, as was their wont.

'Where's our Jack?' Nellie called out.

'He's in the cellar with Fred. They're taking out the empty casks like you told them to,' Nancy answered.

'That was an hour ago! If that little sod is...!'

'Nell, Jack's eighteen now, he ain't a kid any more! Oh, hello Dolly,' Nancy said as she saw the young woman enter the kitchen.

'Are you two at it again?' Dolly asked with a wide grin.

'Always and forever. Nell, Dolly's here!'

Nellie Larkin trundled through from the bar, her grey hair piled untidily on her head. 'Hello, gel.'

'I've come for some advice, Nellie, if you have time.'

'Always got time for you, sweetheart. Nance, tea and biscuits if you please.'

Nancy set the kettle to boil, grumbling under her breath. 'Been here all these years and still treated like a skivvy!'

Nellie and Dolly exchanged an amused smile as they sat at the table.

'Now, how can we help?'

'Oh, it's *we* now is it?' Nancy said quietly.

'It's always been us, Nance, even before you married Fred,' Nellie replied soothingly.

'Let me explain,' Dolly interrupted before a full-blown argument broke out. She told them all about the incident in her bar the previous night and how she'd dealt with it.

'You should have let the Bickley boys leather him!' Nancy said scornfully.

'Oh, ignore her. I think you did the right thing, but you watch this Danny Whitehouse. Make sure he's honest and loyal.'

'I will, but I came to ask the best way to employ some more muscle. Billy and Bobby are good men but they're better working the cellar really, and they don't seem to be cutting the mustard on the door any more. It's difficult not having a full-time cellar man so I thought to move them into that position, with a little sweetener of course.' Dolly rubbed her thumb and fingertips together as she spoke, denoting a raise in wages for the boys.

'Then you won't have anybody in the bar or standing by the door!' Nancy said as she covered the brown teapot with a knitted cosy.

'Exactly, so alongside Danny, I need to know where to hire some other men for those jobs.'

'What about the bread line?' Nellie suggested.

'I wondered about that too,' Dolly concurred.

'Take Fred with you, lovey, he knows everybody, and no one will mess with you if he's there,' Nancy said.

'Thanks, that's a great idea.'

A moment later the man in question came up from the cellar followed by Jack, and Nellie outlined what Dolly needed.

While Nellie talked, Dolly looked at Jack and she could barely believe how much he'd grown since the day they'd first met. He was a handsome young man now. His dark hair was always clean and shiny and his brown eyes held a constant twinkle. The timbre of his voice was deep and pleasant, smooth like cream on coffee. Her mind slipped back through the years to how she and Jack had worked Nellie's bar together, along with Poppy, who was now wed to Noah Dempster, Nellie's doorman. They had been one big happy family back then, and to a degree they still were. It was a little different now with Dolly living and working across the road, but they always had each other's backs in times of need.

'I could move over and work for Dolly,' Jack said, snapping Dolly back to the conversation.

'No, lad, you're needed here,' Nellie said, clearly unwilling to let her son go.

Once more, Dolly's thoughts travelled back to when at ten years old Jack had discovered he'd been left on Nellie's doorstep as a baby. Always believing he was Nellie's boy, it had come as a major shock to discover he was a foundling, but after talking it through with Dolly, he had come to accept it in time.

Pulling herself back to the present, Dolly listened as Fred, who had always looked out for her, agreed to accompany her to seek out workers from the ever-growing bread line.

'We'll go after dinner if that's all right, 'cos I can't miss my Nancy's cooking,' the big man said, rubbing his hands together.

'I don't blame you for that,' Dolly said. 'I'll see you about two o'clock then.'

Dolly left them to their work and sauntered back to Daydream Palace.

Walking through the back door, she was surprised to see Danny Whitehouse sitting at the table waiting for her.

'I didn't expect to see you for a while yet,' Dolly said and nodded to Billy, who stood towering over Danny.

'My mother passed away last night,' the young man said sadly.

'I'm very sorry for your loss,' Dolly responded quietly.

'Thank you. She enjoyed her drop of gin, though.' Danny gave a wan smile before his sadness returned.

'I'm glad for that.'

'I was wondering... would it be possible...?'

'Do you want to start work sooner? I'm guessing you have no money for the funeral.'

Dolly's hunch was proved right when Danny nodded.

'I know it's a lot to ask, but I'd work off what I owe for the gin so my debt to you is paid. You've been kindness itself to me and I know I don't deserve it.'

'What about laying your mum to rest?' Dolly asked.

'It will have to be a pauper's grave,' Danny said, a look of abject misery crossing his face.

Reaching into her apron pocket, Dolly drew out her purse.

Passing enough for a burial over to the forlorn Danny, she said, 'Go and bury your mum. Come back when it's all done and you can start then.'

'I don't know how to thank you,' he said, his fair hair falling over his blue eyes as he bowed his head.

'You can thank me by being honest and loyal like Billy here.' Dolly tilted her head towards the big man who puffed out his chest with pride.

'I will, my oath on it.'

'Then that's good enough for me. Oh, and Danny, before you go, who does your house belong to?'

Danny frowned at the question. 'It was my mum's, why?'

'I was concerned that it may be rented and that you were at risk of being turned out,' Dolly answered.

'Oh, I see. No, I'm all right but I thank you for the consideration. I'll see you next week if the vicar can fit Mum in before then. Thank you again.' With that, Danny left.

'I hope you'm right about him,' Billy muttered.

'So do I, but for now I need to speak with you and Bobby.'

Billy found his brother in the cellar and they stood in the kitchen awaiting their fate. Were they to be yelled at for not protecting their boss sufficiently and allowing her to be put in danger? Was Dolly about to sack them?

'I need to know if you two would take on the cellar work full-time?'

'Is this because of last night?' Bobby asked.

'Well, yes, the idea stems from that. But honestly, I need your strength with the barrels and kegs.'

'What about the bar?' Billy asked.

'I've decided it's time for reinforcements so I'm going to the bread line this afternoon and Fred Dell is coming with me. So what do you reckon? I'd need your answers before I go.'

'I prefer the cellar,' Billy said.

'Me an' all,' his brother concurred.

'Good. In that case I'm upping your wages by a florin a week.'

'Two bob! Thanks, Dolly!' Billy gushed.

'Two shillings will help a lot,' Bobby added.

'Right, away with you,' Dolly said with a grin. She knew the Bickley family was a large one and the boys took a little money from their wages back to their parents to help out. They shared a room at the Daydream Palace in order to be on the premises at night and also relieve the overcrowding at home.

Dolly sat at the table and pondered. She needed doormen and bodyguards, but she also needed more bar staff. Now that Janice had twin boys to take care of, Dolly knew there would be times when they would need their mum at home.

Jack had helped out at the busiest times over the years but she could not rely on him coming to her aid; he worked for Nellie and he was needed there. So, it made sense to employ more staff. Having checked her books with the solicitor Mr Sharpe regularly, she knew she could afford it.

A very wise older man, Mr Sharpe had been hers and Nellie's solicitor for years and had helped them buy and renovate the Palace. She always thought of and addressed him as formally as his greater years demanded.

She wondered whether the men on the bread line would be interested in the bar staff positions also. How many would she need to employ, all told? Dolly thought she would ask Fred when he arrived later.

Going through to the bar, she was pleased to see it was packed, even at this time in the morning. Folk always found the money for their gin, regardless of how badly off they were. Her business was fool proof.

'Here she is!' a man yelled from the crowd. 'Our Dolly!'

She waved and gave him a grin.

'Thank God you're here, we're flat out!' Juliet gasped.

'Go and get a cup of tea, I'll take over,' Dolly said.

'We have to get a live-in cook Dolly, it's too much for the two of us,' the girl responded.

'I've been thinking the same,' Dolly said as she served an eager customer. 'I'll call in at the Servants' Registry later.'

Juliet nodded and went to take the weight off her feet for ten minutes.

The noise in the bar was loud as people talked, argued and sang. The drink was flowing copiously and folk were happy, at least for the time being. The doors were propped open to allow the warm summer wind to circulate and men and women stood six thick waiting to be served.

'Dolly, oh Dolly – I love you,' an old man said in a sing-song voice.

'I'm glad to hear it,' Dolly sang back.

All morning they were rushed off their feet, tots of Cream of the Valley, Royal Poverty and Blue Ruin flying across the counter. Coins rattled into the till constantly, a metal symphony accompanying the call for more gin.

At lunchtime, Dolly grabbed some bread and cheese and a cup of tea in the kitchen, before starting back again behind the bar. She saw Fred come in and was surprised at how quickly the time had sped past.

Promising to be as quick as possible, Dolly grabbed a parasol from the umbrella stand in the scullery and left via the back door with Fred at her side.

The relentless sun was only broken momentarily by a breeze like a soft gentle kiss.

Fred wore his shirt sleeves rolled up above the elbow, his braces holding up his trousers and a flat cap to shield his head from the sun's rays. His big boots thudded on the cobbles as they strode down the street.

'How many men will I need, do you think? I've decided it's time to stop cutting corners,' Dolly asked.

After a moment's thought Fred answered, 'Well, ideally about ten I would guess. Two on the door, four behind the bar to give you ladies a rest, and four walking the floor.'

Dolly nodded. She knew he was speaking sense, and the business could afford it.

Eventually they came to the corner of James Watt Street and saw a crowd of men chatting. One or two were standing on one leg, the other foot and their backs resting on the wall of a pub, their hands in their pockets. Some were smoking pipes, others had hand-rolled cigarettes.

All across the town, many street corners had developed breadlines, groups of men waiting in the hope that some wealthy businessman would come along and offer them work. These men would stand all day, come rain or shine, for the promise of a job. It was thought the term breadline stemmed from the men standing in a neat line waiting to be offered toil enough to earn a crust. In reality, the line spent their time putting the world to rights while they awaited the employers who knew where these breadlines were should they need workers.

As they neared, Fred said, 'Cover your ears.'

Dolly looked up at him and hunched her shoulders, holding out her parasol in one hand and her cane in the other.

'Oh, right. I'll make it quick then,' Fred said awkwardly. Then he shoved his forefinger and thumb in his mouth and sent out a loud shrill whistle.

The talking stopped immediately and the men gathered around.

'Most of you know me but for those who don't, I'm Fred Dell

and I work at the Crown Saloon. This lady is Miss Dolly Perkins and she's the owner of the Daydream Palace, and she's looking for workers.'

'Good afternoon, gentlemen.'

A few grunts greeted her and Dolly looked up at Fred who nodded for her to continue.

'I'm looking for workers, as Fred said. I need to know how many of you are married.' She watched as all but one hand went up. 'And how many of you have children?' All but two raised this time.

Turning to Fred, she whispered, 'How do I choose?'

Fred shrugged.

'I'm thinking to hire ten men,' Dolly went on and was taken aback by the response.

'Me, miss,' one man called.

'We'll tackle anything that pays a wage,' said another.

'I think it fair to hire those with families to feed,' Dolly said. 'I need men to work the door at the Daydream as well as some to throw the trouble-makers out.'

'That's you out then Bert, cos you'm a trouble-maker yerself!' a man at the back said, causing laughter to ripple amongst the gathering.

'Fred, what about if I took them all on? That way I could have a day shift and a night shift. It would mean they could all be earning, too.'

'Can you afford that many, though?' Fred asked.

'Yes, I think so. We were guessing ten, but there's twelve here so we'll just have to sell more gin!'

'It's up to you, Dolly.'

'I can employ all of you if you've a mind to take the work,' she called out.

'Yes, miss.'

'Thank you, miss.'

Dolly smiled. 'Right, come along to the Daydream Palace tomorrow morning at eight o'clock. Doors open at nine so be on time. I expect honesty, loyalty and good work in exchange for a fair wage. Anyone shirking their duties will be out on their ear because I don't suffer fools gladly. Thank you, gentlemen, I'll see you in the morning. Oh, and tell your wives you'll have breakfast with us.'

Flat caps flew into the air and yips and laughter sounded. Shouting their thanks, the men dispersed and Dolly and Fred turned for home.

'I'll have to work out a rota now, I suppose,' Dolly said with a grin.

'You've made a lot of men happy today, Dolly. Their families will be able to eat now too.'

Dolly thought about that as she limped her way back towards the Daydream Palace.

'I have to go to the Servants' Registry, I'm going to get us a good cook and a maid.'

'A couple more people to be grateful to you.'

'I'll be the one being grateful, Fred. I need the help with the cooking and cleaning. We've had a few years of real hard work and now we can afford it, we might as well have someone to take over the domestic chores. I just hope I can find somebody as good as Nancy.'

'There ain't anybody like my Nancy,' Fred said with a beaming smile.

'Well, let's go and see what's on offer,' Dolly answered, matching his grin.

4

'Good morning, I'm looking for a cook and a maid, both to live in,' Dolly said to the woman behind the desk in the Servants' Registry office.

The office was situated in Hill Street, which flanked New Street railway station. The brickwork was covered in grime carried by the steam from the engines. Inside was a dingy room, the small windows letting in little light, and the gas lamps guttered, giving out tiny flashes before settling to burn evenly again for another short while. There were no chairs other than the one the woman occupied so those seeking either work or workers were forced to stand. A notice was pinned to the wall stating the fees. Sixpence for registry and threepence for an enquiry. Clearly this office took a fee from both employer and servant. Those looking for a job would pay their fee giving their name, address, what type of work they were looking for and their skill sets. All this was entered into a large book.

Looking up from her ledger, the woman peered over her spectacles, which were perched on the end of her nose. Her gaze moved from Dolly to the towering figure of Fred.

'I'll need details. Your name?'

'Dolly Perkins.'

'Address?'

'Daydream Palace, Gin Barrel Lane.'

The woman leaned back in her chair and eyed Dolly. 'I'm not sure I have anyone on my books who would wish to work in a place like that!'

'Have you looked?'

'No, but...'

'Then I suggest you do. That's what *your* job is, isn't it? Besides, how would you feel knowing you had done someone out of work because of your prejudices?'

The woman harrumphed and flicked through her thick ledger. Running a finger down the column of neatly written names, she stopped at one. Grabbing a scrap of paper, she wrote down the name, then continued down the column before finding another which she added to the first.

Taking the paper, Dolly paid the fee. 'When can I expect them?'

The woman shrugged her shoulders. 'That's anyone's guess, tomorrow maybe – if I can get a message to them.'

Leaning forward, Dolly said quietly but forcefully, 'Not good enough. I'll see them later today or I'll have Fred here collect that fee you've just taken.'

'Very well, I'll see what I can do,' the woman muttered, her eyes flicking to Fred and back to Dolly.

'Thank you,' Dolly said before she and her companion left the office.

'Well done, lass,' Fred said, laughing, as they meandered back home.

'Bloody woman!' Dolly said.

'You sound just like Nellie,' Fred said jokingly.

'She taught me well, as did Nancy,' Dolly replied.

Fred beamed his pleasure at having his wife complimented.

'Thanks for your help today, Fred.'

The big man nodded, delighted to feel so important.

They parted company at the end of Aston Street, each going to their respective homes.

Entering through the back door, Dolly heard singing, which told her that her customers were happy. Going through to the bar, she saw old Aggie sidle forward.

'Did you know... old Mrs Whitehouse has passed on? Some say she choked on her gin!' Aggie cackled as she placed her empty glass on the bar.

'I'd already heard,' Dolly replied as she pushed the glass back and served another customer, a woman with a sleeping child tied to her chest with a massive woollen shawl.

Aggie frowned, deepening the lines on her face. She was the font of all knowledge in the area and she swapped snippets of information for a free drink. She'd been doing it for years both here and at the Crown, and on occasions had proved herself extremely useful.

'Ah, but did you know Jack Larkin has got himself a sweetheart?' Aggie's eyes narrowed as she studied the shock registering on Dolly's face.

'I don't believe that for a minute, you old bugger!' Dolly retorted. 'Here, have a drink on the house for thinking up a lie in double-quick time!'

'What makes you think it's a lie?'

'Because Nellie works that lad half to death! When would he have time to find and court a girl?'

Aggie gave a curt nod and smiled a toothless grin. Dolly passed over the filled glass and carried on with her work. In the back of her mind the lie lingered, pushing its way forward every now and then, giving Dolly an uncomfortable feeling which she couldn't explain or shake off.

Jack was perfectly entitled to find himself a lady friend. So why did the thought bother her so much? She had known the day would come when he would fall in love and wish to marry, but somehow Aggie's words felt like a slap in the face. If Jack *was* courting – would he tell her? They were close, after all, but something like stepping out with a girl was a private thing, so maybe he would keep it to himself. Was that what irked her, the fact that she finally realised Jack had a life of his own? That they weren't kids any more and didn't tell each other everything as they once did?

Endeavouring to shake off the discomfort, Dolly continued to serve one person after another.

It was around six o'clock when an older woman pushed her way through the crowd.

'I need to speak with Dolly Perkins,' she called out.

'That's me.'

'The Servants' Registry sent me.'

'Come on through,' Dolly shouted, lifting the end of the counter and pushing the little gate open.

The woman followed Dolly into the kitchen and sat down at the table. She glanced around at the shiny pots and pans hanging on hooks on the walls, then her eyes moved to Dolly, who was preparing a pot of tea.

'I've come about the job.'

'Which one?'

'Cook, why, is there another?'

'I'm looking for a maid, too.'

'Oh, well I ain't doing that.'

Dolly grinned, her back to the woman. 'So, tell me your name and a bit about yourself while we have tea.'

Sitting down opposite the woman, Dolly poured the tea and watched her visitor. Her clothes were old but clean, her dark hair showed signs of grey but her brown eyes gleamed with vitality.

'I'm Sadie Kemp and I'm renting a doss-hole of a room over in Freeman Street.'

'Isn't that near to the hide and skin market?'

'Ar, and it bloody stinks, let me tell you! Can't have the winders open 'cos of it. The same winders that rattle in their frames every time the steam train thunders past!'

'I expect you know this is a live-in post?'

'I do, and I thank the Almighty for that small blessing. Just so as you know, I speak as I find.'

'I gathered, but I like that,' Dolly answered and as she spoke she wondered whether, if she hired Sadie, they would have the same relationship as Nellie and Nancy. Would they become firm friends who constantly bickered? That wouldn't be such a bad thing.

'Tell me what you like to cook. And what experience do you have?'

'I worked for Lady Fortington-Smythe at one time but I left.'

'Oh, why is that?'

'The wealthy are just that because they won't pay much in the way of wages. When I asked for a rise, the mistress said the only rise I was getting was to my feet to carry me out and on my way. I told her to stick her job up her arse!'

Dolly stifled a grin, already beginning to like this woman.

'As for cooking, I like faggots – I make my own. Kidney pudding, grey pays and grorty pudding – lots of beef and groats in that, good and nourishing. Bread and butter pudding with plenty of currants, suet roly-poly...'

'That all sounds delicious,' Dolly cut in, afraid Sadie would go on and on. 'The pay for a cook is around seventeen pounds a year, I believe, but I'm paying twenty. How does that sound?'

'Bloody marvellous!'

'Fine, in that case – when can you start?'

'How does now sound to you?'

'Won't you need to collect your things?'

'I have them here.' Sadie nodded to an old shopping bag Dolly had not noticed before.

'Well, that is organised! Fine then, come with me and I'll show you your room. Welcome on board, Sadie.'

Dolly led her new cook up the back stairs and was pleased to see Sadie's face light up.

'Oh, this is lovely,' Sadie said as she dropped her bag on the bed and walked to the window. 'Look at all those rooftops, makes you feel like you're on the top of the world!'

'I'll leave you to settle in.'

Taking off her coat, Sadie hung it in the wardrobe. 'I'm in, and ready to start work.'

Dolly smiled. 'Come on, then, and get acquainted firstly with your kitchen and then with the other staff.'

Downstairs, Sadie rooted around in the pantry and cupboards whilst Dolly went to the bar. Introductions would have to wait, the place was packed with folk screaming for their tots of gin.

It was not long before a young woman appeared, saying she was a maid sent by the Registry. Dolly again ushered her to the kitchen for an interview and noticed with pleasure that Sadie was already working hard on an evening meal.

'My name is Alice Cliff,' the girl said quietly.

Questions were asked and answered, tea was served and Alice showed herself to be clumsy, having upset the milk jug. Trying to clean up the mess with a handkerchief hastily snatched from her pocket, she pushed back her blonde hair with sticky fingers.

Sadie scowled as she took over and refreshed the jug.

Alice was flustered and muttered, 'I'm so sorry.'

'Don't worry about that, accidents happen.'

As Alice's story was slowly revealed, their impatience was soon forgotten as both Dolly and Sadie began to feel terribly sorry in their hearts for the girl who sat at the table.

5

'My mum had problems giving birth to me and after that she couldn't have any more children. She died last year – summat to do with her kidneys, the doctor said.'

Sadie had sat down to listen to the girl's tale and poured herself some tea.

'Anyway, it was just me and Dad then, but he wasn't the same after Mum went and he took to the drink. He got the sack from the pit and we got turned out of our home by the pit boss.'

'Where have you been living?' Sadie asked gently.

'And where's your dad now?' Dolly added with a worried glance at the cook.

'We went to the heath, to the tarpaulin families, and camped out there.'

Sadie drew in a breath. 'You poor lass. And I thought I'd had it bad!'

'Dad got drunk one night, though heaven knows how 'cos he had no money, and he threw himself in front of the steam train.'

'Dear God!' Sadie exclaimed.

'I'm sorry. I heard about that accident, so it was your father?'

The girl nodded. 'I know some maids earn about six pounds a year but I'll do it for five if you'll have me,' Alice begged.

'Of course we'll have you,' Dolly said, then seeing Alice's face light up went on, 'but not for five pounds. I'll pay you ten pounds a year so make sure you do a good job.'

'Oh, thanks Miss…?'

'Dolly. Sadie, could you show Alice upstairs please? Her room will be next to yours.' Seeing the cook nod, she spoke again to Alice. 'Unless there's anything you need to do first?'

'Like what?'

'Maybe gather your belongings and bring them here.'

'I don't have anything but what I stand up in.'

'No spare clothes?'

Alice shook her head. 'No, nothing. Thanks, Dolly, I won't let you down.'

Watching them go, Dolly shook her own head at the girl's misfortune. Hopefully in time Alice would look upon them all as her second family. In the meantime, Dolly would sort out some of her own clothes and hope Alice didn't think it was charity.

A shout from the bar had Dolly on her feet with a sigh. Clearly the next busy wave had begun, with the employed leaving work to grace her premises with their presence.

Day became night, which was just as busy in the bar, and it was gone midnight before Dolly saw her bed.

The following morning saw twelve men arrive on the doorstep of the Palace exactly on time. Dolly led them into the bar and explained what she needed. Each one gratefully accepted the task allotted to them and those who were on the daytime rota were happy to begin work immediately.

Sadie and Alice had been up for quite a while to cook breakfast for everyone and as the kitchen was too small to accommodate them all, they ate in the bar.

Once their hunger was sated, Dolly said, 'Respect is the watch word in this place.' She nodded her thanks as pots of tea were brought out. 'We all respect each other as well as look out for our ladies here. I have extra bar staff to help out so everyone will be able to take regular breaks for a rest and to eat.' Dolly indicated the female staff with a wave of her hand. 'You work hard for me and I'll ensure you are rewarded.'

'We heard what you did for Danny Whitehouse and you have our thanks for that too,' one man said.

Dolly inclined her head in acknowledgement.

'We need to draw in custom as it's my intention to endeavour to open another gin palace should the right property become available.'

'Won't we lose trade here if you do that?' Janice asked.

'Not if the new place is across the other side of the town,' Dolly replied. 'So, if any of you hear of a pub for sale, let me know and I may be able to negotiate a good price.'

A quiet buzz of voices echoed in the room before a man spoke up. 'I heard the pub on Horse Fair – by the Drill Hall – is looking to sell.'

'Ar, but I believe Ezra Moreton could be interested in it an' all,' called another.

'Well then, that might be worth a look,' Dolly said. 'Right, lads, to work please.'

Dolly retired to the kitchen to think on what had been said and her mind took her back to her dealings with Mr Moreton many years ago now.

Nellie Larkin had been indebted to Moreton for a loan she'd had to refurbish the Crown Saloon. Dolly had sold the expensive necklace left to her by her mother and had given Nellie enough money to pay off that loan. Moreton, furious at losing the interest on the repayments and also because it meant

Nellie was no longer tied to only selling his gin, had tried to prevent Nellie from receiving alcohol from elsewhere by threatening all the suppliers in the town. But Moreton had underestimated the women, and Nellie had thwarted him again by finding a distiller further afield who continued to deliver both to Nellie and Dolly. Although he had left them in peace ever since, Dolly knew the man would not have forgotten their dealings.

Now it was looking very much like Dolly and Moreton might cross paths again.

Dolly gave an involuntary shiver as she recalled Moreton's reputation as a gangster, his bully-boy tactics usually getting him what he wanted. Not wanting to go up against this man, Dolly was hoping she could find a way around it, and she prayed that a stand-off with Moreton was avoidable.

Her thoughts were intruded upon by a resounding crash as Alice dropped a plate.

'Bloody hell, Alice! You are a clumsy girl!' Sadie yelled. 'Clean it up, will you!'

'It's all right, it's only a plate,' Dolly said to her distraught maid.

'This time, yes, but next time it could be a pile of 'em!' Sadie retorted.

'I'll be careful, Dolly, please don't sack me!' Poor Alice burst into tears and Dolly placed an arm around her shoulder.

'I'm not likely to do that, Alice, just try to be a little more careful will you, lass. Now fetch the broom, please, and sweep this up.'

Sadie shook her head as Alice disappeared into the scullery. 'You shouldn't mollycoddle her, she'll think she can get away with anything.'

'I've more pressing matters on my mind than a smashed plate,

Sadie. Besides, if Alice doesn't wash the dishes then it will fall to you to do it.'

Dolly smiled as Sadie blustered about the kitchen muttering under her breath. The pecking order always needed to be established, especially with new staff, and Sadie was letting everyone know she was queen of the kitchen – beneath Dolly, of course.

'Gentleman to see you, Dolly,' Janice called from the bar.

Dolly limped through to be faced with a handsome young man. A mop of black hair topped a sun-tanned face and his dark eyes held a mischievous twinkle.

'Good morning, I'm Wilton Burton, my father is your gin supplier.'

'Good morning, I'm Dolly. What can I do for you?' she asked as they shook hands.

'Father asked me to call and see how you were doing and if you are satisfied with our service.'

'Come along into the kitchen and have a sup of tea, and we can discuss it.'

'Could we have some tea please, Alice?' Dolly asked once they were in the kitchen. She indicated Wilton should take a seat.

'It looks like you're busy, there's staff everywhere!'

'Yes, I've just taken on some extra floor-walkers and barmen.'

Pulling out a wad of papers from his briefcase, Wilton selected one and pushed it across the table.

'We heard you were expanding and wondered if you might be interested in our new range.'

Dolly glanced at the paper with its list of names and prices. So this was why this good-looking man was really here.

'It's distilled twice so it's a little smoother on the tongue,' Wilton said with a nod of thanks to Alice for the tea.

'And there are nice names to go with the higher prices,' Dolly said with a knowing smile.

'Cream of the Palace was named after this place,' Wilton said over the rim of his cup.

'I'm very flattered but I'm not sure I can warrant paying this asking price. It would mean putting up my prices and then many of my customers would go elsewhere.'

'May I send you a cask free of charge to try out? It may be that some of your customers are willing to pay a little more for a smoother gut-rot.'

Dolly burst out laughing. 'You do have a way with words.'

'And you have a lovely laugh.'

Dolly blushed scarlet and glanced at Sadie and Alice, who had been intent on listening to the conversation, so quickly returned to their own business.

'Partiality is also new to our range,' Wilton went on, 'another gin which could possibly send you blind – but it takes a little longer.'

Dolly laughed again. She had instantly taken to this young man but guessed he used this charm on all of his clients.

'You could always Strip me Naked,' he said with a grin.

Alice's sharp intake of breath had them both look at her before he went on, 'It's our latest gin.' He watched the maid breathe a sigh of relief.

'All right, enough, Mr Burton,' Dolly said with a grin of her own.

'Wilton, please.'

Dolly nodded. 'Send me a free cask and we'll try it, but I'm not promising anything further.'

'Fair enough. Which one would you like?'

'Which is the best?'

Wilton shook his head then said, 'It doesn't really matter because they're all the same anyway!'

Dolly laughed loudly. 'Have you been to the Crown Saloon

yet?'

'Yes, I saw Nellie. I'm to deliver her free cask tomorrow.'

'I'll see you again, then,' Dolly said as the noise from the bar reached her ears.

Wilton stood, replacing the papers in his briefcase, and shook Dolly's hand once more.

'Good grief!' he exclaimed as she led him through to the bar. 'So many people and so early! Where did they all come from?'

'Far and wide. We open at nine and by half past you can't move for bodies,' Dolly explained, 'and it's like this until we close at midnight!'

Wilton's mouth hung open as he faced her.

With two fingers under his chin, Dolly gently lifted his lower jaw. 'Close your mouth else you'll catch a fly.'

It was Wilton's turn to burst out laughing. 'I'll see you tomorrow, pre-supposing I can get out alive!'

Dolly led him through the crowd who cheered to see her in their midst.

'They love you,' Wilton called over the noise.

'It's because I sell them their blinding gut-rot,' she yelled back. This time they both collapsed in a fit of the giggles.

Having waved as he departed in a cab, Dolly returned to the kitchen where she sat thinking about the very pleasant Wilton Burton. *I bet he's fun to spend time with.* Immediately, though, Dolly lambasted herself for fantasising about making a gentleman friend, knowing he would never be interested in her – her gammy leg would see to that.

However, as the day wore on she found herself smiling as she recalled his little jokes.

Wilton Burton had made quite an impression on Dolly and he stayed on her mind well into the night. She began to look forward to the following day when she would see him again.

6

Up early, work cleaning the bar was in full swing when Wilton Burton arrived – coincidentally at the same time Jack did.

Dolly welcomed both with hot tea in the kitchen whilst the Bickley brothers installed the free cask in the cellar.

'Are you planning to up the price for that one?' Jack asked.

'I'll put a penny on and see how it goes,' Dolly replied.

Jack sipped his tea and listened to the easy banter taking place between Dolly and Wilton. He could hardly believe how his friend had grown in confidence since he found her cowering in the yard of the Crown seven years ago. She was now an astute businesswoman running her own gin palace with a good and loyal crew to help.

He watched the sunlight play over her shiny dark hair, her brown eyes twinkling when she laughed. Dolly Perkins had turned into a beautiful young woman, Jack realised all of a sudden. Then, as she glanced at him, he felt his heart lurch. What was going on? Was he falling for her? Or was he jealous of the relationship beginning to form between Dolly and this salesman? Concern for her welfare trickled into his thoughts – would Dolly fall in love with Wilton only to be spurned because of her leg? Was Wilton just flirting with her in order to sell more gin?

Chastising himself, Jack pushed away the thoughts. It was Dolly's life and she was old enough to make up her own mind. The familiar feeling of wanting to protect her rose in him like a storm, however, and it was a feeling which would not be ignored. Something inside told him Dolly might need his counsel before too long and he wondered how he would deal with that time when it came.

'I'd best get back, otherwise Mum will be screaming for my blood,' Jack said. 'Thanks for the tea.' Jack left his friend and Wilton to it, still unable to fully understand why he felt uncomfortable.

'Are you and Jack...?' Wilton ventured after a moment when Jack had left.

'Goodness, no! We're friends and have been for years. Although we're very close, I don't see him in that way.' Dolly was surprised at the question and a little flustered. Why had Wilton asked that? Could it be he was interested in her? No, surely he was just being nosey. He was here merely to cajole her into purchasing the new range of spirits – nothing more.

The sound of yelling from the bar saved her from the conversation continuing.

'I'm afraid duty calls,' she said, grabbing her cane and getting to her feet.

'I'd better get gone then. You'll let me know how well Partiality sells, won't you?'

'And how will I do that?'

'I could call round again.'

Nodding, Dolly smiled. Then, at another shout from Janice, she rolled her eyes. 'Sounds like it's busy out there. Maybe we could try the new gin today.'

Walking him through the bar to the door she watched him climb into the driving seat of the horse and cart he'd left in the roadway. With a wave, he flicked the reins and the horse walked on.

Dolly waved before going back indoors. The room was filling up quickly even at this time of the morning. Her customers were enjoying their destructive love affair with their gin. Even after all these years, Dolly couldn't understand the attraction; how could they drink the throat-searing stuff? She knew it offered relief from perpetual cold, it sated hunger pangs too, but she couldn't help feeling they would have done better to buy food with what little money they had. Then again, she did understand that the gin lulled them into a world where they could forget the poverty and drudgery of slum life.

In the beginning, Dolly had felt guilty about selling the eye-reddening spirit, taking what little money folk had, but it was as Jack told her – if *she* didn't then someone else would. Her customers would never be abstemious where gin was concerned and so Dolly eventually felt absolved of any guilt and instead took it upon herself to make sure she took care of her customers and ran a safe establishment.

Standing behind the bar, she smiled when someone struck up the refrain of 'Polly Perkins of Paddington Green'. Before long, the whole congregation were singing along. Gin might be a health hazard, but it certainly made people happy – if only for a while.

The staff were coping admirably so Dolly retired to the kitchen, where Sadie was haranguing Alice for some little misdeed or another. Setting the kettle on the range to boil, Dolly sat at the table, her thoughts once again returning to the handsome Wilton Burton.

* * *

In the meantime, Jack had gone home in a foul mood.

'Whatever is up with you today?' Nellie asked.

'Nothing, Mum.'

'Nothing, my arse!'

'Leave him be, Nell,' Nancy put in.

'Nance, summat is wrong and I want to know what it is.'

'Shovin' yer nose where it don't belong again, you mean,' Nancy muttered.

Ignoring the remark, Nellie went on. 'Jack, a problem shared is a problem halved.'

Releasing a deep sigh, Jack folded under the pressure. 'I'm worried about Dolly.'

'Why?' Nellie asked, her brows drawing together in a furrow.

'She's a mite too friendly with that salesman – Wilton Burton, you know, the one that came here too.'

Nellie shot a glance at Nancy who clamped her upper teeth over her lower lip.

'Ah, well, I wouldn't worry about that. I'm sure Dolly knows what she's doing, son,' Nellie said.

'Does she? She ain't had any experience with men and I'm scared he'll break her heart. He's got the gift of the gab, that one.'

'We have to let her go her own way, lovey. You can't wrap her up in cotton wool. All as you can do is look out for her.'

'I suppose.' With that Jack went to the cellar, dragging his feet along the way.

'Oh, blimey!' Nancy exclaimed. 'You don't think Jack's carrying a candle for Dolly, do you? A touch of the green-eyed monster, perhaps?'

'That would be my guess, and a bloody big candle at that! But I ain't sure Dolly feels the same.'

'How do you know?' Nancy asked as she sat at the table with her friend.

'I don't know, Nance, I just feel it in my belly.'

'That'll be wind,' Nancy quipped. 'I suppose time will tell,' she added, as Nellie ignored her little joke.

'Hmm.'

'There could be ructions if Jack interferes with any blossoming relationship atwixt Dolly and that bloke.'

'That's what concerns me, and they've been friends too long to fall out now,' Nellie replied.

'Well, there's nowt we can do about it.'

'Hmm,' Nellie mumbled again, but her mind was telling her she should discover what, if anything, was going on. She needed to mention this to Dolly – discreetly, of course.

Later that morning, Nancy grumbled that they were almost out of bread and she didn't have time to make any. Nellie yelled for Jack and, giving him some money, sent him to the bakers.

Jack ambled down the street mentally grumbling to himself. *A man now and I'm still sent on errands.*

Entering the baker's, he was faced with Daisy Truckle, her blonde curls bobbing and her cornflower blue eyes shining.

'I ain't seen you in an age,' she said.

'Ar well, I'm here now and I need some bread.'

'What's got your gander up?'

'None of your business,' Jack snapped.

'Well, whatever it is, don't you bloody take it out on me!'

Jack looked at the pretty face, thinking how different it was to Dolly's. 'Sorry, I'm out of sorts today.'

Wrapping two freshly baked loaves, Daisy gave a curt nod.

Around Jack's age, Daisy had harboured feelings for the lad for what seemed forever, but it was like he never even noticed her. She knew that if they were ever to walk out together, it would have to be her who instigated it.

'There you go,' she said, handing over the bread and taking payment. 'Ain't it time you asked me out?'

Jack was momentarily taken aback at the girl's forthright manner.

'I ain't got time to go courting,' he responded.

'You could find time if you tried hard enough.'

Daisy was a handsome young woman, there was no denying that, and would make someone a good wife. Could that someone be him? Could he wed another when he had such strong feelings for Dolly? The revelation hit him like a bolt out of the blue. Was his love for Dolly that of a friend and protector, or was it something more?

'Well?' Daisy pushed.

'All right! Sunday afternoon, we'll have a walk down to Park Street Gardens, but don't be expecting anything more.'

'What time?'

Jack sighed. Daisy was not about to give up. 'Two o'clock.' With that he left the baker's. He did not look back, else he would have seen the broad smile on Daisy's face.

Strolling home, he wondered what he'd got himself into. Would stepping out with Daisy give her the impression they were a couple? He had agreed just to stop her from pestering him, but what if she thought he was soft on her?

Mind you, it would do him good to get away from the Crown for a few hours, and the park was lovely. Benches beneath the trees, blue sky, warm breeze – he found himself actually looking forward to it. Now all he had to do was tell his mum so she'd give him time off.

Back in the kitchen, he slapped the bread on the table and Nellie raised her eyes from the accounts she was studying.

'I'm going out on Sunday afternoon, so I need a few hours off,' he said. Having thought about it, he decided to take a leaf out of Daisy's book and be direct.

'Where are you going?' Nellie asked.

'I'm taking Daisy Truckle to the park.'

'Oh, all right then,' Nellie said with a quick glance at Nancy.

'Will you be wanting a picnic basket?' Nancy asked.

'No, we're only going for a walk.'

'You don't seem very keen,' Nellie put in.

Jack shrugged and went to see Fred in the cellar.

'What do you make of that?' Nancy asked.

'I think she bullied him into it, you know how pushy that girl is, but it won't hurt him to get out of here for a while. You never know, he might even enjoy himself.'

Sitting on an upturned cask, Jack watched Fred sweep the cellar floor.

'Want to talk about it?' Fred asked.

'What?'

'Whatever's on yer mind.'

Jack told him what had occurred in the baker's shop.

'She's a nice girl, is Daisy,' Fred said, 'even though she speaks her mind and doesn't care who knows it.'

'I know, Fred, but...'

'You ain't betraying Dolly if that's what you're thinking.'

'It's not that,' Jack mumbled.

'Oh, I see. You'd rather be walking out with Dolly, is that it?'

Jack nodded.

'Have you asked her?'

Jack shook his head. 'She seems too taken up with that Wilton Burton!'

Fred leaned the broom against the wall and sat himself on a barrel, not trusting his weight on a smaller cask.

'Well, the only way you'll know is to ask.'

'What if she says no?'

'At least then you *will* know. It might be that you and Daisy find you really like each other.'

'Maybe.'

'Give it a go and if it don't work out you're no worse off.'

'All right, thanks Fred.' Jack climbed the cellar steps to help out behind the bar. At least it would take his mind off things while he was serving customers.

* * *

Over at the Palace, Dolly was pleased to see, despite the rise in price, that the Partiality gin supplied by Burton's Distillery was selling well. Taking a seat in the kitchen to rest her leg, she was surprised when Janice joined her.

'Dolly, I've got something I need to talk to you about. I've decided I'm giving up work.'

'Oh! Why's that?'

'The twins are three years old now and I want to spend some time with them before they go to school. I've discussed it with Matt and he agrees.'

'I can understand that, but I hope you don't mind me asking – can you afford it? Will you be able to manage on Matt's wage alone?'

'We think so.'

'Fair enough. Well then, we'll all miss you, but I can see how family comes first. Just promise me one thing. If you find yourselves struggling financially, you'll come to me.'

Janice smiled. 'Thanks, Dolly.'

Dolly reached into the table drawer and pulled out enough to cover Janice's pay. 'Go on, there's no time like the present. Get yourself off home and enjoy those boys of yours.'

Giving Dolly a hug, Janice left with tears in her eyes.

'One down in the bar now,' Sadie said. No sooner were the words out of her mouth than a knock came to the back door.

Dolly glanced up with a puzzled look.

Sadie answered and ushered the visitor in.

Danny Whitehouse stood before Dolly. 'I've come to work off what I owe.'

'Your mum's...?'

'Mum was laid to rest this morning. The vicar shoved us in between two other funerals.'

Dolly nodded. 'Well, Danny, your timing is perfect as I find myself in need of a barman. If you go through to the bar, Juliet will show you the ropes. Remember, Danny, loyalty and respect.'

'Yes, ma'am, and thank you.' Danny knuckled his forehead and disappeared into the packed bar.

'I hope he works out,' Sadie said.

'So do I. Now, what's for dinner?'

'Faggots, taters and cabbage with onion gravy if Alice bucks her ideas up and peels them spuds.'

The maid scowled. 'I'm doing my best.'

Dolly smiled and left them to it. She wanted to see how Danny Whitehouse was getting to grips with his new job.

Laughing, joking and serving, Danny seemed to have taken to the work like a duck to water.

'You ain't as pretty as Janice,' a customer called over the noise.

'Maybe not, but I've got the gin so you'd best be nice to me,' Danny responded with a grin.

The Palace was busy all day and the staff were run off their feet. Taking turns to slip away for a meal, they then returned to the melee.

After lock-up that night, as a few sat with a well-earned cup of tea, Dolly piped up. 'I think I'll go over to Horse Fair tomorrow and have a look at the pub for sale.'

'Great idea, but it might be an idea to take somebody with you,' Sadie suggested.

'You're probably right. Danny, you up for a trip out?'

'Certainly, it will be my pleasure. I'll be getting off home now then. Thanks, Sadie, for that good home-cooked meal. See you all tomorrow.'

Once he'd gone, and with a beaming smile, Sadie said, 'Nice lad, that Danny.'

'Dreamy looking an' all,' Alice muttered.

Dolly could barely contain her smile as Sadie sighed and rolled her eyes. Then one by one they retired to their respective beds, feeling weary to the bone.

8

The following morning, Dolly and Danny boarded a cab which set off for Horse Fair. The cab travelled down Corporation Street, passing the county court and the Grand Theatre. Coming to New Street, it circumnavigated the railway station before cutting down narrower streets. Horse Fair was a wide thoroughfare lined each side by trees, giving the impression of being a relatively wealthy area.

On arrival, they alighted and stared up at the soot-blackened building. Dolly looked around her. With a position not far from New Street Station it would bring in custom from passengers. The public house stood on the corner of the tramway and Essex Street, opposite an inn right next to St Catherine's Chapel. It was busy with carts, riders and foot traffic, but everyone was in a hurry to get where they were going, not even sparing the pub a second glance.

Going indoors, she smiled inwardly as the buzz of conversation halted at seeing a woman in a drinking den. Stepping up to the bar, she said loudly, 'I'm here to see the landlord, please.'

The barman nodded and disappeared into a back room. Dolly

glanced around. She counted only six men, quaffing ale and smoking clay pipes, all of whom were most likely retired from working life. They looked at her with disgust on their faces. Women in their local – whatever next!

A tall thin man with a hooked nose and very little hair followed the barman, and said, 'You wanted to see me?'

'Yes, I believe your premises might be up for sale?'

He nodded.

'I could be interested in buying. May we have a look around and then discuss business somewhere more private?'

Nodding again he approached a door which led to the stairs. Ascending, Dolly wrinkled her nose at the smell of dank decay. The whole place was riddled with damp and would need a lot of attention. She was surprised to find it only had four rooms upstairs, all of which were completely empty.

'Clearly you don't have people to stay, then,' she said.

'No.'

Dolly shot a quick look at Danny, who shrugged his shoulders.

Returning to the lower level, the landlord pointed to behind the bar. 'My living quarters.'

'May we see?' Dolly asked.

'No,' the man replied abruptly, and Dolly wondered if he was ashamed of where he was living.

'Well, then, thank you for the tour.'

'So, are you buying it?'

'I'll think on it and consult my financial adviser but I appreciate your time. Good day to you.'

Climbing into the waiting cab once more Dolly blew through her lips. 'Well, that was like trying to get blood out of a stone.'

'He wasn't very forthcoming, he never even told you how much he was asking for it!' Danny replied.

'It's my guess he didn't want to deal with a woman. I should have realised and asked you to take the lead.'

'So, what did you think of the place?'

'It smelled damp, and it's dark and dismal. God knows what the living quarters are like. It would take an immense amount of work and money to make it into a going concern.'

'It's a busy area, though.'

'Yes, but did you notice no one was going in? A few elderly gentlemen having a quiet drink – if it's like that all the time it's no wonder he wants rid of it. No, I don't think it would be a sound investment, in fact it could turn out to be a pig in a poke.'

'Not exactly sociable either, was he? He never even introduced himself.'

'That's another thing that tells me he's had enough of public house life.'

'Oh well, it was worth a look, I suppose.'

'Always. Thank you for accompanying me, Danny, I appreciate it.'

'You're most welcome. It's the least I could do after all you've done for me. I'm sorry about... you know, the knife.'

'It's forgotten, Danny.'

As the cab trundled along, Dolly noted the dirty streets, people ambling about as if they had nothing better to do. Women were washing windows – a thankless task with the smoke from countless chimneys throwing out soot particles. Children with bare feet ran around yelling as they played, heedless of the traffic. Men in flat caps stood in groups, putting the world to rights as they smoked hand-rolled cigarettes.

Birmingham was a poverty-stricken area, Dolly thought, as they passed houses standing cheek by jowl shutting out the sunlight.

The cab slowed to a crawl as it approached the railway

station, where hordes of people spilled out into the street. The hiss of the steam trains could be heard even over the noisy crowds.

Changing direction at Victoria Square, the cab picked up speed to travel along Colmore Row and on into Steelhouse Lane. The plethora of grimy buildings was broken only by St Philip's church, headstones of all shapes and sizes filling the cemetery.

Drawing to a halt outside Daydream Palace, Dolly and Danny alighted and could hear the singing going on indoors. Dolly paid the cabbie and thanked him before they walked around to the back door, not wanting to fight their way through the throng in the bar.

'How did you get on?' Sadie asked as they stepped through the doorway.

'It was pretty awful,' Dolly said.

Danny immediately went to work behind the bar whilst Dolly explained about their little adventure. 'It doesn't matter, though, because something else will come up in time. Besides, I'm in no hurry.'

'That place sounds like it was cack!' Alice said.

Dolly grinned. 'It was, Alice, truly dreadful.'

'Get on with those vegetables and mind your business, girl,' Sadie chastised.

'I was only saying,' Alice muttered.

'I'm doing meat and potato pie, vegetables and gravy for lunch,' Sadie said, ignoring the maid's comment.

'Lovely, we'll all be hungry by then because it sounds hectic out there.' Dolly tilted her head as she spoke. Moving to the doorway, she leaned against it and scanned the crowd. The room was barely able to accommodate another body, it was so full.

Old Aggie crooked a finger and Dolly stepped forward.

'I hear as you'm looking for new premises,' Aggie said.

Dolly smiled but said nothing. How had Aggie found out? It was a mystery how the gossip grapevine was constantly fed.

'I'll keep my ear to the ground,' Aggie added.

'Thank you, Aggie,' Dolly said, giving the old girl a free tot, and tapped the side of her nose, indicating it should be between them. She knew, however, that the town would be privy to the knowledge in no time.

'So, you moving then?' Aggie asked.

'Maybe,' Dolly grinned.

'No you ain't, you're after another Palace, ain't yer?'

'Maybe,' Dolly responded again, unwilling to give away any more of her private business.

Just then a fight broke out, and two of her floor-walkers dived in to separate the battling men. Dolly watched as the fighters were escorted out of the front door before her new workers returned. They nodded to their boss and Dolly smiled.

'We've run out of that Partiality,' Juliet said out of the side of her mouth.

'Already? That went quick. I'll put in a regular order if it's that popular.'

'Better had, folks are complaining when I tell them it's all gone,' the barmaid answered then rushed off to serve a woman yelling for service.

It was late afternoon when Wilton Burton arrived and Dolly was delighted to see him, not least because she needed to place a new order.

'I guessed you might like our new range,' Wilton said when Dolly told him every drop had been sold.

'Not me personally, but the customers certainly do.'

Sadie and Alice went about their business with half an ear on the conversation.

'I'm looking to open another gin house if I can find the right premises.'

'Very good, and I'm assuming you will be dealing with us?'

'Of course.'

'Funnily enough, father was thinking about extending the works. We're struggling to keep up with demand. Our sales of beer are at an all-time high.'

'I'm glad to hear it.' Dolly smiled.

Wilton's dark eyes sparkled. Dolly saw the blue-black jets as sunlight danced over his hair. His voice was smooth and gentle as he coaxed her into trying another of the new gins.

He laughed, which snapped her attention back to the conversation and made her realise she'd been staring, a dreamy look on her face. Had he noticed? Whatever would he think?

'Dolly!' the call came from the bar.

'Sorry but it appears I'm needed,' she said as she picked up her cane from where it had been propped against her chair.

'I'll get off home, then, and get your order set up.'

Shaking hands, Wilton held hers a few seconds longer than was needed and Dolly's heart leapt. Was he trying to tell her something? Or was she reading something into it that wasn't there?

Wilton slipped out of the back door as Dolly limped to the bar, a flush to her cheeks which was not caused by the warm weather.

Alice opened her mouth to speak but Sadie put a finger to her own lips, telling the maid not to say a word. Sadie nodded and Alice grinned. They both had the same idea – their employer was giving out all the signs of being in love.

9

Sunday rolled around and Jack half-heartedly polished his boots. He had on a clean shirt and trousers, and his beloved flat cap was on his head. It was almost time to meet Daisy Truckle for their walk in Park Street Gardens. Why had he agreed to go? He didn't particularly want to spend his time with the girl, and to be honest he would much rather have gone across to see Dolly. Slipping his feet into his boots, he laced them up.

With a sigh, he walked from the scullery into the kitchen.

'You look very smart,' his mother said as she handed over some money in case he should need it.

'You don't really want to go, do you?' Nancy asked.

'Course he does,' Nellie put in quickly.

'He don't. Look at his face, Nell, the poor lad is dreading it.'

'Nance, it's nowt to do with us.'

Ignoring her friend, Nancy went on. 'He shouldn't have to if he...'

'I'd best be off. I'll see you later,' Jack said before the women could argue any more, then left to collect Daisy.

As he strolled down Gin Barrel Lane with his hands in his

pockets, he knew Nancy was right. However, he had agreed and he wouldn't go back on his word. Moreover, he didn't have to step out with the girl again if he didn't enjoy himself. The thought cheered him somewhat and he pushed through the filthy streets to the baker's.

Daisy was waiting outside for him and he forced a smile as he approached her. She did look pretty in a white cotton dress which fell to her shoes. Her blonde curls were caught up by a white ribbon shaded beneath a matching lace parasol.

Side by side, they walked towards the park, Daisy chatting as they went, although Jack wasn't really listening. He was wondering what Dolly was doing today.

'Are you hearing me?'

Jack nodded.

'Well, what do you think?'

'About what?'

Daisy sighed audibly. 'You've not heard a word I've said, Jack Larkin!'

Wisely he kept his counsel. Entering the park gates they stepped onto the gravel path that wound between trees and around well-kept lawns.

'What's up with you?'

'Nothing,' Jack muttered.

'You shouldn't have come if your heart ain't in it.'

'You asked me, remember?'

'Yes, I do remember but I'm beginning to think I've made a mistake.' Daisy stopped and plonked herself on a bench beneath a tree where a squirrel scampered to the high canopy of leaves.

Jack sat beside her, his hands still in his pockets. He was feeling wretched. Try as he might, he couldn't summon the will to make an effort to show Daisy a pleasant afternoon.

He heard a woodpecker hammering a tree in the distance

then a cuckoo called. Birds chirped and flew across the grass in search of worms.

Everything was different now he was older. When he was a kid, he and Dolly had laughed as they worked together behind the bar of the Crown. He recalled how excited she had been when he bought her some books for her birthday. She still loved to read and Jack thought he'd visit the market to get her some more. The newly built central library was not in use as yet, its grand opening was scheduled for next year.

Daisy was tapping her foot on the gravel, making a pattering sound. There was an awkward silence between them which was suddenly broken when Daisy said, 'Right, I'm going home. I don't think I like you very much, after all.'

Jack walked beside her, his head down. He didn't argue with her decision, for that was what he wanted too, but he still felt ashamed.

They halted outside the baker's and Daisy waited for Jack to speak. When he said nothing, she turned on her heel and stamped down the passage to the back door.

Breathing a sigh of relief, Jack hurried home but as he neared, he changed his mind and crossed the road. His heart beat faster as he made for the front entrance to Daydream Palace. He was going to see Dolly instead.

* * *

Sitting on a chair carried outside by one of her workers, Dolly looked Jack up and down. 'Going somewhere nice?' she asked, taking in his neat appearance.

Jack shook his head, not knowing what to say.

'Come on, Jack, you know I'm a good listener.'

Unable to hold his tongue Jack spilled the whole story of his awkward morning but made no mention of his feelings for Dolly herself.

'I know what you're thinking,' he said. 'I should never have agreed to the outing in the first place.'

Dolly kept her counsel. Her eyes remained on the roadway, watching folk passing by.

'I'm dreading having to go back to the baker's.'

'At least Daisy knows how you feel now and she can move on,' Dolly said at last.

'What about you? Are you and that salesman...?'

'No, Jack, we're not.' Dolly cut across his question.

Changing the subject before the conversation could get awkward, Dolly told Jack about her jaunt to the old pub with Danny Whitehouse.

As he listened, he felt the pangs of jealousy bite again. There was a time she would have asked him to accompany her, but she was totally independent now. It appeared she no longer needed his help, and a feeling of redundancy crept over him.

'So I've decided I'll keep my eyes open for another pub for sale,' Dolly concluded.

'How can you run two places at once?'

'I'll just put a manager in the other one.'

'It would have to be someone you trust,' Jack said. 'Who do you have in mind?'

'I don't know, anyway, it's early days yet.'

'Well, it sounds like an exciting plan, but I'd better get back, otherwise Mum will be calling for my head. *Where have you been? We're snowed under here and you've been gallivanting round the park!*'

Dolly laughed at his imitation of Nellie's voice and it brought back memories of when they were younger. She laughed harder when Jack mimicked Nancy. '*Leave him alone Nell, he's only a kid!*'

Then, out of the blue, he asked, 'Do you still think of Nancy as your second mum?'

'I'd say we're more friends now.' Dolly's mind returned to the past when Nancy needed a child and Dolly needed a mother, her own having passed away.

'Enjoying the sunshine, I see.'

Dolly turned to see Wilton standing in the doorway and she beamed.

'I've brought your order; the boys are unloading it as we speak.'

Jack curled his lip. *Smarmy git!*

'Hello, Jack, not working today?' Wilton asked.

'No.' Jack's sharp answer drew a cursory glance from Dolly. 'I'm away, I'll see you later, Dolly.' With that, head down and hands back in his pockets, he strode across the road to the Crown Saloon.

Once he was back, Jack made his way straight down to the cellar where Fred was sweeping the floor.

'How did it go with Daisy?'

'Dismal.'

'That bad?'

'Worse. We took a turn round the park and I couldn't find anything to talk about. In the end she said she d'aint like me much after all and I took her home.'

'Ah, well, it's done now.'

'I feel awful, Fred. I treated her summat rotten and she didn't deserve it.'

'Why don't you take her some flowers and tell her you're sorry?'

'I don't want her thinking there could be another outing in the offing!'

'Tell her that. Explain you only want to be her friend.'

'I won't be able to get out again now. Mum will want to know everything.'

'Have you got any money?' Fred asked.

'Yes, why?'

'Right, nip to the market for those flowers and take them to Daisy. On way back, bring me a half ounce of baccy.' Fred handed over a couple of coins. 'That way we can say you've run an errand for me and we won't be lying.'

'Thanks Fred,' Jack said and raced up the cellar two steps at a time.

Dashing to the market he bought a bunch of flowers, and on his way to the baker's he purchased Fred's tobacco, which he shoved in his pocket.

At the baker's he saw Daisy serving in the shop and he knocked on the window. When she looked out, he crooked a finger. A moment later Daisy stood before him.

'What do you want?' she asked sharply.

'I've come to apologise and give you these.' He produced the flowers from where he'd hidden them behind his back.

'Oh, well, thanks,' Daisy said, her surprise evident.

'Daisy, I treated you really badly and I'm sorry.'

'Does this mean...?'

'No,' Jack jumped in quickly. 'Look, I can't be your sweetheart, but I can be your friend.'

Daisy nodded and said, 'All right. At least we know now it wasn't meant to be.'

'Thanks. And I'm sorry again to have spoilt our walk.' With a smile, he left her standing with her nose buried in the flowers.

Back at the Crown, Jack went again to the cellar and handed over the tobacco and Fred gave him a questioning look.

'Thanks, Fred, all's well now.'

Meanwhile, at the Palace, Wilton carried the chair around the back and into the kitchen for Dolly, where he greeted Sadie and Alice.

Dolly could hear the Bickley brothers stacking new barrels in the cellar and rolling out the empty ones to be loaded onto Wilton's cart.

They chatted over tea, Dolly enjoying the young man's company, much to the amusement of the cook and maid.

Mentioning her idea to open another gin palace again, Dolly was surprised when Wilton said, 'We supply ale to the Coach & Horses in Dean Street and I know for a fact the owner is looking to sell.'

'Interesting. Well, then, maybe I'll take a trip over to see if it's suitable.'

'It's a small place, about the size of this.'

'Still room for customers, though,' Dolly quipped.

'Ezra Moreton has just purchased that old place on Horse Fair, so we've lost that client.'

It wasn't unexpected that Ezra, who owned the brewery on Nova Scotia Street, had moved in to buy so quickly. He was a man not to be crossed and those who did often ended up floating in the canal, although it could never be proved he'd had a hand in it.

'So if you're interested in the Coach & Horses, I suggest you get over there sharpish,' Wilton concluded.

'Thank you, I'll go today.' Dolly smiled at the man, who was staring at her unashamedly.

'Don't you be going on yer own, though,' Sadie said as she cleared away the tea things.

'I won't.'

'Cellar's all done, Dolly,' Billy Bickley said as he came into the kitchen.

'Thanks, boys,' she answered as she spotted his brother Bobby right behind him. 'Get yourselves some tea and cake before you start on the yard, then.'

Rubbing their hands together they sat at the table waiting for their treat.

Wilton said his farewell and left via the back door.

When he had gone, Dolly thought about what had been said about the pub for sale. She would take a look and she knew just who to take with her.

10

'Nellie, do you mind if I borrow Jack for a couple of hours? I'm going to Dean Street to look at a property for sale.'

'I think I can spare him. Jack! Get your arse in here!'

'What now?' he asked as he rushed into the kitchen. 'Oh, hello Dolly.'

'I wondered if you would do me a favour,' Dolly said before explaining her request. 'I'm off to see a pub that's up for sale.'

'Better hurry up afore Ezra Moreton gets his grubby hands on it, then,' Nancy put in. 'I hear as he is buying up as many old inns and taverns as he can – greedy bugger!'

'It's just business, but you're right, I should go sooner rather than later,' Dolly responded.

Nellie and Nancy would presume she was asking Jack to mind the Palace while she was on her jaunt, and Dolly had no intention of telling them otherwise – yet. A plan was forming in her mind but letting the two women in on it would come later.

Out on the street, Jack whistled for a cab and in a moment they were on their way.

Taking them by way of Moor Street to avoid the busy tramway, the cabbie kept a steady speed.

Dolly nodded, drawing Jack's attention to Park Street Gardens as they passed by and he scowled at being reminded of the disastrous outing with Daisy. Skirting the Bull Ring, they then emerged onto Jamaica Row.

Arriving at their destination, Dolly asked the cabbie to wait, and they wandered over to the building in question.

Dolly wrinkled her nose at the smell emanating from the public slaughterhouse a little further down the street. Looking to her right towards Jamaica Row, she noted Smithfield Market.

'Bloody hell, it stinks round here,' Jack put voice to her thoughts.

'Not a very salubrious area, that's for sure,' Dolly remarked.

'I know folk don't care about anything much once they're full of gin, but...' Jack left the sentence hanging.

'There's a bank up there and another down there, both of which we can see from here,' Dolly said as she pointed. 'Between those stand three public houses, which tells me there must be enough trade for them all to stay open.'

Delighted to have been asked to join her, Jack felt obliged to give his honest opinion. 'It's a doss-hole, Dolly.'

'Maybe. Should we take a look nevertheless?'

'If it were me, I wouldn't take it on.'

Dolly sighed. It was her intention to offer the management of her new premises to Jack, but if he felt this way then he would undoubtedly refuse. To tempt Jack out from beneath the clutches of his mother, Dolly knew her venture would have to meet with his approval. She loved Nellie Larkin dearly and would not upset her for the world, it was just unfortunate she still saw her son as a boy. At eighteen, Jack was a man now, and being under Nellie's thumb prevented him from growing into the astute businessman she knew he could be.

Of course, Jack had no idea of Dolly's true plan, only that she was striving to expand her own business.

'Right, we'll not bother then,' she said as she climbed back inside the cab.

'I'm sorry if I put you off,' Jack muttered as the vehicle bumped over the cobblestone roads.

'Don't be. I think we were right. I'm not sure I could live with that dreadful smell day and night.'

'You wouldn't have to if you're putting a manager in.'

'No, but you would have to.'

'Me?'

'Yes. I'd like you to take over the running of the next gin palace – if we ever find suitable premises that is.'

'Dolly, I don't know what to say!'

'Just say yes.'

Immediately Nellie's voice came from Jack's lips. *'How am I to go on without our Jack? He ain't old enough to be taking on that responsibility!'*

Once she'd stopped laughing, Dolly said, 'Then it will be up to me to persuade Nellie otherwise.'

'Ooh, who'd have thought it, me being a gaffer.'

'I think you will make an excellent boss,' Dolly replied.

'Thanks, Dolly, but I'm keeping my head down when you tell Mum!'

* * *

The weather began to change from summer into autumn and leaves turned yellow and brown. A slight chill in the early morning saw to it that jackets were donned and woollen shawls brought out from storage. Hazy mists hung low in the streets, giving the town an eerie quality, and horses pulled carts warily on their way to their destinations. The fog was eventually burned off by the weakening sun, only to reappear the following day.

There was an urgency about how people traversed the streets, as though they were rushing to complete their tasks before winter set in. Market traders were more insistent about selling their wares and women were the same regarding their purchases. Fruits and vegetables were bought for bottling to fill pantries and so provide a treat during the long cold months. Jams bubbled in pans on ranges and more coal was ordered for fires, many of which had only been lit for cooking but were now burning all day.

Dolly sat in Nellie's warm kitchen sipping hot tea and wondering how to broach the subject of Jack becoming her manager if and when the time came.

Nellie Larkin had taken her in at a time when she most needed help and Dolly always kept in mind how readily she was accepted. She had become one of the family and could not bear the thought of hurting any of them.

'Nellie, you know I'm looking for new premises...'

'You ain't moving away, are you?' Nancy said before Nellie could speak.

'No, I'm hoping to have another gin palace in the area.'

Nancy was visibly relieved and sat at the table to join in the conversation.

'Can you afford it?' Nellie asked.

'Yes, I think so, if the price is right.'

'Have you had Mr Sharpe go over your books?'

'Yes, and he's of the opinion the business will stand it. I will have to apply for a new mortgage facility, but he thinks the bank would agree to it.'

'Fair enough. The question now, then, is where?'

'I've looked at a couple of properties already, but they weren't really what I'm after.'

'You gonna run it yourself?' Nancy asked.

'That's the thing, I'll put a manager in as I want to stay at the Palace.'

'You'll need somebody reliable, someone who won't steal from you or cheat you,' Nellie said.

'Indeed, and I was wondering if you could recommend anyone.' Dolly had put the notion forward in the hope that if Nellie suggested Jack then she would think it was her idea.

'Not offhand. Ain't any of your staff suitable?' Nellie asked.

'I'm not sure they are, a lot are new workers and I need to keep an eye on them.'

'You could put an advertisement in the paper.'

'I would still have the same problem of not knowing them properly though. I need someone I can trust without breathing down their neck every minute of the day.'

'What about Jack?' Nancy asked.

Dolly had not expected Nancy to come up with the idea and her face showed genuine surprise.

'Don't be daft. I can't do without him,' Nellie said sharply.

Dolly smiled inwardly, recalling Jack's imitation of his mother.

'You can, Nell, most of the time he's piddling about looking for summat to do,' Nancy returned.

'He ain't old enough for a position such as that!' Nellie snapped.

Again, Dolly remembered Jack's words.

'He's eighteen, for God's sake! Dolly was only fourteen when she took over the Daydream!'

Nellie couldn't deny the truth of that statement and Dolly saw the mixed emotions play across Nellie's countenance.

'He's got to leave home sometime Nell, but at least this way he'd have a decent job,' Nancy pushed.

'I suppose there is that.'

'Well, then! Why don't you ask him? It might be he would rather stay here but if you don't ask, you won't know.'

Dolly kept her counsel as the conversation went back and forth.

'I ain't sure.'

'Look, Nell, you d'aint tell him you found him on the doorstep as a babby until he was ten years old and look what happened then. It took him a long time to accept it cos he felt you'd kept him in the dark!'

'What the bloody hell does that have to do with it?'

'If Dolly puts a manager in without considering Jack first because you wouldn't let him go, how's he going to feel about that?'

'He'll be all right...'

'He won't, Nell! He'll blame you for holding him back!'

'He wouldn't – would he?'

'He might, Nellie,' Dolly put in. 'He's the perfect choice to work with me, and if you deny him the chance it could cause a rift and nobody wants that.'

Nellie was quiet for a while as she thought over the suggestion. Nancy was right, as was Dolly, and Jack would be the ideal person for the job. On the other hand, she had brought him up as her own and the thought of him leaving home would be an enormous wrench.

'Right, then,' Nellie said, slapping her hands on the table and making the others jump, 'let's ask him.'

11

'Jack! Get yer arse in here a minute, will you?' Nellie yelled.

Knowing Dolly was here, having heard her voice even over the noise of the bar, Jack had been true to his word and kept his head down.

'Whatcha want now?' he asked as he entered the kitchen.

'Sit down, lad. I've summat to ask you,' Nellie said.

Doing as he was bid, he saw Dolly give him a quick wink. Knowing what was coming, he debated whether to say he'd known about the idea, or let Nellie think he had no clue. Wisely, he opted for the latter.

'Now then, Dolly is after another palace and needs a manager and we thought of you.'

'*I* thought of him,' Nancy said sharply.

'Nance thought of you,' Nellie corrected herself. 'How would you feel about that?'

'I'd love it!' Jack said, feigning surprise, and saw Dolly release a relieved breath.

'Right, well, my advice would be for you to go with her when she finds what she's looking for because you'll be the one who has to live and work there.'

'That's an excellent idea, Nellie,' Dolly said, and she and Jack shared a knowing smile.

'Dolly's already checked out a couple of places but didn't like them, so you be ready when she calls for you.'

'Yes, Mum. Thanks, Dolly, I won't let you down.'

'I know you won't. I'll let you know when another pub comes up for sale.'

'That's that, then. You can get back to work now,' Nellie instructed.

Jack gave a little jump, clicking his heels together, and the women smiled at his excitement.

'I'll miss him around the place, though, Dolly,' Nellie said a little sadly.

'Me an' all, but he's a man now and has to go his own way,' Nancy said resignedly.

'He won't be far away, Nellie, maybe only a short cab ride. We'll have to see, but you can always visit him and give him the benefit of your experience.'

Nellie nodded but it was all she could do to stem the tears pricking her eyes.

Dolly stood to make a strategic withdrawal. 'I'll see you both later, and thanks.' Her plan had worked out better than she could ever have hoped.

When she'd gone, Nellie finally allowed her tears to fall, as did Nancy at seeing her friend's distress.

'I don't want him to go, Nance,' Nellie sobbed.

'I know, Nell,' Nancy replied as she wrapped her arms around the woman who had taken her in off the street so very many years ago. 'He'll be right, you'll see.'

With their arms around each other, they cried quietly at the thought of the boy they both loved so much finally leaving home.

* * *

Over the road, customers were spilling out of the doors of the Palace as fast as others rushed in and the bar was packed.

Dolly made her way around the back to enter the kitchen and was surprised to see Wilton Burton enjoying tea and cake and chatting with her cook, Sadie.

'Ah here she is, the queen returned to her palace,' Wilton quipped.

Dolly smiled and blushed scarlet. 'What brings you to my door again so soon?'

'Merely checking you are happy with our gin.'

'My gin – it belongs to me now I've paid the bill.'

'Of course, my apologies, your majesty.'

Sadie howled at the banter and Alice gazed dreamily at the handsome young man.

'It's selling well and I'm very pleased, thank you.'

'Good, we can't have our best customer unhappy now, can we?'

Dolly shook her head at his blatant sales pitch. 'My cellar is full, so I have no need to place another order as yet.'

After a short time of playful chat, Wilton took his leave, waving over his shoulder as he left.

'I think that lad has an eye on you,' Sadie said.

'Hmm. Only so that he can get me to buy more gin,' Dolly responded. However, she wished it was true, that Wilton could be interested in her and not just her business.

'There's more on his mind than that,' Sadie went on.

'I'd take him on in a flash!' Alice added.

'You need to get that pastry made and keep your thoughts to yourself!' the cook remonstrated.

It crossed Dolly's mind that the cook should do the same, but she said nothing. Instead, she limped her way into the bar where her staff were run ragged.

'Juliet, go for a break, I'll take over.'

Glad of the chance to rest her aching feet, the barmaid scuttled away to the kitchen.

Immediately Dolly's attention was called for by a woman wanting to be served. The woman had a sleeping baby strapped to her chest and Dolly wondered how the noise didn't wake the child. A little gin on the end of a finger perhaps? Having no time to dwell on the matter, Dolly moved on to her next customer.

'Dolly!' The shout came from Aggie, who pushed her way to the counter.

'One minute, Aggie.' Then a moment later Dolly said, 'What can I do for you?' *Other than fill a glass.*

Aggie spoke from the corner of her toothless mouth in a surreptitious manner. 'I know where there's a landlord selling up!'

'Do tell.'

'Well, I would, but my mouth is too dry,' the old woman said before making a sound like a cat vomiting.

Dolly passed over a glass of Partiality and waited while Aggie took a slurp.

'That's better. Over behind the cattle market on the corner of Great Barr Street and Watery Lane. Bloody big place it is an' all. It ain't common knowledge as yet so if you'm interested I suggest you stir your stumps.'

'What's the name of it?'

Aggie coughed pushing her empty glass across the counter. Dolly filled it again.

'The Bricklayer's Arms but it's known locally as the Bricky.'

'Thank you, Aggie. That deserves another drink.'

Aggie grinned, showing pale gums, and after serving her, Dolly went to the kitchen and called Danny Whitehouse up from where he was helping in the cellar.

'Would you do me a favour and fetch Jack from the Crown and also whistle for a cab, please?'

'Will do. Back in a mo.'

Five minutes passed but in no time Jack and Dolly boarded the waiting cab. Giving the address, Dolly then updated Jack about where they were going and why.

On arrival, Dolly saw with pleasure that Aggie was right – the building was huge. She stayed outside in the cab whilst Jack went to speak with the landlord. Then the cab door opened and a large man with a deep voice spoke. 'You wanted to see me?'

Dolly noted he was an older man, his hair beginning to turn grey. Blue eyes stared back at her as she nodded.

'I believe you are selling up?'

'I am, but how did you know?'

'I make it my business to know. I'm Dolly Perkins and I co-own Daydream Palace.'

'And you're looking to buy my pub.'

'I could be interested if the price is right. Of course, Jack and I would need to see the whole place before I decide if it's right for me.'

'Come along in, then. I'm Lucas Freeman but everybody calls me Luke.'

As he helped her from the cab, she could see that the man noticed her stick, but he remained tight-lipped.

Once inside, Jack and Dolly were given a guided tour. The bar was a massive room with only a few curious customers. Next they were shown a kitchen, scullery, dining room, and then stairs down to an impossibly big cellar, and stairs leading to bedrooms and private quarters.

'There's a strange smell in this bedroom,' Dolly mentioned as they stood in one of the doorways. The room was piled high with spare furniture so it was impossible to go in further.

'Ar, it's the sewage I think. I've informed the council, but you know how slow they are to get anything done. The night soil men come regular as clockwork, though, and I've had a word with them an' all. It'll be sorted out soon, I'm sure.'

Once they had seen everything, Dolly had to admit that she was impressed. Sitting now in Lucas's own living room, Dolly broached the subject of the sale price.

'That's how much I paid for it and that's how much I want for it,' Lucas said, passing two documents to Dolly to peruse. Handing them to Jack to read, Dolly nodded.

'You paid two thousand pounds, which seems a low price if I may say, and you are asking three thousand. I wonder what Mr Sharpe, my solicitor, would have to say about that.' Dolly watched the landlord squirm under her scrutiny.

'It's a going concern, now! It was dead on its feet when I took it over.'

'A few elderly gentlemen in the bar does not, in my opinion, constitute a going concern. I'm interested, but not at that price.' Dolly pointed at the documents in Jack's hand.

Wanting rid of the property, Freeman considered his options. He could stand his ground and watch this woman leave his premises without having come to an agreement, or he could reduce the asking price and ensure a buyer.

'I'll come down by two hundred and fifty pounds,' he said at last.

'Five hundred,' Dolly argued.

With a loud sigh, Freeman nodded.

Looking at Jack, who returned the papers to their rightful owner, she said, 'I'd like your opinion.'

'I think it would be ideal.'

'Would you be happy here, do you think?'

'I reckon so.'

'Do we have an accord, then, Dolly Perkins?' Lucas asked.

'We do, Lucas Freeman.'

Shaking hands, Dolly added, 'I will return in a couple of days with my solicitor and the necessary documents to be signed. Once that's done, I will instruct the bank to make payment. All that will be left to do then will be for you to move out and Jack to move in.'

'Let's celebrate! Tea everyone?' Lucas laughed.

Calling into the solicitor's office on the way home, Dolly and Jack enthused about their proposal to buy the Bricky and requested the man draw up the paperwork.

Mr Sharpe listened attentively then said, 'I will, of course, but I'd like to ensure you are not paying over the odds.'

'I told Lucas Freeman you would do due diligence,' Dolly replied.

'Then leave it with me. I will accompany you there the day after tomorrow and we'll take a good look around.'

Giving her thanks, Dolly and Jack returned to the Crown. Dolly paid the cabbie and they went indoors to the kitchen to share their news.

'Dolly's going to buy the Bricky!' Jack burst out, unable to hold his excitement in check.

'Bloody hell, that was quick!' Nellie said.

'I haven't got it yet. Mr Sharpe is accompanying us when we go again to make sure it's a sound investment.'

'Oh, bab! I'm that pleased for you!' Nancy said, giving the girl a hug.

'Thanks, Nancy, let's hope it all goes through without a hitch.'

'How about you, Jack? I bet you're excited,' Nellie asked.

'It'll be great, Mum!'

Nellie's eyes brimmed with tears. 'I'll miss you something rotten, though,' she mumbled.

Folding her in his arms Jack said, 'You taught me well, Mum, now it's time to show you what I've learned.'

Nancy blubbered into the corner of her apron and Dolly felt a lump in her throat.

'I must get back to work, I'll be needing the money more than ever now.'

Back at the Palace, Dolly informed her staff of her possible new acquisition, but asked them not to breathe a word until the sale was finalised.

'I don't want anyone to pip me to the post,' she explained, 'so let's work hard and see how it goes.'

Two days later, Mr Sharpe arrived almost at the same time as Jack and all three climbed into the cab and set off.

Jack was very excited, explaining he'd barely slept for thinking of this new adventure.

Dolly had worried about whether her finances could stand the expense, not only of buying the property, but also the renovations it would need.

Mr Sharpe assured her all would be well with the bank and a new mortgage facility. 'They're not likely to turn you down, my dear, after all, you have almost paid off your existing loan.'

Once they had arrived at the pub, they were welcomed by Lucas Freeman and given another tour, the same explanation given for the foul smell to Mr Sharpe who commented on it too. Once in the living room, the landlord said sheepishly. 'Now then, I'm sorry to tell you that I've had another offer for the place.'

Dolly was dumbstruck for a moment then asked, 'From whom?'

'I don't rightly feel I should say.'

'Lucas, we had an agreement!'

'I know, lass, but I was offered more than the asking price.'

'We shook hands! It was a gentleman's agreement!' Dolly was becoming distressed and was close to tears.

'Forgive me for saying, but – you're a woman.'

Anger at his flippancy replaced her disappointment and Dolly rallied herself. Suddenly a thought struck her. 'Lucas, who offered you more?'

'I...' the landlord began.

'Were you coerced into accepting the offer?'

Lucas lowered his head clearly feeling wretched.

'Ezra Moreton?' Dolly asked and Lucas nodded. 'I knew it!'

'Did you sign anything, Mr Freeman?' Mr Sharpe asked.

'No, but...'

'Then nothing is binding. You are not obliged to accept Mr Moreton's proposal.'

'If I don't he's likely to burn the place down!'

'Your insurance would cover that,' Mr Sharpe informed him. Seeing the man shake his head the solicitor went on, 'You have no insurance?'

'No.'

Dolly and Jack exchanged a worried glance.

'I'm in fear of my life!' Lucas said.

'But you will be again from me if you sell to Moreton!' Jack raged. Mr Sharpe interrupted him with a calm voice.

'Now then, I may have a solution, but it would mean keeping our lips tightly sealed.'

'What's that then?' Dolly asked.

'Well, Mr Freeman can sign these papers as can you and then

they will be witnessed by Jack and myself. Then we go directly to the bank and explain the situation. You will have to request they pay Mr Freeman as soon as possible. In the meantime, you, Mr Freeman, will discreetly pack your belongings for a quick getaway.'

'It's risky,' Jack said. 'Where will you go, Lucas?'

'My sister married a chap from the Americas and I had planned to go to live over there.'

'Then I suggest you book your passage on the next available ship. This all needs timing to perfection.'

'The thing is, Mr Moreton offered me more, so it would make sense to take his offer. Plus, that way he won't do for me!'

'Mr Freeman!' Dolly yelled.

Again, Mr Sharpe's calm voice put in, 'I'm sure Miss Perkins could make it worth your while to accept her offer with – let's say, a little financial remuneration.'

'I can do that. When was Ezra Moreton coming back to see you?' Dolly asked.

'Not till next week,' Lucas answered.

'Then we have time, but it will be tight,' Mr Sharpe said.

'I ain't sure. If Moreton finds out what's happening then the only place I'll be going is face down in the cut!'

'The canal will not be your final resting place, Mr Freeman, believe me. Now you have to decide who will take over your public house.'

Lucas looked at each in turn, his mind obviously wrestling with the decision of whether it was worth taking the gamble. He didn't want Moreton to be the new owner of his beloved pub, but the man's reputation preceded him. True or not, Lucas was afraid. He needed to be certain he could be aboard a ship and sailing before Moreton got wind of what he would see as treachery.

'I'll sign, but I need more money! I'll settle for the asking price of three thousand to get it over and done with quickly, and God help me if I ain't on my way to my sister's afore Moreton comes calling again!'

The papers were signed by Lucas and Dolly and witnessed by Jack and Mr Sharpe.

'What if the bank won't give her that mortgage?' Lucas asked.

'Then we return here immediately and you tear these up,' Mr Sharpe said, waving the documents in the air.

13

At the bank, Mr Sharpe, Dolly and Jack were shown into the manager's office. Mr Sharpe, in his wisdom, had had the foresight to book an appointment in the hope the visit to the pub had been fruitful.

'Nice to see you again, Miss Perkins,' Jonah Blessep said.

'Likewise, Mr Blessep. This is Jack Larkin and Mr Sharpe.'

'Mr Larkin. I haven't seen you in a while, Andrew,' Blessep said to the solicitor.

'Jonah and I go way back, Dolly, in case you were wondering,' Sharpe explained.

What she was actually thinking was that in all the years she'd known him she had only now discovered her trusted adviser's Christian name.

'What can I do for you today?' Blessep asked, his grey eyes twinkling beneath white bushy eyebrows. His silver hair shone in the light from the window as he gestured to them to take a seat in his huge office.

Dolly outlined her request and after retrieving her file from a cabinet, the man looked over the figures.

Andrew Sharpe explained the need for expediency and why the transaction should be dealt with as quickly as possible.

'Ezra Moreton again!' Blessep snapped.

'I'm afraid so. That's why the landlord, Mr Lucas Freeman, wishes to have the matter done and dusted so he can head straight to his sister in America,' Sharpe said.

'At least he'll be safe over there,' Blessep said as he rang a little hand bell kept on his desk. 'Ah, Evelyn, would you be kind enough to bring me a set of mortgage papers, please? Thank you.'

Two hours later, they left the bank and Dolly had a new mortgage agreement and a banker's draft for Lucas Freeman. The cabbie took them back to the Bricky where Lucas was pacing the living room floor.

'Well?' he asked eagerly as they entered via the back door.

'This is for you,' Dolly said as she handed over the banker's draft, 'and now I need the deeds to the property.'

Lucas stared at the paper and grinned. Rushing to a dresser against one wall, he pulled open the drawer and lifted out a sheaf of papers before handing them to Dolly.

Shaking her hand, he said, 'Pleasure doing business with you. I've a passage booked on a ship bound for America tomorrow morning. I ain't waiting around for Ezra bloody Moreton to slit my gizzard!'

'Very wise, if I may say so,' Andrew Sharpe put in.

'The place is yours now, Dolly, look after her for me.'

'I will, Lucas, and if you should return to this country, then do come and visit us. Good luck for your new life.'

'And to you an' all cos you'll need it when Ezra finds out what's occurred here today!'

They left the man packing his belongings and returned to the Palace, dropping Mr Sharpe at his own workplace on the way.

As they celebrated later with tea and cake, Dolly and Jack discussed what should be done with the new premises.

'I can't believe how swiftly the business was concluded!' Dolly said, looking over the deeds.

'It's my guess Mr Blessep dislikes Ezra as much as everybody else does,' Jack replied, 'so he decided to help you rather than see the Bricky in Moreton's hands.'

'If Lucas is away on his voyage tomorrow, then you'll need to go over and sort out staff. Let them know what's occurring if Lucas hasn't already.'

Jack nodded. 'It's really happening! I can't believe it. Thanks to you I'm going to be a boss!'

'And I'm sure you'll do a grand job. Now, if you two don't mind I've meals to cook so clear off out of my kitchen!' Sadie blustered.

Dolly and Jack left to tell Nellie Larkin the good news.

'She sounds just like Nancy,' Jack said referring to Sadie the cook as they crossed the road.

'I know and it's wonderful!' Dolly grinned. 'It's almost like being back at the Crown.'

'Mum! We're home!' Jack called as they entered.

'How did you get on?' Nellie asked.

Dolly waved the deeds, saying, 'All signed, sealed and delivered!'

'Well done!'

'Ooh, congratulations,' Nancy said. 'I'm so proud of you both.'

'Me an' all, Nance,' Nellie added.

Dolly told the women the whole tale as tea was served, until eventually Nancy asked, 'What you gonna call it?'

'Oh, that takes me back. I remember you asking the same thing about Daydream Palace,' Dolly said with fondness.

'Nance all over that is, lace curtains up afore the floorboards are down,' Nellie said.

'There you go again, I was only asking. She'll need a name, won't she?'

'Maybe we could all give it some thought, but there's work to be done refurbishing the place first,' Dolly said, trying to prevent all-out war.

'I think I'll move in tomorrow, Mum, after Lucas Freeman has departed, that way I can be right there to help work get started,' Jack said excitedly.

'So soon? I thought...' Nellie's eyes glistened.

'We can't leave the place unattended in case it's vandalised.'

'I know, son, it's just all happened so quickly!'

'Who will you get to do the work?' Nancy asked.

Dolly looked at Jack. 'Eli Hodges?'

'Why not? He did an amazing job on the Palace and I'm sure he'll be glad of the work,' Jack replied.

'That's your first task as manager, then, go and ask Mr Hodges to call at his earliest convenience.'

'Thanks, Dolly,' Jack said before striding from the kitchen.

'I'm worried what Moreton will do when he finds out who the new owner of the Bricky is,' Nellie said once her son had gone.

'I am, too. That's why I'm going to put some of my new workers in there to help Jack until such time as he hires his own staff. However, he'll need a cook and maid straight away. None of my workers are qualified to help with that.'

'The Servants' Registry?' Nancy asked.

'That will be his next step – interviewing applicants,' Dolly said with a grin as Nellie rolled her eyes. Nellie would rather nothing ever changed...

* * *

Lucas Freeman had only two barmen because although the Bricky was a huge place, it was not a busy one. He told his staff that he had sold up and was moving to America, but he didn't say who had bought the building. Instantly the rumours started that Ezra Moreton was to be the new owner, and both barmen dreaded the thought of working for *him*.

With a bag packed full of his meagre belongings, Lucas left the Bricky for the last time – in the middle of the night. He was taking no chances at being seen and the knowledge finding its way back to bully-boy Moreton.

He'd already ordered a cab to wait for him at the corner of Great Barr Street, which would take him to the railway station to board the milk train to Liverpool. Only when the cab was rolling did Lucas feel a little safer, but he knew he could not fully relax until he was in his berth on the ship, way out on the ocean. Moreton had eyes and ears everywhere.

* * *

The following morning, whilst her customers were drinking their breakfasts, Dolly and Jack took a cab to the Bricky. There they were to meet Eli Hodges, the builder who, along with his sons, had transformed an old pub into the Daydream Palace.

Nellie and Nancy said they would be along later with Jack's things to help him to settle in. Dolly had also arranged for two of her best men from the breadline to help Jack out for the time being, which they were happy to do.

Lucas's barmen, who lived at the property, let them in when they arrived and, over tea, Jack reassured them their jobs were safe. They were elated to know they wouldn't be working for Ezra Moreton after all, even when Jack explained what the plans were and how they would be destined to live in dust and upheaval for the time it took to renovate the old place.

'Who supplies your beer?' Jack asked.

'Moreton's Brewery,' one answered, and Jack exchanged a glance with Dolly.

'Well, no more orders are to be placed. Once we're up and running the gin will come from Burton's,' Jack said.

'What do we do with what we have?'

'Sell it cheap. Get rid of it before Mr Hodges gets going,' Jack answered.

'Did I hear my name mentioned?' the builder asked, strolling into the bar where the meeting was taking place.

'You did, thanks for coming.'

Dolly sat at a table at the back of the bar, determined to let Jack as the new manager make his mark. Everyone needed to understand he was their gaffer now and show him the respect the post deserved.

'Tea?' Joey, the barman, asked.

'Porter would be better,' Eli said with a grin. 'Now, Jack, what do you have in mind for this bloody great monstrosity?'

'Much the same as Daydream Palace, we thought, didn't we Dolly?'

Dolly nodded.

'Lamps, mirrors, chandeliers, and big windows,' Jack went on.

'Right, then.' Swigging the beer the barman had given him, Eli wandered around, pencil tucked behind his ear and paper tucked in his pocket.

Nancy and Nellie arrived, puffing and blowing, with bags of Jack's clothes.

'I'll show you upstairs,' Joey said as he and the other barman Frank took the bags. They showed the women the room which

Lucas had vacated and would now become Jack's. It was clean and tidy and Nancy enthusiastically expressed her approval.

'He'll be able to settle in nicely,' she said, pleased to be able to help Jack get organised.

Whilst the women poked around upstairs, Joey and Frank returned to the bar.

All morning, people moved from room to room, upstairs and down, to the cellar and back to the bar.

Eli Hodges left to assess the numbers for the cost of the work to be undertaken and as the afternoon wore on, everyone met in the bar for more tea and discussion.

'There's a hell of a stink in that one bedroom,' Nellie said.

'There is, isn't there? Lucas said he'd reported it to the council, he seemed to think it might be the sewer,' Dolly replied.

'Well, it wants sorting – and soon!' Nellie said with a grimace.

The front door burst open and the figure of a tall man was silhouetted against the daylight.

14

'Might I ask what the bloody hell is going on here?' the man's voice boomed out as he strode purposefully into the room.

'Hello Ezra,' Nellie said.

'Nellie,' Moreton replied waspishly as he cast a glance at each face in turn.

'What can we do for you, Mr Moreton?' Dolly asked.

'You can tell me what's occurring. Where's Lucas?'

'Mr Freeman has gone to live with his sister,' Dolly informed him, although she made no mention of where that was.

'And where does this sister live – exactly?'

'I'm afraid I have no idea,' Dolly answered truthfully.

Ezra frowned as he digested the information. His hazel eyes scanned the little gathering again and Dolly noted the grey creeping into his dark hair. Impeccably dressed as always, he tapped his silver-topped cane on the floor.

'He's up and gone – just like that?'

'Yes,' Dolly said.

'Did he leave any documents for me?'

'Not that I know of.'

The conversation between Dolly and Moreton was being watched with interest by the others, who were eagerly awaiting the outcome.

'Ah well, he should have left me the deeds to this place, so I'll need to find those immediately.'

'Why would he have left you those?'

'We had a deal. He was selling this,' Ezra swung his stick around the room with a grimace on his face, 'to me.'

'I'm afraid I can't shed any light on that, Mr Moreton. Mr Freeman didn't mention it.'

'I must confess I'm at a loss as to why you are all here.'

'Yes, I was thinking the same thing about you,' Dolly said bravely.

'I'm here because I own it,' Ezra snapped.

'I'm afraid that's incorrect. You don't own it, Mr Moreton, because I do,' Dolly replied coolly.

The look of shock on Moreton's face was priceless and Nellie and Nancy could barely contain their laughter.

'That's not possible!'

'It is. The business was conducted yesterday.'

'How? I mean, where did you get the money to...?'

'Well, that's none of your business, Mr Moreton. All you need to know is that this building belongs to me now. Jack is the manager and these men are his staff.'

The two big bodyguards who had followed Ezra indoors tittered nervously, and their employer shot them a look which could fry bacon.

'What do you want with a pub?'

'Again, sir – that is my business.'

For a moment, the only sound was Nellie tapping her foot on the flagstone floor.

'I see. It's to become yet another gin palace, I presume!'

Dolly shrugged.

Moreton took a step forward and pointed the top of his cane at her. In the same instant, the men surrounded her in a protective huddle.

Ezra looked at the men and lowered his cane.

'You have not heard the last of this!'

'I guessed as much, which is why I have the constabulary on my side.'

'What?'

'The police will be keeping a keen eye out for any, let's say, wrongdoings.'

Dragging a deep breath in through flared nostrils, Moreton turned on his heel and stamped away, his two guards following closely behind, a grin splitting their faces.

'That ain't strictly true, about the coppers I mean,' Nellie said.

'Ah, but Ezra doesn't know that does he?' Dolly replied with a smirk.

Spontaneous applause broke out as Dolly was congratulated on how she had dealt with the precarious situation, but out in the street Ezra Moreton fumed.

Climbing into the waiting cab, full of fury, Ezra snapped at the two men who had accompanied him, 'You two can walk!' He slammed the cab door and banged his stick on the floor twice.

The bodyguards looked at the cabbie who shrugged and flicked the reins, then they turned their gaze to each other.

'That's bloody nice ain't it?' one said.

'Miserable old sod!' the other answered.

Then, with a sigh, they began to walk back to the brewery on Nova Scotia Street.

* * *

'Well, you certainly told him!' Nellie said as the applause melted away.

'I learned it all from you, Nellie,' Dolly replied. 'Jack, don't you think it's time to ask your barmen to open up? Then I suggest you visit the Servants' Registry to hire a cook and maid.'

'Oh, blimey!' Jack said to everyone's amusement. Then he confidently began issuing orders to his staff. 'Throw open the windows for some fresh air. Sweep the floor, wash the glasses...'

Nellie and Nancy said farewell before returning to the Crown, and Dolly pulled Jack aside. 'We'll work out the wages tomorrow, shall we?'

'Yes, I've enough to be thinking about right now. Will you help me with, you know, a cook and maid?'

'Of course. Ask them to send the applicants here tomorrow and we'll interview them together.'

'Thanks. I'd better get on, then.' With that he raced away, leaving Dolly to supervise the cleaning.

Looking around her, she smiled. This was hers now and it was all down to her mother. Dolly's mind slipped back to when she had inherited a necklace which she had sold to help Nellie pay off what was owed to Ezra Moreton. Then, between them they had a mortgage and the rest of the money from the sale to buy what had become the Daydream Palace. Now she had a second property, and finally this one was all hers.

'Place is all ready, miss,' Joey said, breaking Dolly's reverie.

'Thank you, and the name is Dolly.'

The barman knuckled his forehead and went to open the doors wide.

Dolly went to the kitchen to wait for Jack and began nosing into cupboards to ensure there was everything a cook might need. Satisfied with what she found, she limped up the stairs to take another look at the rooms where the cook and maid would be living once they'd been appointed.

She moved to the window of one room which looked out onto the yard below, and she was horrified to see a rat scuttle away. With a shudder, she made her way back downstairs.

'Joey, do you know where the rat-catcher lives?'

'Yes, Dolly.'

'Would you be kind enough to have him call round straight away, because I've just seen one in the yard.'

'Will do. Some of 'em are as big as 'osses,' he quipped.

'I suggest you get hold of a couple of cats – good ones – or terriers, they would do the trick.'

'I'll put it to Jack, shall I?'

'Of course, but in the meantime – the rat-catcher, please.'

It was one of the men who was a barman for Freeman, called Frank, who ran the errand and swiftly brought back a stick-thin man dressed all in black. He wore a tailcoat, breeches and a top hat, which he lifted in greeting.

'I hear as you've a problem with rats,' he said with a raspy voice.

'That's correct. Out in the yard,' Dolly answered, barely able to suppress a shiver.

'I'll do the necessary, then,' the man said with a grim smile. 'Powder, that'll do the trick. Poison in powder form so they haves to eat it there and then. Can't carry it back to the nest, see? Then the thirst gets 'em and they have to find water. So, any of 'em lurking about will move away, do anything for a drink by then they will.'

This time Dolly could not hide the shudder and the rat-catcher laughed before going about his grisly business outside.

'Joey, let everyone know so they steer clear of whatever he's doing and wherever he's doing it.'

'Righto, Dolly.'

Another shiver took her and Dolly moved to the fireplace. A nice fire would take the chill off and make the room feel more homely and inviting. It wasn't long before roaring flames leapt up the chimney and she began to relax and imagine the look of the place once it was finished.

A shout and a satisfied holler, followed by a clang, had her on her feet, and in a quick hobble she made her way to the scullery. There she was faced with the thin man in black holding up a dead rat by its tail, a gratified smile on his face.

15

The following day saw a flurry of activity, starting with a visit from Ezra's draymen arriving to collect the empty barrels.

Jack, having spent his first night in his new home, was woken early by the rattle of the cart and clip-clop of horses' hooves.

'Is this usual?' he asked Joey, who stood rubbing the sleep from his eyes.

'No, boss, they normally only come to deliver and collect the empties at the same time.'

'I thought so. Ezra's making sure all his property is returned. Get the kettle on, I'm parched.'

Hot tea was soon made and Jack, cup in hand, watched the cart roll away.

After a breakfast of bacon and eggs floating in a sea of grease cooked by Frank, they set to cleaning the bar. The doors were propped open in readiness for any customers who might grace the premises with their presence that day.

Jack was out the front, gazing at the façade, when Dolly arrived by cab. 'I was just trying to imagine what it will look like after the Hodges have finished with it,' Jack said to his friend by way of greeting.

'It will be grand, I'm sure. Any customers yet?'

'No. Not a single one.' Jack shook his head.

'That will change once it's transformed, I'm sure of it.'

'I bloody hope so!' Jack replied with a laugh.

Going indoors, Dolly asked, 'How was your first night away from home?'

'Strange. It took me forever to get to sleep, but once I did, I slept like the dead. Ezra's cart woke me early, though; they came for the empty barrels.'

'He's just letting us know he's not best pleased that we pulled a flanker and beat him to the sale.'

'Yes, I thought that too.'

'It's cold in here,' Dolly said with a shiver.

'I'll get a fire going. Everybody else is busy in the cellar and the yard.'

It didn't take long for the hearth to become a place of heat and brightly dancing flames, and Dolly sat close to it to warm her cold hands.

'I'm looking for Jack Larkin.' A woman's voice sailed across the room.

'That's me.'

'I've been sent by the Registry. I'm a cook. I'll need to see the kitchen and my bedroom before I decide whether to accept the post.'

'You ain't been offered it yet!' Jack retorted with a snort.

'You can please yourself. Do you need a cook or not?'

'Yes, but the more pressing question is – do you need a job or not?'

'Don't play games with me, young man!'

'I'm not. I need a cook who can feed us men well, who can live with the mess while alterations are underway and who won't give me any grief. Now, how desperately do you need this job or do I wait for the next person to apply?'

Dolly watched with a smile on her face, amazed at the difference in Jack's confidence in such a short time. In just a couple of days he had shown his mettle, now he was no longer living with his mum, and he was already acting like a boss. Dolly had always known it was within him and he had simply needed the opportunity for his talents to shine out.

'I'm here, ain't I? Don't that tell you as I'm in need?' the woman said curtly.

'I don't know how you think you'll get a job with an attitude like that!'

'I will because you need me!'

Jack sighed and glanced at Dolly who shrugged and smiled. Turning back to the woman, who wore a self-satisfied smile, he said, 'Let's start again, shall we? What's your name?'

'Bess Knight.'

'Tell me about yourself, Bess,' Jack said, having bitten back his surging frustration.

'I'm here, I need the job and the room.'

'Where do you live now?'

'Across town.'

Jack's sigh was loud enough to reach Dolly, who was listening from the fireside.

'Jack, maybe Bess would appreciate a cup of tea in the kitchen? I'd be happy to help out,' Dolly said.

'Good idea,' he replied, leading the way.

'Who's that? I hope it ain't the maid. I can't have a hoity-toity wench working under me.'

'That lady is Dolly Perkins, and she is the owner of this establishment,' Jack enlightened her.

'Oh, right. This ain't a bad kitchen, nice and big, but I'd have to change it around a bit.'

'All good chefs arrange their surroundings to suit themselves and we would expect no less from you,' Dolly said with a smile.

Bess plumped up her ample chest and directed her next words to Jack. '*That* is how to treat a person who you need on your staff!'

'Dolly, I'll leave you to it. I'm going to check on the rat problem,' Jack said, looking to frighten the woman now sitting at the table.

'Rats don't scare me,' Bess said with a grin.

No, but I'd guess you scare them! Jack marched away with steam coming out of his ears.

'Jack is my new manager and he's just settling in, but he is excellent at his job,' Dolly explained.

'A bit young, ain't he?'

Dolly sighed. Here was another woman who spoke her mind. What was it with cooks? She could see Sadie and Bess getting on famously.

'We all have to start where and when we can, don't you agree?'

'I suppose so.'

Dolly continued to put Bess at her ease, informing her of the changes they were making, and saying she needed a reliable *chef* to feed the workers well.

Bess, in turn, related how she was lodging in a room which was cold and damp, how her savings were all but gone, and how she desperately needed to find live-in work.

'Can I ask what the wages are here?' Bess asked at last, much softer now.

'Same as my cook over at the Daydream Palace, twenty pounds a year.'

'Bloody hell, that's good!'

'I like to reward hard work and loyalty. Come with me and I'll show you your room,' Dolly said.

'You mean I've got the job?'

'Yes, welcome to your new family.'

Bess left soon after to collect her few paltry belongings and her seat at the table was taken up by a young girl called Gwen Calvert. Gwen had arrived to apply for the post of maid and Jack again deferred to Dolly, preferring instead to be in the cellar with the other men.

Dolly explained carefully and gently that the building would be transformed and that she was paying ten pounds a year wages, as she did with her own maid. 'It's a live-in position and our new cook Bess has gone to fetch her things.'

'Ten quid a year, blimey!'

'It's more than average because I only employ the best.'

'I'll work ever so hard if I'm given the chance,' Gwen said, her blue eyes glistening.

'What's your story, Gwen?'

'I live at home, but with fourteen brothers and sisters I think it's time to move out and lessen the stress of my folks trying to feed us all.'

'Goodness, that's a big family,' Dolly couldn't help but remark.

'Mum and Dad love each other – what else can I say?' Gwen grinned, seeing Dolly catch her meaning.

Dolly showed the girl to the room next to the one Bess had chosen and Gwen marvelled at the size. 'Will I be sharing?'

'No, Bess is next door and the men are at the other end of the landing. There's a lock so you can feel safe at night.'

'Thank you. I can't imagine having all this space to myself.'

'Fetch your things and get settled in then, and we'll all get acquainted later over lunch.'

After Gwen had left, Dolly began preparing food. She was sat peeling potatoes when she heard Bess's voice. 'Yoohoo! I'm back!'

'In the kitchen,' Dolly returned.

'Here, now, you shouldn't be doing that.'

'I thought I'd get started.'

'Ar, well, you make a brew and I'll do the spuds.'

Dolly obliged and then set to telling Bess about the new maid, Gwen.

'I got some sausages from the market on my way and a couple of cabbages. With a nice onion gravy – what do you say?'

'May I stay for lunch?' Dolly said, prompting Bess to laugh loudly.

Gwen returned a short while later loaded down with bags, and Bess helped her to take them to her room.

The two men Dolly had brought across to help were returned to the Palace, where there was plenty for them to do. Gwen arrived back in double-quick time and with no customers as yet, all sat around the kitchen table to get to know each other.

'Frank and Joey are the barmen, Jack is the manager, Bess is the cook and Gwen is the maid. Respect the women, gentlemen, and they will look after you well,' Dolly said to the gathered group.

Jack shot Bess a sour look, which she sent back tenfold.

'You must all get along because you're a family now. There can be no fallings-out – you have to watch each other's backs and work together.' Dolly had caught the black look between Jack and Bess and felt she could not allow it to fester. Their initial meeting had not gone well, but if these people were to gel then it must be understood that silly misunderstandings would not be tolerated. So she told them so.

It was mid-afternoon when Eli Hodges turned up with papers full of sketches and calculations of costs.

That was when Dolly wished she drank gin.

16

'It's a lot of work,' Eli said as he watched Dolly and Jack look over his sketches.

'It's a lot of money an' all!' Jack replied.

'Speculate to accumulate, ain't that what folks say?'

'It is, Mr Hodges, that it is,' Dolly answered.

'Eli, call me Eli. I'll leave all that with you and you can let me know what you think.'

'Before you go, Eli, would you be kind enough to come to one of the bedrooms with me? There's something I want your opinion on.'

Jack stared open-mouthed and Frank and Joey laughed and whistled. For a moment Dolly wondered what was going on, then Eli's words gave her an explanation.

'That's the best offer I've had in an age, lass!'

The penny dropped and Dolly flushed scarlet. 'No, no – I meant...'

'It's all right, gel, we're only having a little laugh at your expense.'

'Oh, I see,' Dolly said before she joined in the hilarity.

Eli and Jack followed her to a room right at the back of the building which was stacked with spare furniture.

'Can you smell that?' Dolly asked.

'I can. I did notice it before when I had a quick gander around the place,' Eli said as he moved further into the room, shifting chairs as he went.

'What is it, do you think?'

'Sewerage, maybe?'

Dolly grimaced. 'Is it somehow getting into the building?'

The thought of ordure seeping into the walls or beneath the floor was a major worry and if it was proved to be the case, then that would have to be where the work began.

Eli shook his head. 'No, the sewage is all pumped into the River Rea now, has been these past thirteen years.'

'Then what can be causing that dreadful smell? And more to the point, why has no one complained about it before?'

'Lucas said the night soil men come regularly,' Jack reminded her.

'They've no need to now,' Eli said, shaking his head.

'So, he lied to us!' Dolly exclaimed.

Her eyes followed Eli as he scrambled past the spare furniture and began sniffing the walls and floorboards.

'It's stronger this end of the room,' he said as he stood close to the window. 'Whatever it is, it needs fixing.'

'You'd best start there, Eli,' Dolly said, then she asked Jack, 'don't you think?'

'Yes. That needs putting right before we do anything else. We can't live with that stink, we'll be ill.'

'I agree. We'll need to shift this furniture out to give Eli room to work.'

'I'll get the lads on it right away,' Jack said.

'What about the bar?'

'I've shut the doors, we only had two blokes in yesterday so it ain't worth the effort,' Jack said in an authoritative manner.

'Right then, get your lads to clearing a space while I fetch my boys to give me a hand with this,' Eli wrinkled his nose and waved a hand before his face, 'pong!'

Jack nodded.

'Of course, it could be that summat has crawled in the space between the bricks and died there, a rat maybe,' Eli said as he trundled downstairs behind Dolly and Jack.

The barmen were given their new instructions and Frank asked, 'Where are we going to put all that stuff?'

'Shove it in another spare room for now until we decide what to do with it,' Jack answered.

As the men went to do Jack's bidding, Dolly asked, 'What do we do with all that beer in the cellar?'

'I don't know. I was thinking to ask you. I wonder if Ezra would take it back?'

'I wouldn't give him the satisfaction because he would only pay under the odds, if anything at all,' Dolly said.

'We'll have to get it moved to make way for the gin barrels.'

'That's a way off yet, but I agree. How much does it sell for?'

'Porter is five pence halfpenny a quart.'

'How about putting it at two pence a quart until it's all gone? Then Ezra can fetch his empties and the cellar can be cleaned out and whitewashed.'

'Good idea, at least it will get rid of it and we'll be earning even if it's only a bit.'

'I'll let Aggie know, that way the news will spread quickly,' Dolly said and they both smiled.

'Good plan. The sooner the better.'

'I'll leave you to it, then,' Dolly said. 'Let me know how Eli gets on.'

Dolly said her goodbyes and stepped out to find a cab. She waved her stick at a cabbie waiting for a fare and waited while he drew up.

On her way home, Dolly pondered the tricky issue of choosing a new name for the old building.

In the meantime, over in Nova Scotia Street, Ezra Moreton was pondering too. He had been informed that Hodges had been spotted at the Bricky, which could only mean one thing – Dolly Perkins intended to renovate the whole building. Where the hell was she getting her money from? Clearly she had bought the place on a mortgage facility from the bank but how had she obtained that? Was Daydream Palace pulling in that much money? He began to wonder if he was in the wrong business and whether he should turn one of his old pubs into a gin palace of his own. But he quickly shook his head. No, that would mean paying out to refurbish and he wasn't about to spend good money on what could turn out to be a pipedream. The risk was too great; he liked his money where it was – in his bank account.

Returning his thoughts to Dolly and her new venture, he wondered if she was overstepping herself. Could Birmingham stand three gin palaces? Were there enough gin drinkers to support them all?

Ezra sighed as he frowned. Only time would tell and if it turned out to be a failure, then he could step in with an offer to buy the place, at a vastly reduced price, of course.

He had set a couple of his men to watch the goings-on and report back to him. He wanted to keep a keen eye on the situation in order to be first in should Dolly's plans fall foul of her grand ideas.

A knock on his office door broke him free of his thoughts. 'Hodges has been booked to move in to start work on the Bricky, boss, and the roof's leaking again in the works,' a voice said.

Ezra nodded and dismissed the messenger with a flick of his fingers. He smiled as he snipped the end of his cigar with the cutter. He struck a match and puffed hard, sending clouds of blue-grey smoke into the air. Tossing the match into the cut-glass ashtray, he leaned back in his chair.

Good luck, Dolly Daydream, you're going to need it.

* * *

Over at the Palace, Dolly had told old Aggie about the porter going for two pennies a quart at the *Bricky*, but only while stocks lasted. A free tot of gin ensured the message would be spread rapidly.

'You got the place, then?' Aggie asked.

'Yes, thanks to you I did.' Dolly grinned as Aggie pushed an empty glass across the counter. Dolly filled it again, saying, 'You're coming too often with this.'

'I earned it though, d'aint I?'

'You did,' Dolly replied.

Just then there was the sound of a ruckus breaking out, and Dolly saw two of her floor-walkers move into the fray. The situation was calmed almost immediately as the culprits were forcibly ejected. She watched as a child with a tin jug was served, and as the girl wove her way through the crowd she dipped her finger in and sucked the liquid off, then shuddered at the sharp taste. A woman too drunk to stand unaided draped herself over a man standing next to her. Unable to hold himself and the woman upright they both crashed to the floor, howling with laughter.

Dolly smiled at the spectacle and shook her head at her floor-walkers, which told them to leave the drunkards where they were. They were causing no harm and would soon be back on their feet once their laughing had ceased.

The smile still on her face, Dolly retired to the kitchen, where Sadie and Alice were working hard.

'Something smells good,' Dolly remarked.

'Steak and kidney pudding,' Sadie replied.

'And rice pudding to follow,' Alice added.

'How's it going at the Bricky?' Sadie asked, providing tea for her employer.

'All good, thank you, but there's a horrid smell coming from one of the bedrooms. Eli Hodges is investigating it now.'

'It'll be the lavvies,' Alice said.

'And how would you know that?' Sadie asked.

''Cos my dad knew a night soil man who said the shit was always seeping where it shouldn't go.'

Dolly could barely contain her smile.

'I'm sure Mr Hodges will let us know as soon as he discovers what the problem is. It is, however, an added expense I hadn't planned for.'

'It's better sorted now, though,' the cook said sensibly.

'Definitely, 'cos shit that's set in will stink the place out forever,' Alice answered with a mischievous grin.

'I wasn't speaking to you!' Sadie barked.

'Well, excuse the hell out of me!' Alice returned just as harshly.

Dolly let go of the grin she was holding back. It was like being at the music hall watching these two, and it brought back memories of Nellie and Nancy doing the same thing. It brought her comfort as she watched the cook and maid bicker, it was like being home.

'Hellooo!' The call preceded the man as Wilton Burton stepped into the kitchen and Dolly felt her heart lurch.

'Back again? What brings you here this time?' Dolly asked happily.

'Good food,' he sniffed, 'and the best company,' he added with a bow.

'You should be on the stage,' Dolly said.

'Ar, sweeping it,' Sadie mumbled, and Alice burst out laughing. Dolly was relieved to see Wilton join in.

'I hear on the grapevine that you have invested in new premises.'

'Now, how would you know that – and so quickly?'

'I have a spy,' Wilton said, glancing around surreptitiously.

'Let me guess – Aggie!'

He nodded.

'I wondered where she was getting her money from,' Dolly said with a laugh, 'but you know you could save your coin and just ask me instead.'

Over tea and cake, Dolly related the whole tale of the purchase of the Bricky, including the news that Ezra Moreton wasn't best pleased.

'You really shouldn't mess with him, Dolly. He's the worst kind of person.'

'I know, I've had dealings with him before, which is how Nellie came to be ordering her gin from your father.' She explained how Ezra had threatened the local distillers should they decide to supply Nellie at the Crown Saloon. Nellie, not to be outdone, had sought out Burton's instead.

They had just finished lunch when a runner came from the Bricky with a message for Dolly to come back straight away. The urchin runners were situated all over the town and ran messages for pennies in order to buy food or second-hand clothes. It was a vast network of orphans and runaways who came together to form an extremely efficient service. No one seemed to know where they all lived, but if you wanted a runner you only had to whistle and one would arrive in a matter of moments.

The boy was dressed in rags and was barefoot. His hair was a matted mess and his face was filthy dirty, and when Dolly asked the boy what was so important, the street urchin said, 'I don't know, missus, but Jack said to move your arse!'

Giving the child a sixpence, Dolly saw his eyes light up before he turned and ran.

Grabbing her cane, Dolly wondered what the fates had in store for her now.

17

Wilton insisted on accompanying Dolly to the Bricky in case it was something he could help with, and they hailed a cab.

'I wonder what it is that has Jack sending for you so urgently?' he asked as the cab lurched its way through the busy streets.

'We'll find out soon enough,' Dolly replied, looking worried.

Any other time she would have enjoyed a carriage ride with Wilton Burton, but today she had other things on her mind. Whatever had happened had clearly made Jack feel he couldn't cope alone, hence the call for her to return immediately, and that couldn't mean anything good.

Dolly was pleased to see a crowd of people in the bar, the notice outside seeming to have worked. On a chalk board was scrawled: *Porter twopence a quart – till it's all gone!*

'Two pennies a quart! Dolly – Jack's giving it away!' Wilton remarked.

'I know, I told him to. I need the cellar emptied.'

Wilton blew out his cheeks and shrugged. Clearly Dolly had a plan but he hoped she knew what she was doing.

'Thank God you're here!' Frank said as Dolly approached

the bar.

'What's going on?' she asked, then looked around as the buzz of conversation halted. She saw men exchange looks which clearly meant, *what's a woman doing in a public house?*

'Jack's upstairs with Eli Hodges, you'd best get your ar... go up right away,' the barman said, looking agitated.

Dolly led the way, with Wilton right behind her.

'Whatever is that awful smell?' he asked as they neared the room where voices could be heard.

'Sewers, we think.'

Entering the bedroom, which was now devoid of the old furniture, Dolly gagged and held onto the door before she collapsed. There, at the back of the room, was a woman, clearly long dead, and hidden behind the wall. The corpse was somehow still standing in the small cavity and its eyes stared back accusingly. Teeth showed in the open mouth as if the woman was asking for help. Dolly turned and fled down the corridor to the stairs as fast as her gammy leg would allow with Wilton hot on her heels, closely followed by Jack. Sitting in the kitchen, Dolly's complexion turned from white to green and she just made it to the privy outside before her food and stomach parted company.

Given a glass of water when she returned to the kitchen, she asked urgently, 'Have you sent for the constabulary?'

'Not yet, I thought...' Jack mumbled.

'Do it, Jack, do it now!'

Joey was despatched to inform the police that during renovations, something very disturbing had been found and he was told a bobby would call round when he could spare the time.

'We need a detective for this,' Joey said to the duty sergeant.

'Oh, really? And why would that be?'

'Because the something we found is a body!'

'Right, lad, get back there and don't touch anything! We have a sleuth here and he'll want to inspect everything!' the sergeant said, all business now.

Joey raced back to inform Dolly and Jack that the police were on their way and to leave things as they were.

'No wonder it was smelling so bad!' Dolly said shakily as they all awaited the arrival of the police.

'But who could she be is the question I keep coming back to?' Eli asked.

'And how long has she been there?' Jack added.

Bess and Gwen had been eager to go up and have a look at what everyone was talking about but had been forbidden by Jack. 'You don't want to be looking at that.'

In short order, Inspector James Conroy arrived with a constable and was shown the grisly scene by Eli. And just a while later, Inspector Conroy positioned himself in the kitchen to ask his questions, having sent the constable to fetch the coroner.

Naturally, having the police there had caused a buzz of excitement amongst the patrons in the bar, and Jack was instructed to send them home and close up.

'Who is the owner of this establishment?' Conroy asked.

'I am, Dolly Perkins. I bought the place a couple of days ago from Lucas Freeman.'

'And where is Mr Freeman now?'

'I believe he went to live with his sister in America, but I don't have a forwarding address for him.'

'How very unfortunate.'

'Unfortunate? Why?'

'Well, I have a lot of questions for him.'

'Of course,' Dolly said quietly.

'Does anyone know how long Mr Freeman lived here?'

'Ten years or so.' Joey supplied the answer.

'And you are?'

'Joey Piggot, I'm the barman, along with Frank Davies.'

'How long have you worked here?'

'Twelve months. Me and Frank started at the same time.'

Inspector Conroy glanced at Frank who nodded. 'And in that time did you witness anything untoward?'

'Like what?' Frank asked.

'Like somebody hiding a corpse behind a wall!'

Frank shook his head frantically.

'Was Mr Freeman married?'

'Yes, but apparently she left him,' Joey said.

'When?'

'I don't know, it was before we came here.'

'Bugger!' Conroy muttered.

A banging on the front door heralded the arrival of the coroner and his assistant. There was a clatter as a gurney was dragged out of the official-looking carriage and was pulled inside when the door was opened by Jack. The constable had held on to the back of the coach during the journey to the Bricky, and now showed the way to the bedroom.

'It's unusual for a woman to own a pub, may I ask why you bought it?' Conroy asked Dolly pointedly.

'I intend to turn it into a gin palace,' Dolly replied.

'Not another!' Conroy said with a curl of his lip. 'We have two in the town already!'

'There are also a lot of inns, taverns and public houses. There's one on almost every corner,' Dolly said, her gander up now.

Conroy chose to ignore Dolly's remark and turning to Wilton asked, 'Mr Perkins?'

'Goodness me, no!' Wilton said. 'Wilton Burton, supplier of fine ales and spirits.'

'Hmm. And you?' Conroy jabbed a finger in Jack's direction.

'Jack Larkin, manager.'

Turning back to Dolly, Conroy asked, 'So where's your husband?'

'I don't have one.'

The inspector harrumphed and was about to speak again but was interrupted by the bustle heard on the stairs as the body was transported to the carriage.

'So, what can you tell me, doc?' Conroy called out.

The coroner followed the voice, arriving at the kitchen. 'Ah, there you are, James. We have the body of a woman in her middle years.'

'How can you be sure it's a woman?' Conroy asked.

'The dress rather gave it away.'

Everyone in the kitchen suppressed a smile at the quip despite the grim circumstances.

'Any idea what killed her?' Conroy pushed.

'Another person would be my guess.'

Titters sounded and Conroy huffed. 'Funny man today, ain't yer?'

'Just trying to make light of a grotesque situation, James. An autopsy will tell us more.' With that, he left to help lift the gurney back into the carriage.

'He can be a real smartarse at times,' Conroy said. 'I think that's all I need in the way of information for now, so I'll get back to the station.'

'What about our renovations, can we proceed?' Dolly asked.

'I don't see why not, unless you find another body, that is.' Conroy was the only one to chuckle this time so, clearing his throat, he added, 'Yes, although it's a crime scene, we have no hard evidence to point towards a perpetrator. Therefore, in my professional opinion, your work can continue.'

Jack saw Conroy and the constable out, and instantly the

chatter and gossip began over tea.

'I ain't so sure I want to live here now!' Gwen, the maid, wailed.

'Don't be so daft, girl! The dead can't hurt you, it's the living you have to watch out for!' the cook snapped.

'Quite right, Bess, but if you feel you need to leave, I understand,' Dolly said.

'But I need the wages.'

'Then button your lip!' Bess barked.

'Do you think Lucas Freeman murdered his wife and walled her up?' Jack asked.

'I don't know, maybe Inspector Conroy will discover more in the fullness of time,' Dolly answered. 'In the meantime, we need to get rid of that disgusting smell and get back to work.'

'Leave that to me,' Eli said, 'we'll clean it out and fix the wall so you'll never know anything happened.'

'Thank you. I expect it won't be long before the news gets out,' Dolly said.

'It might draw the punters in,' Jack said with a grim smile.

'Indeed. People are fascinated by anything macabre,' Dolly concurred.

'I'll get the doors open again then.'

'Wilton and I will return to the Palace, they'll want to know what the fuss was about.'

With all the commotion, it had not registered with Jack that Wilton had accompanied Dolly, and now he shot the other man a sour look. Why was he here again? Was he trying to court Dolly? Did Dolly know what he was up to?

Jack bid them farewell, but he was not happy Wilton Burton was visiting so often. Unable to do anything about it, he threw open the doors and was almost knocked off his feet in the crush as men rushed in to hear the gossip.

18

Nellie and Nancy were waiting in the kitchen of the Palace when Dolly and Wilton arrived back. They had heard about the coroner's wagon being called to the Bricky and wanted to know all about it.

It still amazed Dolly how quickly gossip travelled, but then again with people like Aggie around, it was no wonder.

'Bloody hell, Dolly! Of all the pubs in the town, you have to go and buy that one!' Nellie said.

'Was it his wife? The landlord's, I mean,' Nancy asked.

'It was a woman, but more than that we don't know,' Dolly answered.

'I must get on now, Dolly, but if there's anything I can help with, let me know,' Wilton said.

'Thank you,' Dolly answered with a beaming smile.

'He likes you,' Nancy said, once the young man had left.

'He's nice.' Dolly blushed to the roots of her hair.

'Never mind all that, tell us about this body and what the coppers think,' Nellie snapped.

'First of all, Jack was incredibly efficient. He dealt with everything like he was born to it.'

Nellie smiled proudly and listened intently as Dolly told her everything she knew. As quickly as Dolly had finished, the speculation started.

Had Lucas Freeman killed his wife and hidden her in the wall? Had he got someone else to do it for him? Was Ezra Moreton involved? Had Lucas paid Ezra or one of his goons to dispose of his wife? But why then would they hide her in the wall of the pub? Why not drop her in the canal with concrete boots on? If Lucas *had* committed the murder, why had he done it? What had he gained from it? How come Mrs Freeman had not been missed? Why had no one investigated the source of the foul smell before this?

The questions flew around the kitchen, but no answers were forthcoming.

'Will the coppers let you know anything more, do you think?' Nancy asked.

'I doubt it. I don't suppose there's any way of discovering the identity of the poor woman,' Dolly answered.

'No wonder Freeman was in a hurry to get gone!' Sadie said as she provided yet another pot of tea.

'Well, he's a free man now!' Nancy said and only joined in the laughter when her pun was explained to her.

'I doubt the police will ever get to the bottom of it all.'

'Why, Dolly?' Nellie asked.

'Because we have their permission to continue our renovations. It's a crime scene but Inspector Conroy just gave it a cursory glance over before asking his questions and sending for the coroner. It was like he couldn't be bothered.' After a moment's thought she added, 'If the crime was an old one, which it appears to be, and the perpetrator is thought to be no longer in the country, then maybe Conroy thought it not worth his time pursuing it.'

'Well, now it's all over you can get on with the changes and with luck you'll be up and running in no time,' Nellie said in her inimitable no-nonsense manner.

'Hopefully, yes.'

Nellie and Nancy bid them goodbye and returned to the Crown Saloon to pass on what they'd learned, and Dolly went to help in the bar.

'I hear they've found poor old Mrs Freeman,' Aggie shouted over the noise.

'News travels fast. A woman was found, yes, but as yet they don't know who she is – was,' Dolly said.

'It'll be her. They was always fighting, according to my spies.'

'You should work for the government, Aggie.'

'Not unless they pay me in gin!'

Dolly laughed before settling in for a hard day's toil.

* * *

As Dolly worked, over in his office in the brewery, Ezra Moreton was listening carefully to the news of the murder brought by one of his men.

Sloppy work, we could have made a better job of it, Ezra thought as he dismissed the messenger.

He knew the Bricky would draw in custom now. Folk would be curious and could boast of taking a drink in a place where a murder had been committed. He chastised himself for not being quicker off the mark in buying the pub, and cursed Dolly Perkins for outsmarting him.

He had thought another gin palace would not take off with there being two already, but the wheel of fate had turned again in

Dolly's favour. Her new gin house would become infamous now and he feared people would travel for miles to visit.

Was there anything he could do to thwart Dolly's endeavours? He could burn it down, but he dismissed that idea, there were staff living there now so the building was always occupied. He could get his men to trash the place, smash the windows and wreck the yard. The damage would be repaired but it would cost, and it would only slow things down rather than prevent the grand opening.

Face it, Moreton, you missed out on that one!

Snipping the end of his cigar, he threw the cutter onto his desk. Bloody women! First Nellie Larkin and now her protégé! Women are the bane of my life!

Ezra scowled as he puffed great plumes of grey smoke into the air, then swore as hot cigar ash fell onto his trousers. Brushing it off quickly, his mind blamed Dolly for that too, for if he hadn't been thinking of her it wouldn't have happened. Stabbing the cigar out in the ashtray, he left the office to tour the works. He was in a temper and needed to find someone to take it out on, even if it took the rest of the day!

*   *   *

The following morning saw Jack arrive at the Palace, feeling full of excitement. 'I've had an idea!'

'Sit and have a sup,' Sadie said.

'Yes ta, I will.'

'What's this idea?' Dolly asked.

'Well, at the moment Bess only has to cook a meal for Frank, Joey, me, Gwen and herself, so I thought we could turn one of the downstairs rooms into an eating place!'

'Jack, it will be a gin palace – eventually!' Dolly said aghast.

'I know, but news of the murder will bring in the hoi polloi! You know yourself how the toffs love anything like that. If we had a dining room they could eat in comfort and learn all about the gruesome find!'

'It's certainly a thought,' Sadie put in.

'It would be a lot of work for Bess and Gwen. You may have to hire a waitress or two and a cook's assistant.'

'Yes, maybe, but think of the money it will bring in.'

'Have you spoken to your staff about it?'

'Not yet. I thought to ask you first.'

Jack waited while Dolly thought over the suggestion. It was a good one, provided Bess could manage. The cook could draw up a menu and they could advertise in the local paper. It would mean more expense she hadn't planned on, but the more she considered it, the better she liked the idea.

'Sound it out with Bess, then, and see if she's willing to take on the work, and Jack – be nice. Tell her she would be head chef and she could interview an assistant herself.'

'Don't you trust me?'

'Yes, of course, but Bess will know what to look for in a good kitchen worker.'

'Right, yes, I didn't think of that. So, you agree then?'

'We can try it out and see how it goes. Firstly, however, we need to get the bar finished and open.'

Jack beamed his pleasure.

'Oh and Jack, don't forget you'll need tables and chairs, cutlery and crockery, table cloths and napkins, maybe candles for the tables too.'

'That's gonna cost,' he answered, and some of his initial excitement drained away.

Dolly nodded. 'That's why the bar has to come first. Once we show a profit, we can then invest in a dining room.'

'That makes sense.'

'Good, then we're agreed. How's the work going?'

'Well, the smell has gone and Eli's boys have re-plastered the wall. The new lights and windows are on order and Eli is busy ripping out the bar as we speak.'

'What about the customers?'

'All the porter went yesterday so we shut the doors so work could start.'

'Send a message to Ezra to collect his empty barrels.'

'Already done. I'll get back and make sure Eli doesn't find anything else we should worry about.'

Dolly smiled. 'Well done, Jack, I'm proud of you.'

With a grin from ear to ear, Jack skipped out of the back door.

'That lad idolises you,' Sadie said.

'We've been friends a long time,' Dolly replied.

'There's more than friendship on that boy's mind, you mark my words.'

Dolly frowned as she sipped her tea. Was her cook correct? Did Jack feel that way about her? If so, it could prove awkward for she knew her feelings lay in another direction, and explaining that to Jack would be a sensitive task.

19

Over the next weeks, Dolly visited the Bricky every day and was astonished at how quickly the work was progressing. The double doors had a fresh coat of paint and new gas lamps had been installed either side of them.

Indoors, all the furniture had been stacked in what would eventually become a dining room, and wall lamps and chandeliers had been installed.

The long counter had been left in situ, having been sanded and polished to a high shine, and behind it hung large mirrors. A robust shelf had been put in place to hold empty casks, displaying the names of the gins on offer.

The windows had been replaced by sheet glass and sparkled in the autumnal sun. The cellar was empty and was being whitewashed, the gas lamps throwing out pools of yellow light.

'We need a name plate for over the front doors now, Dolly,' Jack said one morning as Dolly looked around.

'Indeed, and I've been thinking about that.' Telling Jack her thoughts, she was delighted when he agreed to it enthusiastically.

'I'll get off to the sign-writer, then,' he said.

Crowds of people gathered every day to watch the work being done, and they peered through the windows to learn what they could, ready to pass on the information to others.

Neither Dolly nor Jack heard anything more from the police regarding the body found in the wall cavity, but they hadn't really expected to. With no witnesses to the gruesome crime and the remains unable to be identified, the poor woman was committed to a pauper's grave paid for under the Poor Law. The newspapers had regaled the whole town of the incident, but she was soon forgotten.

Wilton Burton had been a regular visitor over the weeks, much to Jack's annoyance. He watched dismayed as the relationship between Dolly and Wilton grew and he became more despondent as the days passed. He was happy enough overseeing the work at the Bricky but his mood swung dramatically on sight of Wilton. He couldn't shake the feeling Dolly was being taken for a ride, although he had no evidence to support it. The couple weren't exactly walking out together, but they appeared to be drawing closer each time he saw them together.

Jack had been pondering this very thing when a banging sounded on the front doors early one morning. The new sign had arrived and Jack stood outside in the chill wind watching it being erected.

The Bricky was no more. In its place stood the Emporium of Dreams. All that was needed now was the cellar to be stocked, and the gin barrels were due to be delivered that same day.

Dolly arrived mid-morning and was thrilled to see the name plate over the door.

'We will need to advertise the grand opening,' she said as she settled in the kitchen.

'I would think everybody in Birmingham knows about this place by now,' Jack returned.

'The murder will have ensured that,' Bess put in.

'It would be nice, though, if only to celebrate all the hard work it's taken to get to this point.'

'I suppose you're right. So, when do we throw open the doors for business?'

'It's Thursday today so how about Saturday? That gives us time to bottle up and make sure we have everything ready.'

'Saturday it is, then. I'll get a notice in the newspaper announcing it.'

'You've worked wonders with this place, Jack. You should be proud of all your work.'

'It was the Hodges who did all the hard work, I just supervised,' he replied. He felt gratified at the praise, nevertheless.

'What's happening with those empty rooms upstairs?' Jack asked.

'We could offer overnight accommodation,' Dolly suggested.

'That's a thought but they'll need tidying up a bit; new bedding and curtains and the like.'

'Gwen and I could do that,' Bess said.

'I'm not a bloody chamber maid!'

'Well, you're paid well for your work, bear in mind!' Bess snapped.

'You would be doing us a great favour, and if the idea takes off then a rise in wages would be due,' Dolly said with a warm smile.

'In that case...' Gwen began.

'Kids today!' Bess said with a sigh.

'The gin is here!' Joey called through from the bar before going to open the huge gates at the back of the building. The barrel-laden cart trundled into the yard and the unloading began. One after the other, large barrels were rolled carefully down the ramp into the cellar, where they were stacked neatly by Joey and Frank. Jack went to help and when he spotted Wilton, he gave only a nod of greeting as they passed each other in the doorway.

Bess and Gwen had spent days scalding bottles, which were standing in rows on shelves erected especially for that purpose in the cellar. Now the gin had arrived they could be filled and brought to the bar.

When Jack returned to the kitchen, Dolly and Wilton were laughing and Jack's hackles rose.

'Cellar's full,' he said churlishly. 'We're going to need more workers, Dolly. Floor-walkers, cellar-men and a couple on the door.'

Dolly nodded. 'You're the manager, Jack, so that would be up to you.'

'Fair enough.' Jack felt he was being pushed aside. Up until now he and Dolly had made the decisions together, but today she seemed more interested in laughing and joking with Wilton bloody Burton! Turning on his heel, Jack stamped out of the back door. He needed a distraction so he was going to find the nearest breadline to employ some workers.

'Jack seems upset about something,' Wilton proffered when Jack had left.

'I can't imagine what that could be,' Bess said sarcastically and received a sharp look from Dolly.

'He's just busy, there's a lot on his mind right now,' Dolly answered.

'There most certainly is,' Bess mumbled, ignoring another sour look sent her way. 'I'd best get the dinner started,' she added as she began to clear the table of the tea things.

'I think that's my cue to be leaving,' Wilton said with a smile.

Once he'd gone, Dolly rounded on Bess. 'That was a little insensitive, don't you think?'

'No, I don't think,' Bess answered.

'Pardon me?'

'No. You dismissing Jack like you did was insensitive. The poor lad is head over heels for you and you can't or won't see it!'

'Bess, it's not your place to...'

'You knew when I started here – I speak my mind. Now, if you can't cope with that – sack me!'

Dolly's mouth dropped open in shock at being spoken to in such a manner. 'I don't wish to sack you,' she managed after a moment.

'Right, then,' Bess cut across, 'just bear in mind what I've said. All of us can see what you can't. It's tearing Jack apart every time he sees you with that Wilton.'

'It's not really your business, Bess!' Dolly snapped, the anger rising in her.

'No, it's not; I'm merely trying to save you heartache, that's all. I'm endeavouring to warn you that if you go on like this, you will lose Jack – both as a manager and a friend!'

'Why would you say such a thing?'

'Because you're breaking the lad's heart!'

'I...' Dolly began.

Bess sat at the table and took Dolly's hands in hers while Gwen looked on, her ears cocked. 'Jack loves you to distraction, Dolly, and he can only watch you and Wilton for so long before he will have to move on. Can you imagine what it would do to him if you and Wilton were to wed?'

'There's been no mention...'

'Not yet, but what if there was? I don't think Jack would ever get over it.'

'Oh, Bess! I had no idea!' Dolly's eyes filled with tears.

'I know and that's why we're having this conversation now – before it's too late.'

'I must get back to the Palace,' Dolly said and in a rush she grabbed her cane and fled as fast as her bad leg would allow.

'What will happen now?' Gwen asked.

'Buggered if I know. I've done all I can, it's up to them now,' Bess said with a sad shake of her head.

20

While Bess was reading Dolly the riot act, Jack stamped down the street, taking his temper out on the cobbles. *If that Wilton Burton is still there when I get back, I'm gonna punch him on the nose!*

A group of men were standing chatting outside the vinegary brewery on Westley Street and Jack approached them.

'Anybody looking for work?' he asked.

'All of us,' one spoke up.

'I'm the manager of the new gin palace on Watery Lane – Jack Larkin's the name. I'm looking for two cellar-men, two floor-walkers, two doormen and a couple of barmen.'

The clamour almost knocked him over.

'Blokes with families to feed?' He watched six hands go up and he nodded. Seeing two big burly men he pointed to them, they would be excellent on the door. 'That's all I can employ for now,' he said as he saw the disappointed looks from those not chosen, 'but I'll bear you in mind if I need extra help.'

Turning to his eight new workers, he said, 'Eight o'clock sharp in the morning.'

'Yes, boss!' they chorused and Jack left them being congratulated by their pals.

Back at the Emporium, he was glad to see Wilton had left, but sorry Dolly had gone too.

'Joey and Frank are filling bottles in the cellar,' Bess informed him.

'Hmm.'

'Bull's balls and snake belly for dinner?'

'Hmm.'

Gwen burst out laughing, breaking Jack's thoughts.

'Why don't you tell her?' Bess asked.

'Tell who what?'

'Dolly – how you feel about her.'

'It's that obvious, is it? Well, the truth is, I ain't sure how she'd take it.'

'At least she would know.'

'Hmm.'

Gwen tittered as Bess shook her head.

'Did you find any workers?'

'Hmm.'

'Bloody hell! It's like pulling teeth!'

'What is?' Jack asked.

'Getting a word out of you!'

'Sorry. Yes, eight blokes coming in the morning.'

'Thank you. Eight more to feed then, Gwen,' Bess said with a grin.

'I hope they're young and handsome,' Gwen said dreamily.

'Oh, blimey! I'm glad I'm too old for all this nonsense,' Bess laughed.

Jack wandered away to the cellar without another word, and Bess sighed. 'Poor bugger,' she muttered.

Dolly had rushed away with Bess's words still ringing in her ears. Now she sat at the kitchen table, mulling over what had been said. She couldn't help how Jack was feeling about her any more than she could help how she felt about Wilton. Of course, she had no idea whether Wilton returned those feelings, but he certainly appeared happy in her company. There was also the fact that he visited more often than was strictly necessary, to her way of thinking, anyway.

Turning her mind from thoughts that would surely give her a headache, Dolly instead concentrated on the grand opening of the Emporium of Dreams.

Scratching out an advert on a slip of paper, she asked one of her staff to run it down to the newspaper office along with a handful of coins. All that was left to do now was wait for the time when the doors could be opened officially.

The following morning, after breakfast, Jack looked over the furniture which had been in the bar and was now stacked in the other room. Tables, chairs and stools, and all were in pretty good condition as far as he could see.

Calling Bess and Gwen, he asked, 'How would you turn this into a fashionable eating place?'

'Nice table linen for a start,' Gwen said.

'I agree, it would cover a multitude of sins. Good cutlery and glassware as well,' Bess added.

'It's dark and dingy in here, how can we remedy that?'

'Do as you've done in the bar, lots of lights and mirrors,' Bess suggested.

Jack nodded. 'Good idea! That would brighten it up a lot. We need to set out these tables and chairs to the best effect.'

'Why don't you have a word with Eli Hodges about décor and leave this lot to us?' Bess asked.

'It wouldn't hurt to see how much it would cost to get it done, I suppose.'

'Won't you have to ask Dolly first?' Gwen asked tentatively.

'No. Like she said, I'm the manager so I'll make the decisions.'

Gwen and Bess exchanged a glance as Jack walked from the room.

Enlisting the help of Joey and Frank, Bess got them organised shifting furniture and before long the room looked more like a nice place to eat.

At eight o'clock on the dot, the men hired from the breadline arrived and were given breakfast in the large kitchen. While they ate, Jack instructed them in their duties.

'The doors will open at nine in the mornings so you need to be here an hour earlier. We'll all eat together, then you take up your allotted tasks. Respect, gentlemen, to each other in this family and to our customers. You be nice until it's time to not be nice.'

A chuckle sounded and Jack went on. 'Any trouble-makers are to be escorted off the property – nicely. You treat Bess like you would your mum and Gwen like your sister and any problems you bring to me. Any questions?'

'Will we have to work a week in hand, boss?'

'No, you'll get your wages on Friday, same as Joey and Frank.'

'Any chance of a sub, boss? Only I have kids to feed.'

'For all of you?'

Nods affirmed it to be a good idea.

'Right. Two quid today, the rest on Friday, how does that sound?'

'Bostin'!' came the reply.

Jack left the room and returned not long after with the money which he handed out to each man. 'I'm trusting you, don't let me down.'

'We won't, will we fellas?' another said.

'God's honour, boss.'

'Right, I'll see you all in the morning. It's the grand opening so tidy yourselves up as best you can. Thank you, gentlemen.'

Jack watched them leave, each one thanking Bess and Gwen for their breakfasts. He prayed he'd done the right thing in giving out the money before they had even started work. He didn't think they would take his coin and run, but one could never be sure.

'I'm away to pester Eli Hodges if anyone should want me,' Jack said, grabbing his jacket.

'Dolly, you mean?' Bess asked.

'Tell her whatever you like!' Jack snapped and walked out.

'There'll be trouble there before long, you see if I ain't right,' the cook mumbled as she sent Gwen to the linen cupboard in search of tablecloths.

21

Saturday morning saw crowds of people waiting for the Emporium's doors to open. The newspaper had sent a reporter to write an article, and Ezra Moreton was sat in a cab watching the gathering customers. He wanted to see what had been done with the old place, and certainly from the outside it looked quite impressive, which caused him to scowl.

The church bell began to toll the hour and Dolly and Jack appeared, having walked from the back of the building.

'Welcome to the Emporium of Dreams!' Dolly called out.

So over dramatic! Ezra thought.

'Get your money ready and come inside to sample our new range of gins!' With that, Dolly and Jack flung open the double doors and were almost crushed in the rush.

Aggie was one of the first in and Dolly smiled. The old girl wasn't about to miss out on the grand opening.

Ezra alighted from his carriage and donned his top hat. Stepping inside, he used his silver-topped cane to move people out of his way. He glanced around and to his dismay he was impressed.

Gas lamps and chandeliers were lit bouncing the light against huge mirrors behind the counter, which then reflected back into the room. The walls had been whitewashed and the counter polished so you could see your face in it. The casks along the back wall had the names of the different gins burnt into the wood.

'Come to see how we've transformed the Bricky?' Dolly asked.

Ezra turned to face the girl who was standing behind him.

'Hmm. A little gaudy for my taste but I can see the necessity of such decoration. It is a gin palace, after all.'

'Indeed, and judging by this crowd, a popular one.'

'Ah, but this is the opening day. I wonder how busy it will be in – say – six months' time.'

'You'll have to stop by again then and see for yourself, you'd be most welcome,' Dolly said with a smile.

'Quite, but for now I have business to attend to. Good day, Dolly.'

'Good day to you too, Ezra.'

Climbing back into the cab, Ezra fumed. Dolly could well be on the way to making herself a fortune from that place, a fortune he'd missed out on.

As the cab rolled away, he wondered how long this gin craze would last. Men would always want ale after a hard day's work, but gin?

Daydream Palace had been doing a roaring trade these past seven years and the Crown Saloon a lot longer than that, but it would all come to a halt eventually, he was sure. Then Dolly Perkins would have two properties on her hands which were doing little or no trade. What would she do then? Would she sell up? Might he have the opportunity to buy from her at a vastly reduced rate?

The thought cheered him a little as the cab entered the open gates of the brewery. He smiled. All this belonged to him. He also had money coming from the public houses that were 'tied' to him. In return for his loaning them money to refurbish their buildings, they were only allowed to sell his beer.

Paying the cabbie, Ezra stood a while staring up at the huge building, the smell of hops pungent on the air. He was proud of what he'd achieved, and humming a little tune, he walked inside to his office.

Back at the Emporium, Jack watched Dolly chatting with customers, thinking bitterly that she was playing the lady bountiful. He could not have been more wrong. Dolly was in fact singing his praises, saying it was all down to the manager Jack Larkin that the place was open so quickly.

His mood darkened further when Wilton arrived to offer his congratulations, and Dolly took her visitor to the kitchen for tea.

The long counter accommodated three barmen easily, and they were all working flat out, and Jack and one of his new men went to the cellar to bring up more bottles to replenish the shelves.

Satisfied all was running smoothly, Jack then retired to the kitchen for his well-earned cuppa.

'Congratulations on your huge success, Jack!' Wilton said.

'Thanks,' Jack mumbled over the rim of his cup.

Dolly didn't appear to notice his black mood and continued to chat happily with Wilton for a while. Then, saying farewell, Wilton left them all to their work.

Dolly returned to the Palace and Jack heaved a sigh of relief. He was finding it harder and harder to see his best friend in the company of another man.

Called to the bar, Jack helped out serving the gin-starved public. The time fled past and he was surprised when Bess shouted him for his lunch. After a quick bite, Jack went back to the bar, knowing it was going to be a long time yet before he saw his bed.

An older man was entertaining the customers with a tune on a battered trumpet and then the singing began. Drunken women hitched up their skirt hems and danced as songs, one after another, filled the air. There was laughter and gin-induced happiness as more of the throat-searing spirit was bought and consumed.

By midnight, when the last customer was persuaded to go home with a smile and a shove, the staff were almost dead on their feet. Before saying goodnight, Jack said, 'Thank you one and all, you've done a marvellous job. I'm thinking, however, that we need more workers so we can use a rota system, otherwise we'll be burned out before the week's end.'

His staff muttered their agreement before they left to trudge home on very tired feet.

Bess and Gwen had long since sought their beds, and Jack, Joey and Frank lingered over tea in the warm kitchen.

'What a bloody day!' Frank said.

'It was never that busy when it was the Bricky,' Joey concurred.

'It's hard work and no mistake, but like I said, I'll get some more help tomorrow.'

Frank and Joey said goodnight and dragged themselves to bed, leaving Jack to ponder whatever was on his mind.

True to his word, first thing the next day, Jack employed a further eight men from the breadline on Westley Street, and over breakfast he drew up a rota. Half the men would work nine to five, the rest would then take over until midnight. This would be for a month, then they would swap hours to ensure everyone worked the evening shift. All were happy enough with the new arrangements and Bess drew up a chart which she pinned to the kitchen door so there would be no arguments about who was on duty and who was off.

The front doors were opened and people flooded in.

The new day had begun.

22

The next couple of weeks saw a marked change in the weather. The chill wind in the mornings had mufflers tied about necks, jackets donned and shawls wrapped tightly around cold shoulders. The sun, when it appeared, shed its weak rays onto the populace as they hurried about their business. Fires were lit and the smoke from hundreds of chimneys lay low over the town. Kitchens everywhere were busy as stews and broths were cooked, ensuring a hot meal for those families who could afford one. The temperature at night dropped rapidly, promising ice, and the doormen at the Emporium did their duty inside the closed doors.

Everyone had plenty of work to do and the gin was selling fast. Each Saturday morning the draymen delivered full barrels and took away the empty ones. Business was booming and the money rolled in.

Jack was happy enough being the manager, but always at the back of his mind was what he saw as the blossoming relationship between Dolly and Wilton. Whenever he saw them together, his mood fell flat.

There were no outward signs to say they were sweethearts,

and Jack often wondered if he was imagining things that were not there. Then he would see them laughing and having fun and his heart ached.

One morning, while he was over at the Crown visiting his mother, Wilton arrived. Dolly was enjoying tea with Nellie and Nancy too.

'I wondered if you would like to visit the distillery, Dolly, then you can see how your gin is produced.'

'I'd love to!' Dolly replied excitedly.

Grabbing her hat and coat and her cane, she said cheerio and was helped up onto the cart which had delivered Nellie's new stock.

'I'm surprised Wilton didn't ask you to go an' all,' Nellie said.

'I ain't,' Jack muttered.

'Why's that, then?' Nancy asked, although she suspected she knew the answer.

'Two's company, three's a crowd.'

Nancy and Nellie exchanged a concerned look. Quickly changing the subject, Nellie asked, 'How are you liking being your own boss?'

'I like it well enough.'

'You're a miserable little bleeder today!' Nellie snapped.

'Mum, don't start!'

Nancy was startled by his outburst, which was most unlike Jack, and so she asked gently, 'What's up lad?'

'Nothing. I'd better get back and make sure they ain't wrecked the place.' Giving the two women a quick peck on the cheek, Jack left.

'What's all that about, do you think?' Nellie asked.

'Dolly,' Nancy answered.

Nellie frowned and Nancy sighed.

'Bloody hell, Nell, I'm sure you walk round with yer eyes closed!'

'What?'

'Jack is in love with Dolly! A blind man could see that!' Nancy explained.

'Oh, blimey,' Nellie mumbled.

'Precisely.'

* * *

Jack walked back to the Emporium briskly but in truth he didn't notice the cold air nipping his nose. He had other things on his mind, like Dolly going off with Wilton without a second thought.

Arriving home, he pushed his way through the crowd and glared when a man yelled, 'Hey, who are you shoving?' Seeing Jack's sour look, the man added, 'Sorry guv, I d'aint know it was you.'

Jack moved on and made for the kitchen.

'Ah, you're back. Cup of tea? How's your mother?' Bess's questions were fired at him as he sat at the table.

Bess glanced at Gwen, who shrugged. Something had obviously happened because Jack was in a foul mood – yet again.

Pushing a cup of hot tea towards him, Bess said, 'I have a good ear if you need to talk.' Then she went back to preparing the vegetables for a lunchtime stew.

Jack said nothing and sipped his tea. When he had finished, he went to take his turn behind the bar.

Gwen opened her mouth to speak but seeing Bess raise a finger, she thought better of it.

In contrast to Jack's black mood, Dolly was thoroughly enjoying the ride on the cart despite the cold weather. Coming into Darlaston, the cart rolled up Church Street. Dolly recalled how Nellie had made this same journey so many years before when she'd had to seek out a new distiller.

The large gates stood open and Wilton expertly guided the horse between them. Dolly gazed up at the red brick buildings and sniffed the aroma of hops which pervaded the air. Helped from the cart she followed Wilton inside to the office.

'Dad, this is Dolly Perkins. Dolly, meet Ned Burton.'

'We meet at last. Welcome, my dear, take a seat.'

'It's nice to meet you, Mr Burton.'

'You too. How is Nellie? I hope she is well.'

'She is, thank you for asking.'

Tea was brought by the secretary and all three chatted about the Emporium and how well it was doing.

Eventually Dolly said she really should be going home. Wilton offered to escort her but Dolly said she would be fine if he would be kind enough to fetch a cab. Wilton wouldn't hear of her travelling alone, and bidding Ned goodbye they went to the distillery part of the works for a swift tour before Dolly headed back.

Dolly was amazed at the huge copper vats with pipes, valves and gauges attached. There were sacks of barley grain and juniper berries, massive water vats as well as barrels and casks.

'The gin is made from barley grain mash. The cold water is run through the condenser here and this is where we add the alcohol and botanicals. The bottom of the still is heated to seventy-three degrees Celsius so the alcohol turns to a gas. This gas rises up through the top of the pot still, then passes through the condenser, which is filled with cold water. The gas then becomes a liquid once more and the final distillate then trickles into a barrel. Burton's distillery does this all over again for a higher proof solution of water and alcohol.'

'So giving a smoother gut-rot,' Dolly said with a smile.

'Indeed. I'm surprised you remember that.'

Dolly relished the opportunity to learn more about the distillery but eventually they hailed a cab. Dolly peppered Wilton with questions for the whole journey back to the Palace.

Once they had reached Gin Barrel Lane, Wilton did not linger after seeing Dolly inside the Palace, and headed straight back to his work.

'You're back, then,' Sadie said as Dolly took a seat in the kitchen.

'Yes, I've been to Darlaston to see the distillery.'

'It's all right for some, gallivanting round the countryside while others have to work.'

'It's a perk of being the boss, Sadie,' Dolly replied.

'Ain't it just. We have liver and onions for tea tonight.'

Dolly smiled. 'My favourite.'

'Have you had a word with Jack yet?' Sadie asked.

'No, I... I haven't found the right time,' Dolly said. When she had returned from the Emporium in such a lather, she had confided to Sadie about what Bess had told her and her cook had agreed with every word.

'You'd better find time, else ordure and wind will come together in one mighty shit-storm!'

Alice collapsed in a fit of giggles and Sadie shot her a look of disdain, silencing her in an instant.

'I'll do it tomorrow.'

'Make sure you do because I'd hate to see you two fall out.'

Dolly nodded and went to take her turn behind the bar, her mind on what she would say to Jack the following day.

23

Dolly took a cab early the next day, wanting to be at the Emporium before it opened its doors to its thirsty customers. She had no idea what she would say to Jack or how she would broach the subject, but she knew something had to be said.

Entering via the back door, she spoke quietly when she saw her friend. 'I need to speak with you, Jack, somewhere private.' She ignored the glances from Bess and Gwen and followed Jack into the room set aside for diners.

'I need a word an' all,' Jack said as they sat at one of the tables already set with glassware and cutlery to see how it might look when the room was opened to the public.

'Jack, I...'

'Hang on, Dolly, what I have to say is important.'

Dolly nodded, glad of having a short reprieve before she had to speak.

'I've worked my arse off getting this place up and running for you.'

'I know.'

Jack held up a hand to forestall her. 'Hear me out before you say anything else. I've decided it's time for me to move on. I'm quitting Dolly, I've had enough.'

The colour drained from Dolly's face as Bess's words echoed in her mind. *If you go on like this, you will lose Jack – both as a manager and a friend!* She'd left it too late! Jack was leaving – her one true friend in all the world was deserting her.

'Ain't you got anything to say?' he asked, watching Dolly play with a fork on the table.

'I... Why?' Dolly was in shock at his decision.

'You know why, Dolly, you've known for a while.'

'Jack, you can't give all this up just because...' Still Dolly could not voice her thoughts. How could she tell him about her feelings for Wilton? She would never be able to find the words.

'What will you do? Where will you go?' Dolly felt a myriad of emotions assaulting her brain.

'I don't know but not back to the Crown that's for sure. I couldn't put up with Mum hanging out of my ear every minute of the day.'

'Jack, she'll be devastated! It was hard enough for her to let you come here!'

Looking at the girl he loved with all his heart, he wondered why *she* wasn't devastated.

'I'm a man now, Dolly, and it's time to make my own way in life.'

'Please, you can't go! You should speak to Nellie...'

'No! Can you imagine what she'll say? *You're a bloody fool, Jack Larkin! Get your arse back there and stop clartin' about!*'

Dolly could not raise a smile at his imitation of Nellie. Instead, she closed her eyes tight to prevent her threatening tears from forming.

'I've made up my mind, Dolly. I'll be leaving today.'

'No! Jack, please don't! Think on it some more,' Dolly begged as she opened her eyes and looked at him earnestly.

Shaking his head, he said, 'What was it you wanted to say to me?'

'That's not important now. Jack, please don't leave me! What will I do without you?'

'You'll find another manager easily enough.'

'I don't mean that! You're my friend, Jack, and I...'

'That's just it Dolly – I'm your *friend*.'

The meaning was clear to them both. After a moment, Jack stood and strode from the room, leaving Dolly in a state of shock which had her glued to her chair. Silent tears rolled down her cheeks as she stared into space. She had failed him, and she felt wretched. It wasn't even as though she and Wilton were stepping out. Yes, they had become friends over the months, but Wilton had given her no reason to think it was anything more than that. She had let her heart rule her head and now because of that she was losing her soulmate. The thought hit her like a sledgehammer. How had she not stopped to wonder if Jack could be the one for her? Had she been too tied up in her musings about Wilton Burton to see what was right under her nose?

Dolly thought of the implications Jack's leaving would bring. Nellie would blame her and that could cause a rift between them. How could she tell Nellie that her son had upped and left? She wouldn't be able to answer the questions Nellie would rail at her: *Why didn't you stop him? Why didn't he talk to me? Why didn't he come home here to us?*

A sob escaped her throat. It was all going wrong. Everything was being spoiled because she had let her feelings take over.

It was then that Bess came into the room.

'Oh, Bess! I've made such a mess of everything!'

Sitting in the seat Jack had vacated, the cook said, 'I'm sorry to say this, love, but you have. You wouldn't listen. I warned you this might happen.'

'I know and that's why I came this morning. I was going to talk to Jack!'

Bess nodded sadly. 'Well, you left it too late, lass, the lad's gone.'

'What? Already? He said he was leaving today but...'

'Yes, had his bag already packed it seems.'

'Did he say where he was going?'

'No, he just said his goodbyes and thank yous, and off he went.'

Dolly's tears burst their banks now and, grabbing her cane, she rushed out to see if she could catch him before he disappeared from her life entirely.

Out in the street, she sobbed as she looked both ways, but she could see no sign of Jack. If he'd caught a cab he could be anywhere by now.

She stretched her body in an effort to see over people's heads, but she wasn't tall enough. Her eyes scanned folk passing by, searching for sight of Jack's cap but it wasn't there. Stepping into the middle of the road she looked first one way then the other but could see no sign of him.

A carter called out, 'Get out of the 'ossroad!'

Dolly stepped back to allow the cart to roll past. Bess was right – she had left it too late!

Going back indoors, she told everyone rather sharply they would have a new manager in place in an hour. Other than that, she said nothing. She didn't need to, Bess would explain, she was sure.

Leaving the staff staring in disbelief, Dolly hailed a cab back to Daydream Palace.

The moment she arrived, she called for Danny Whitehouse. 'I need you to take over as manager at the Emporium.'

'But I thought Jack...'

'Will you do it?' Dolly snapped.

'Yes.'

'Right, you'll need to live in so I suggest you rent out your house, it will bring you a little extra money.'

'Fair enough. When do I start?'

'Now. I have to go across the road to see Nellie.'

Dolly left Danny wondering what the hell was going on. He shook his head at the questions coming from the others as he pulled his jacket on.

'I haven't a clue,' he said over the noise of the bar, 'but I'm to take over immediately.'

With that, he left for the Emporium.

Over at the Crown Saloon, Dolly did her best to explain what had happened, and as she suspected, Nellie shot questions at her one after another. Nancy wept into her apron and Fred tried his best to console her.

'Fred, take a couple of men and get out there. See if you can find my boy!' Nellie said urgently.

With a nod, Fred moved as fast as his lumbering frame would allow.

'Now then. Tell me again exactly what's gone on,' Nellie said sternly. She wasn't going to let it rest until she had the truth.

24

Dolly tearfully related again what had transpired in the soon-to-be dining room at the Emporium.

'You had no idea? Really?'

'Bess and Sadie both told me Jack was sweet on me and was jealous of Wilton Burton, but I didn't really believe them.'

'A blind man could see that he is in love with you!' Nancy snapped.

'Maybe he is and that's why he's left,' Dolly said quietly. 'Bess warned me this might happen.'

'And you did nothing about it?' Nellie asked sharply.

'That's why I went over there this morning. I was going to talk it out with him, but he didn't give me the chance!'

'Have you any notion as to where he might have gone?'

Dolly shook her head.

'Christ, what a mess!' Nellie dragged her hands down her face and Dolly was shocked to see how old her friend suddenly looked. Why had she not noticed this before?

'I'm so sorry. I never meant for any of this to happen.'

'It ain't your fault, gel,' Nancy said, trying to make the girl feel a little better.

'It is though, Nancy. If I hadn't encouraged him to leave here... I should have been more considerate where his feelings were concerned!'

'Well, it's too late now, ain't it?' Nellie thundered.

'Nell!' Nancy boomed.

'Oh, bloody hell! I'm sorry, Dolly, it's just – I'm scared for the lad. God knows what could happen to him out there.'

'Fred will find him, you'll see,' Nancy said, laying a comforting hand on her friend's arm.

'I hope to God he does!' Looking up at the other two women, Nellie's emotions overcame her and she burst into tears. Before a moment passed, all three were sobbing their hearts out.

A couple of hours later, Fred returned.

'No luck, Nellie, I'm sorry. I've sent out the urchins with messages to as many pubs as I could think of. Hopefully someone will have seen him.'

'Thanks, Fred,' Nellie answered sadly.

Dolly left, saying she should check on Danny Whitehouse, who she'd put in charge of the Emporium in the meantime, and see if there had been any word of Jack.

They agreed to let each other know if anything was heard of Jack's whereabouts.

Hailing a cab, Dolly made the journey to Watery Lane, feeling the worst she'd ever felt in her life. She'd lost a real true friend, all because she'd been wrapped up in herself. She had been too cowardly to talk to Jack and now he'd gone, added to which everyone held her responsible, which of course she was.

Entering the Emporium, she saw Danny was busy working the bar, so she sidled into the kitchen.

Bess and Gwen gave her a cursory glance as she dropped onto a kitchen chair.

'So, we have a new manager,' Bess said.

Dolly nodded.

'He seems nice enough.'

'He is,' Dolly said quietly.

'Any news on Jack?'

'No.'

'It's no use you moping about, you need to get on with your work. News will come sooner or later.'

'I can't work! I'm worried sick!'

'If you make yourself bad, that won't help anybody!' Bess snapped. 'Stop feeling sorry for yourself and buck your ideas up!'

Dolly burst into tears yet again and Gwen rushed to put an arm around the sobbing girl's shoulders.

'Look at what you've done now! Can't you see she's a mess? Leave her be!'

Bess, feeling suitable chastened, put the kettle to boil. Tea, the best panacea in the world, was what was needed now.

25

When Jack had walked out of the Emporium and his life within it, he had no idea where his feet would take him. With just his wages and a few clothes in a bag, he went from pub to inn to tavern looking for work. He found nothing and his spirits dipped. He had genuinely believed he would be able to walk into another bar job somewhere easily, but no one was hiring.

All morning he searched the town and by lunchtime he realised he was out on a limb. He had a little money, but no home and no work. The chill wind reminded him he needed to find shelter before the evening set in.

Buying a pie and a bottle of lemonade for his dinner, Jack found a bench to sit and eat his food. As he chewed, he pondered his predicament. Hardly stopping to think what he was doing, he had left a comfortable life behind and now found himself alone, homeless and unemployed. He chided himself for being so rash; he should have thought about it more before he made his move. Then again, it was breaking his heart to think Dolly might be in love with Wilton Burton. How could he have stayed and watched their relationship grow into something more than friendship? If he had stayed, then resentment towards Dolly would have set in and he couldn't bear that thought.

His mind turned to Nellie, the only mother he had ever known. Taking him in from her doorstep she had raised him as her own and he loved her dearly. She would probably be going out of her mind with worry and he felt badly about that. However, he knew that if he'd spoken to her about his intentions, they would have argued. She would have tried to cajole him into staying and when that failed she would have bullied him.

He'd been gone only a few hours and already he missed everyone, and his heart ached to be back amongst them all. But he was an adult and had made his choice. How could he return with his tail between his legs now? He could not crawl back begging to be forgiven, apologising for the hurt he had caused. What about the hurt he was feeling? Would anyone understand that?

Finishing his drink, he took the empty bottle back to the shop and was given a halfpenny refund. Looking around, he wondered which way to go next.

* * *

Back at the Emporium, Dolly wailed, 'I need to go and search for him!'

'And where would you look? You have no clue which route he took,' Bess said sensibly.

'He'll come back when he's tired and hungry,' Gwen added.

'No, he won't. He's too pig-headed to do that.'

'Dolly, you have to resign yourself to the fact that he's gone. It's up to him now to decide his own fate,' Bess said.

Knowing the words were true didn't make Dolly feel any better. She just wanted Jack home, and she said so.

'Is it because you were the cause of him leaving? Or because Nellie holds you responsible? Or is it something more?' Bess asked.

Dolly looked at the cook and the woman nodded. 'I thought so. Dolly, my wench, you ain't in love with Wilton Burton; your heart belongs to Jack Larkin! I'd guess that it always has.'

26

'I've always thought of Jack as my brother until...' Dolly began.

'Until now. Put it this way. If Wilton Burton disappeared from your life tomorrow, how would you feel?'

'I'd be sad, he's a lovely man.'

Bess nodded. 'Sad. Now look at Jack. He's done just that and you feel – what? Bereft? Lost, lonely?'

'Yes, all of those things,' Dolly mumbled.

'There you go then! You can do without young Mr Burton, but Jack...?'

'Oh, Bess! I didn't think... I had no idea until today!'

'Love don't always hit you between the eyes like a poleaxe gal, sometimes it grows slowly, and if you ask me that's the best way because then it usually lasts a lifetime.'

Dolly drew in a shuddering breath. 'It's too late now.'

'It's never too late. Someone will know where that lad went, so we just have to find out who that person is.'

'How?'

'Ask around.'

'Fred has sent the urchin runners out already.'

'Then that's the first step. The next is for Gwen and me to ask around the other servants.'

'I'd be very grateful if you could.'

'Leave that with us. What you need to do now is to stop fretting. There's enough of us and Birmingham ain't so big as to hide him for long.'

'What if he's not in Birmingham? Maybe he caught a train to another town!'

'Then somebody will have seen him at the station.'

'Do you really think so?'

'I do. Now quit worrying and get off home and have a rest. Wait for word, it will come eventually.'

'Thank you, Bess, you too, Gwen.'

Dolly left quietly, hoping there would be news of Jack on her return, but she wasn't holding her breath.

Bess sent Gwen to the neighbouring public house kitchens with a message to be given to the cooks and maids to let them know if they discovered Jack's whereabouts they were to pass a message back.

On her return, Gwen asked, 'Do you think anyone will have seen where Jack went?'

'I don't know,' Bess answered.

'But you told D—'

'I had to say something, the girl was beside herself!'

'I wish he'd come back so everything could go back to being normal again.'

'So do I, Gwen, but it's not likely. He's too proud to come skulking back with his tail between his legs.'

They sighed in unison as they returned to their work.

Whilst Dolly was getting sound advice from Bess, Jack had been considering the options open to him. The conclusion he kept coming back to was that he needed to find a job in a pub. It was work he knew and he was good at it. So, as he had earlier in the day, he walked from inn to tavern enquiring at each one he came to.

As the afternoon wore on, Jack was feeling more and more despondent. No one was looking to hire a barman or cellar man. He knew he would have to find shelter by night-time and he began to worry he would never find work.

Coming to the end of a street he didn't know the name of, he realised he was totally lost. He'd never been to this area before and he recognised nothing. The buildings were unfamiliar to him and there were no landmarks from which to get his bearings. What to do now? Which way to go? Should he back-track to the shop he'd bought his food from? Could he even find his way back there?

Looking around, he saw houses crammed together. A sharp odour hung in the air and he guessed the fish market must be somewhere near, but he didn't know in which direction. *I need to keep walking, then maybe I'll find somewhere I know.*

Miserable, tired and hungry again, he wandered on, wishing he was at home with Dolly and his mum.

'You all right, lad?' a woman asked as he walked towards her.

'I'm lost.'

'Where are you looking to get to?'

'I'm actually searching for work.'

'Ah, well, you'll not find any of that round here.'

'Can you point me in the direction of the Bull Ring then, please?'

'Oh, bless your cotton socks. At the end of this road you'll see St Martin's Church and the Bull Ring is at t'other side.'

Thanking the woman, Jack moved on. As he walked, he recalled how the Bull Ring had acquired its name. An area previously known as Corn Cheaping had a green in the centre of it, which was used for bull baiting. The ring was a hoop of iron to which the bulls were tied before they were taken for slaughter. The Cruelty to Animals Act of 1835 had put a stop to that, though, as it forbade the keeping of a place for baiting or fighting bulls, bears, dogs or any other animal.

Coming to the end of the street, Jack saw the church and heaved a sigh of relief, at least now he knew where he was. He was still, however, out of work and had no home.

Finding an inn on Moat Lane, not far from the Bull Ring, which rented rooms, Jack booked in for the night. Ordering hot stew and fresh bread, he settled himself beside the roaring fire. At least he would have a good meal and a bed tonight, but he would need to be careful with what money he had left.

Overnight the temperature plummeted and the little puddles in the road froze solid. Lacy patterns crawled over windows and icicles hung from eaves looking like crystal stalactites which glittered in the light from the gas-lit streetlamps. The winter had come early, which meant it would be a long one.

Jack was delighted to find a stone bottle filled with hot water in his bed when he retired, and snuggling down beneath the thick blankets and eiderdown he pondered his fate. He watched the moonbeams cast pretty designs on the ceiling, lighting the room brightly, looking like a kaleidoscope. The sky was clear and the stars shone like diamonds on black velvet.

Tomorrow was a new day and he wasn't looking forward to trudging the streets in the icy weather. Having left his socks on, he rested his feet on the hot bottle. Tonight at least he was warm and dry. Tired from walking the day away, he drifted into a fitful sleep.

The following morning, after a good cooked breakfast, Jack set out into a frost-covered world. He shivered as the cold blasted his warm face and nipped his nose and ears. Walking carefully lest he slip and break a bone, he wandered away down Bradford Street and crossed the Deritend bridge which stood over the River Rea. There were at least sixteen pubs in the area but not one of them was looking for staff, he found out as he visited each. So, Jack moved on.

His fingers and toes were cold so he stamped his feet and blew on his digits. He began to realise how desperate his plight was and he thought of others in the same situation. There were families having to live outdoors in this freezing weather, many of whom would not see the spring. Diseases such as pneumonia would carry off the old, the weak and the very young. Graves would be scraped out on the heath with bare hands by those left behind, for there would be no money for funerals.

Coming to Bordesley Street, Jack ducked into yet another public house to ask for work.

The landlord, a man in his fifties Jack guessed, had hair as grey as a badger and he looked through thick spectacles, saying, 'Aye, I could do with a good barman who won't thieve from me. What experience do you have?'

'I was raised in the Crown Saloon and was manager of the Emporium of Dreams for a while.'

'How come you ain't there now?'

'A woman.'

'Ah! Well, I don't pay much but there's bed and board if'n you've a mind to take it.'

'I will, thank you. My name is Jack Larkin.'

'Will Jeavons. Welcome to the Hole in the Wall.'

They shook hands and Jack was led up the dark stairs to his room overlooking the yard. He shivered as the cold hit him.

'You can light a fire as long as you're careful to put the guard up. Plenty of coal in the bunker at the back, help yourself,' Will said pointing to the window.

'Thank you, I'm grateful.'

'Aye, well, get it lit then and come down and I'll show you the ropes.'

Jack hastily built a fire in the small grate and placed the guard securely in front, then went downstairs, counting his blessings. He knew he had been extremely fortunate in finding a job so soon, and Will Jeavons seemed a nice bloke.

Shown where everything was, he now stood with Will behind the bar. The few customers were sat around the fire making their drinks last. It was clear they had no money for more and Jack wondered how the place could survive amongst the many pubs in Birmingham. One day he would count them, but for now he was just happy to be working again.

'The last fella was pinching money out of the till, so before I sacked him I gave him a sound thrashing,' Will said.

'I don't blame you,' Jack answered.

'I ain't got a cook or maid so we have to do all that ourselves.'

'I can cook.'

'Good, 'cos I can't. I can burn water, lad, so that'll be your department.'

Jack smiled.

'We ain't busy as you can see, so why don't you nip to the kitchen and find something for us for tea?'

With a nod, Jack did as he was bid. The old brownstone sink was piled high with dirty dishes and Jack sighed. The range threw out plenty of heat and he filled pans of water to wash the crocks once they boiled. He shoved the kettle onto the range, and searched for tea, sugar and milk. The pantry was well stocked and he found bacon, eggs and sausages on the cold slab, which would make them a good meal along with some fried bread.

Taking a cup of tea through to Will, who smiled his thanks, Jack returned to the kitchen and set to at the sink. Before long, the smell of bacon filled the kitchen and floated through to the bar.

The aroma reminded the customers it was probably time to go home and once they'd left, Will locked the doors and joined Jack in the kitchen.

'Bloody hell! You've been busy, lad!' he said as he took in the sight of a clean and tidy kitchen.

'Sit, your tea's ready,' Jack said, producing a plate of steaming hot food.

'Ta lad, any more tea in that pot?'

'Freshly brewed,' Jack answered as he sat down too.

'Bostin'!'

Jack grinned. As he tucked into his meal, he felt blessed to have fallen on his feet and to have found a safe place to stay.

27

Over the next couple of weeks, nothing came back from the messages sent out as to Jack's whereabouts. Both Dolly and Nellie were inconsolable with worry. No one had seen Jack or knew where he was, and Dolly convinced herself he must have moved to another town, but which one she had no idea.

Nellie was more short-tempered and snappier than usual so Nancy kept her tongue behind her teeth lest they have a real fall-out.

The work in the gin palaces went on as usual but there was no joy in it, for everyone feared something bad might have happened to the boy who was so well liked.

However, over in the Hole in the Wall, Jack was settling in nicely and proving his worth both behind the bar and in the kitchen. He had given Will Jeavons scant explanation as to how he had ended up on the landlord's doorstep, and Will had not pushed the matter. If the lad had his secrets, then let him keep them.

Will had told Jack he was a widower and had no other family; he and his late wife had not been blessed with children.

The pub was not a busy place but had enough custom for it to tick over, and Jack learned fast how to tap and vent barrels of ale. He got to know the regulars and spent many hours listening to their tales of bygone days.

'We need to get the empty barrels out today 'cos the draymen are coming,' Will said early one morning.

'Righto, I'll make a start after breakfast,' Jack replied.

'We'll do it together, lad; can't have you straining yourself and being fit for nothing.'

Between them, they rolled the empty barrels out of the cellar and lined them up against the yard wall ready for collection, and mid-morning the dray cart arrived.

Jack supervised the restocking of the cellar, then he and the men from the brewery went inside for a drink, Jack for his tea and ale for the others.

It was as he walked through to the bar, tea in hand, that he stopped dead in his tracks.

'Jack! My God, everyone's been so worried!'

'Hello, Wilton.' Jack sighed. Of all the people to come across it would have to be Wilton Burton.

'Your mum and Dolly will be elated to know you're all right.'

'How did you find me?'

'I wasn't looking – not as such, anyway. Will's pub is one of our regulars.'

'I'd rather you didn't tell anyone you've seen me.'

'But Jack...!'

'I think you two should be having this conversation somewhere more private,' Will Jeavons said, cocking his head in the direction of his few customers who were listening avidly.

Jack and Wilton moved to the kitchen and conversation in the bar settled to a quiet buzz.

'I don't want Dolly or my mum to know where I am because they'll be on the doorstep causing a ruckus.'

'Whyever did you leave? Everybody is still in shock at how you just walked out.'

'You know why, Wilton.'

'Me? How would I know?'

'Wilton, don't play the innocent with me!'

Wilton frowned at Jack's outburst. Was he supposed to have done or said something that was the cause of all this?

'Jack, I have no idea what you're talking about.'

'Then let me spell it out for you! All the flirting with Dolly! The little jaunt out to your brewery...'

'Hold on there!'

'No, Wilton! You and Dolly – it was plain as a pike staff!'

'You have it all wrong, Jack.'

'Do I? I don't think so. How do you think it made me feel having to watch you two laughing and joking?'

'I had no idea you had feelings for Dolly.'

'Would it have made any difference if you had?'

'Does she know? Have you told her?'

Jack shook his head. 'How could I? I know she's in love with you.'

'No! We have a good relationship, I'll grant you, but it's strictly business.'

'I don't think Dolly sees it that way.'

'My dear fellow – I'm a married man!'

The words hit Jack like a slap in the face.

'What?'

'Yes! I'm married and my wife has just given me a healthy baby boy!'

'Does Dolly know this?'

'Why would I discuss my private life with her?'

Jack dragged his hands down his face and groaned.

'You left the Emporium because you thought Dolly and I...?'

'Yes. It was tearing me apart and I couldn't stand the hurt any longer.'

'You idiot!'

Jack's eyes shot fire and he jumped up from his seat at the table, his fists raised.

'Sit down and listen to me,' Wilton said quietly.

The gentle tone disarmed Jack and he dropped back onto his chair.

'The way I am with Dolly is the way I am with all of my clients. It's business, Jack, nothing more. I'm sorry if you got the wrong impression.'

'Oh, so it's all my fault now, is it?'

'No. Calm down, for goodness' sake. What *is* your fault is not telling Dolly how you feel about her. She's not a mind-reader, so how would she know?'

'I couldn't, not when I thought you and she... oh, God! I've made such a mess of things!'

'You have, rather, but it's not like you can't put it right. All you have to do is take your courage in both hands and tell her.'

'She'll kick my arse to hell and back.'

'For worrying her? Probably, and rightly so.'

'Wilton, I'm sorry for holding you responsible,' Jack said humbly.

'You're forgiven, but you have to sort this out because that girl is going out of her mind with worry, to say nothing of your mother.'

'Oh, blimey! Once Dolly stops kicking my arse, my mum will take over!'

Wilton laughed and Jack gave a crooked smile.

'What will you do now you know the truth of it all?'

'I don't know. Will Jeavons took me in and gave me a job when I most needed it and I would feel I'd be letting him down if I go home.'

'Does Will know anything about you?'

'Not much.'

'Then your first task is to explain it all to him and see what he says.'

'I feel a right fool.'

'That's because you are.'

'Wilton, do me a favour. Please don't tell anyone you've seen me, not yet. I have a lot to think about so I can decide what to do next.'

'I can't lie for you, Jack. If I'm asked, I will have to divulge that I've seen you.'

'I respect that. Give me a couple of days?'

'All right, but after that I will visit Dolly and get everything straightened out from my perspective. I think it's time I told her my good news – that I have become a father – and put a stop to any rumours and misunderstandings.'

'Congratulations on that, Wilton, and I hope Dolly understands. For my part I'll talk things over with Will Jeavons.'

The two young men shook hands and returned to the bar where the landlord was leaning on the counter reading the newspaper in the dim lamplight.

Wilton left them to their discussions.

'So, you gonna be leaving then, Jack?'

'About that, Will,' Jack said sheepishly.

28

Will and Jack slipped into the kitchen, knowing the customers would bang their coin on the counter if they needed their glasses refilling. Will doubted they would, though. Those four men would sit by his fire all day over a single glass of ale.

When Wilton went he had given a promise to wait at least two days before visiting Dolly again.

Jack made a fresh pot of tea and once they were settled at the table, he related his tale to his new friend.

When he had finished, Will said, 'As far as I see it, you should be getting back and whisking that girl down the aisle.'

'You've been so good to me though, Will, and I don't want to let you down.'

'You won't be doing that, lad. To be truthful, there ain't really enough work here for the both of us.'

'Then why did you employ me?'

'I felt sorry for you, lad. You looked so lost and forlorn and I wouldn't have been able to live with myself if I'd turned you back out onto the street.'

'You're a good man, Will Jeavons.'

'And you'll be a stupid one if you let Dolly get away from you, so take my advice and go home, and as soon as you get there, ask her to marry you. You thought you'd lost her once, don't let it happen again.'

'Thanks, Will.'

'Go on, get going before it freezes over and is too risky to walk safely on the streets.'

Jack went to his room to collect his things and then shook hands with the landlord who had been so kind to him. Will gave him his wages and Jack said, 'I can't take that.'

'You can and you will, lad. You've earned it. Now get on with you.'

'Thank you. If you need anything I'll be at the Crown Saloon, I expect. I may not be given my job back at the Emporium but my mum will take me in again.'

'Good luck to you, Jack.'

'To you too, Will.'

Leaving the Hole in the Wall, Jack walked towards home, praying he would be forgiven for making everyone so unhappy.

Wrapped up warmly against the cold wind, he trudged through the dirty streets where palls of smoke from household chimneys swirled high about the rooftops.

As he dodged around hurrying people Jack wondered what he should do first. Would it be wiser to visit his mum and stand fast against the inevitable ear-bashing? Or should he see Dolly first where no doubt he would receive a severe tongue-lashing? Either way, he was in ordure up to his eyeballs.

The nearer he got to Gin Barrel Lane, the slower his steps became. He was dreading having to face up to the people he loved. His heart hammered in his chest and sweat formed on his brow despite the icy cold. He tried to find the words he could use to explain his actions, but he failed miserably. Walking out had been far easier than trying to go back.

Spotting the Crown at the top of the lane, he felt his pulse quicken. He stopped and stared at the building which had been his home for nearly all of his life and a warm feeling crept over him. A dog barked somewhere close, making him jump, and Jack started walking once more.

Going around to the back, Jack stood by the door. Should he knock? Would it be appropriate to just walk in? Making a decision, he knocked first then strode in.

'Jack!' Nancy gasped. 'Oh, lad, it's so good to see you! Thank God you're all right! You had us so worried!' As she spoke, she wrapped her arms around the young man she'd loved since he was a baby.

'It's nice to see you too,' he mumbled from where his face was hidden deep in Nancy's bosom.

'Nell! Nellie!' Nancy called as she let Jack go and he hauled in a great breath.

'What? What's all the racket? Bloody hell, Nance, I'm up to my armpits in customers!' Nellie yelled back.

'Nellie Larkin, you get your arse in here now!'

Jack grinned. How he'd missed this.

'What's so important...?' Nellie left the question hanging as she spied her son. 'The prodigal returns.'

'Hello, Mum.'

'Is that all you have to say for yourself – hello Mum? Do you have any idea what you've put us all through? We've been to hell and back while you've been doing God knows what!'

Jack stood and took his mother's anger, knowing he deserved it. Wisely he kept his mouth shut.

'I've not been able to sleep for fretting! I couldn't eat...' Nellie went on.

'That's not strictly true,' Nancy mumbled, and Jack fought against a smile beginning to form.

Nellie ignored the remark and continued with her tirade. 'Fred is beside himself and Dolly – well Dolly is a shadow of her former self!'

'I missed you an' all,' Nancy said quickly while Nellie took a breath.

Jack clamped his teeth together before the threatened grin broke through.

'We've had runners out looking for you, we've sent messages to all the pubs and inns and what came back? Nothing, that's what! We d'aint know if you were alive or dead!'

Whilst Nellie paused, Jack said quickly, 'I'm sorry, Mum.'

Nellie was undone and rushed to her boy. 'Thank the good Lord you're home safe and sound!' Tears rolled down her face as she hugged him and it was all Jack could do not to cry along with her.

Nancy's apron was soaked with tears as she set the kettle to boil.

'Sit down and tell me where you've been. Have you seen Dolly yet? What have you been doing?'

'Give the boy a chance, Nell, otherwise he'll turn tail and go off again!' Nancy said sharply.

Nellie threw her friend a look which could sour milk then returned her attention to Jack.

'I came here first, I'll see Dolly later. I've been working in a pub in Bordesley Street.'

'That's just over the way!' Nellie said flapping a hand in the air.

Jack nodded.

'So close yet so far,' Nancy muttered as she provided tea.

'Shut yer cake-hole, Nance!' Nellie snapped.

Nancy pushed a plate of cake in front of Jack and pursed her lips. The gesture was too much for him and he burst out laughing.

'I've missed you two so much,' he managed at last.

Over hot tea, Jack explained how kind Will Jeavons had been to him. 'I wanted to come back as soon as I left,' he said.

'Well, why didn't you?' his mum asked.

'Pride.'

Taking a deep breath Jack explained his confusion. He told of his love for Dolly and how he'd been found by Wilton.

'I d'aint know he was married either,' Nellie said.

'Nor me,' Nancy put in.

'Well, you have to go over the road now and see Dolly,' Nellie said.

'Do you want a tot of gin – 'cos I've a feeling you might need it!' Nancy said with a grin.

'No, thanks!' Jack grimaced at the thought.

'Come home to us when she kicks your arse out,' Nellie said.

'I told Wilton that might happen.'

With another deep breath and fingers crossed, Jack left the kitchen of the Crown and headed for the Palace.

'Oh, my God! Jack, where *have* you been?' Dolly gasped as Jack stepped into her kitchen.

'I'm sorry, Dolly,' he mumbled.

'I'm so glad you're all right!' she said as she hobbled over to give him a hug.

Jack's heart melted as he folded Dolly in his arms. He could smell the soap she was so fond of and he kissed her hair, delighting in its silkiness. Then the moment was gone as she pulled away and his joy was replaced by sadness.

'Welcome back,' Sadie said, holding up the teapot.

Jack nodded with a smile. He would not risk offending her by refusing.

'Come and sit down and tell me everything.' Dolly indicated a chair as she sat down herself.

'I don't know where to start.'

'Try the beginning.'

Jack thought about that and decided to start from the end instead; with Will Jeavons and his meeting with Wilton Burton.

'Wilton has a wife and baby son, Dolly,' he said.

'I did wonder,' she replied quietly.

'I'm sorry, I know how much you liked him.'

'I did, yes, but I wasn't sure he felt the same. But what I want to understand is why you left.'

'I think you know already, you just won't accept it.'

Dolly flushed scarlet and she nodded.

'We all told you but you wouldn't have it,' Sadie put in despite it clearly being a private conversation. A look from Dolly had her add, 'If you d'aint want us to hear then you should have gone elsewhere to talk.'

There was a large living room, but Dolly had hated it from the moment she had moved in. She felt uncomfortable in there and it always made her shiver. Dark and drab, it had no windows and seemed as though the builders had stuck the room on the end of the building as if to simply use up their excess bricks. Eventually it had become a lumber room, and everything that didn't have a place of its own was shoved in there. Dolly didn't use it so no one else did either. The door firmly shut, it was forgotten about.

'My feelings for you drove me away. I couldn't bear seeing you with Wilton, I thought...'

'No, Wilton never gave me cause to think there was anything between us. He was ever the gentleman.'

'I know that now and it makes me feel like a fool. Dolly, I have to know one thing. Could there ever be a chance for you and me?'

Dolly's blush came red hot to her cheeks and her eyes glistened with tears. Now she wished they'd gone somewhere more private.

'I see. It's all right, I understand. Mum said I should go home when I'd finished here.' Jack stood to leave but Dolly rushed to him as best she could without her cane. Flinging her arms around his neck she kissed him with a fierceness that almost frightened her.

Sadie and Alice exchanged an astonished glance at the unexpected turn of events.

Jack was in heaven and if he'd died at that moment he wouldn't have cared.

When their kiss ended, Jack mumbled, 'I love you, Dolly Daydream, I think I always have.'

'Oh, Jack! My love, don't you ever go away again!'

'I won't, I promise.'

Sadie and Alice broke into spontaneous applause and Dolly laughed loudly as Jack helped her back to her seat.

Will Jeavons' words came back to him: *As soon as you get there, ask her to marry you. You thought you'd lost her once, don't let it happen again.*

Dropping to one knee, he said, 'Dolly, will you marry me?'

Dolly looked at the man she had loved all along without even realising it, and whispered on a breath, 'Yes.' This prompted more applause.

'Then I'd best find a job.'

'You could go back to the Emporium. Danny Whitehouse is standing in as manager at the moment.'

'No, I wouldn't take that from him. Besides, I'd rather stay close to you.'

'Aww, ain't that nice?' Alice said.

'It's bostin'!' Sadie bawled, wiping tears on her apron.

'Should we go and tell Nellie?' Dolly asked.

'Better had, before Aggie beats us to it!' Jack replied.

The cook and maid watched the happy couple go hand in hand to share their news and Alice said, 'Blimey, that was a bit quick, wasn't it?'

'I think once he'd declared his feelings for her, Jack wasn't about to let Dolly slip through his fingers again.'

'I wonder when the wedding will be?'

'Christ, Alice, he's only just proposed!'

'Ar, well, there don't seem to be any grass growing under his feet.'

'I can't argue with that.'

The two women chatted on as they took up their duties once more.

'Do you think we'll be invited to the wedding?' Alice asked.

'I doubt it, we're only staff, remember.'

'That's a shame, I would have liked that.'

'Hmm, me an' all.'

Over the road, Dolly and Jack were given hugs of congratulation once they had shared their news.

'I was beginning to think it would never happen!' Nellie said tearfully.

'So was I,' Nancy sobbed joyfully.

'When's it to be, then?' Nellie asked.

'Maybe in the spring when the weather warms up?' Dolly suggested.

'I don't care when as long as we are together, but in the meantime I need a job. I have a wedding ring to buy.'

'I told him to go back to the Emporium but he won't,' Dolly explained.

'Well, you can work for me again,' Nellie put in.

'As long as you pay me, and not in gin!' Jack joked.

'Let's go and let them all know at the Emporium that you're home safe,' Dolly said.

In the cab they cuddled together, delighting in their closeness, as well as warding off the cold. They were greeted happily by the staff and congratulated heartily when they shared the joyful news of their engagement.

'You'll be wanting your job back, then?' Danny Whitehouse asked.

'No mate, I didn't come here today for that.'

'Oh.'

'You don't sound very pleased.'

'It's just that – well I don't think I'm really cut out to be a manager.' Turning to Dolly he went on. 'I'm sorry, Dolly, but I was happier back at the Palace with my pals. Please don't think I'm ungrateful because I'm not, what with all you've done for me.'

'But where will you live if you go back?' Dolly asked.

'I never got round to renting out my house, so I'm all good.'

'Right, then, get your stuff together and you can accompany me home,' Dolly said with a smile.

'What about this place?' Danny asked.

They both looked at Jack and with a sigh he said, 'Oh, all right then!'

He smiled at the cheers from the staff. He had walked out on them without a word, and now they had welcomed him back without questions or recriminations.

He knew that the gossip would travel, but he didn't care. He was back in the fold and more importantly, he was betrothed to Dolly. Whistling a little tune, Jack took his rightful place behind the bar and Dolly and Danny left him to it, laughing as they went.

30

Ezra Moreton threw the newspaper onto his desk in frustration. There was an unholy row going on in the corridor outside his office between two of his guards and they were interrupting his peace.

Flinging the door open, he marched towards the arguing men. 'What the bloody hell is going on here?' he demanded.

'I heard summat in the pub last night and he's saying it ain't true!' one said.

'That's 'cos it ain't!' the other remonstrated.

'Shut it, you!' Ezra snapped. 'Now, what was it you heard?'

'There's talk of Dolly Perkins looking to buy another pub.'

'What? She won't be able to afford that.'

'That's what I said, boss,' the other man said before wilting beneath a look of anger from his employer.

'Mr Moreton, sir, I was only coming to tell you what I heard,' the first said.

'Right, well you've told me so now you can both get out there and see if it's true. Don't come back until you know more.'

The two men walked away and Ezra sighed and shook his head as the disagreement began again.

Going back to his newspaper, Ezra found he'd lost interest in it. Laying it on his lap, he stared out of the window at the frost-covered street.

Was Dolly looking for new premises? Surely not, because the Emporium had only recently begun to trade. Where had the rumour started and why? Had Miss Perkins mentioned something along those lines in passing? Was she actually on the lookout for another building?

Surely she didn't have designs on opening yet another gin palace. That would make four! It was a ludicrous idea. It wouldn't work – the town couldn't stand another of those gaudy, glittering palaces. Although, whenever he passed them, they were always bustling with life. She must be making a packet.

He tried to imagine where she would look next if she were to open another gut-rot doss-hole. It was bad enough having three – but four! He thought about how many pubs and inns Birmingham sported; there must be at least a hundred, and all but a few were thriving. So what was another gin house? It was certainly no threat to his business, which was mainly brewing beer, although some gin distilling was done.

He snorted as he realised Dolly Perkins couldn't hurt him or his business. He could, however, hurt her if he could discover whether the rumour was true. If it proved the case then he could buy up any property she showed an interest in, just to spite her.

For the moment he would wait and see what news his men brought back. With a chuckle, Ezra picked up his newspaper once more.

* * *

Back at the Emporium, Eli Hodges was having a meeting with Jack about the changes planned for the dining room.

'As you can see, the ladies have laid it out so we can get a better idea,' Jack said.

'Mirrors and lamps, then. They will make all the difference and it won't cost as much as if we were knocking down walls.'

Jack grimaced as his thoughts immediately went to the bedroom where the body was found.

'I agree. When can you start?'

'I'll put the order in for the mirrors today, and we'll start installing the new lamps as soon as I get them,' Eli said. 'I'm grateful for the work, Jack.'

'I'm pleased you can take it on. I reckon it will be smashing when it's finished and we have folks in for food.'

'Fingers crossed it takes off for you.'

Eli left the Emporium to place the order for mirrors and collect the lighting ready for starting work as soon as possible.

'Looks like we'll be going ahead with it then?' Bess asked.

'Yes, and with Eli's track record, it'll be done in no time. Now you have to come up with a menu.'

'What are you looking for? I hope it ain't lark's tongues and the like,' Bess said with a wrinkle of her nose.

Jack laughed. 'No, just good wholesome home-cooked food like you give us.'

'I'll get on to that right away, then you can see what you think.'

'Thanks, Bess, you're a diamond.'

'Speaking of which, shouldn't you visit the jeweller and buy Dolly a ring?'

'As soon as I have enough money. I thought I'd take her to choose one for herself.'

'That's a good idea, then at least you'll know she has one she loves.'

'I have to pop out for an hour, so I'll leave you to it.'

'Where are you off to now?' Bess asked.

'I'm going to see a man about a joanna.'

'Where on Earth will you put a piano?'

'In the bar!'

Jack left Bess shaking her head. *The schemes that boy comes up with!*

Jack whistled for a cab and called out the address. 'Theatre Royal, New Street, please.'

The cabbie nodded and waited for his passenger to climb aboard.

Jack tapped his pocket where he had put the money taken from the 'accounts' drawer in his bedroom. This was where petty cash was kept for any eventualities that might arise. He had left a note in place of the money saying what it had been used for. He would add the amount once a deal had been struck.

He had noted from the newspaper that the Theatre Royal had invested in a brand-new grand piano and he was hoping their old upright one might be for sale. If he was lucky, he could buy it and get it installed in the bar. Then all he had to do was find someone who could play it.

On arrival, the cabbie nodded when asked to wait and Jack hammered on the doors of the theatre. In just a moment, his knock was answered by a little man who was almost bent double with age.

'Waddya want?' he snapped.

'I'd like to see someone about buying a piano.'

'Get in, then! Standing there letting all the cold inside! You kids have no bloody respect!' The old man continued to mutter as he led Jack down a corridor and further into the theatre. He shuffled along slowly, his slipper-bound feet making a swishing sound as he dragged them over the wooden floor. 'Folk coming to the door making me walk all this way. Some people have got no respect!'

Jack smiled while following along. Coming to an office, the old man pointed. 'See him in there, that's the fella you want.' Turning with tiny steps the man began to mutter again as he moved on. 'Now I have to walk all that way back again. My old bones ain't up to all this gallivanting about!'

Knocking on the office door, Jack walked in, a smile still on his face at the old man's grumbling.

'Yes? Can I help you?'

'I hope so. I saw in the paper the theatre has a new piano and I was wondering if the other one might be for sale.'

'Ah, a pianist, are you?' the young man behind the desk asked, his long fingers wriggling along its edge and he smiled.

'I'm afraid not,' Jack answered.

'Oh, a learner then?' The man's eyebrows drew together as he spoke.

'Erm, no.'

'Then why, may I ask, are you interested in buying a piano?' The man's cultured voice rose a tone.

'I'd like one for my premises,' Jack answered honestly.

'Ah, drawing room? Music room? A soiree taking place maybe?' A hand waved in the air daintily and Jack almost laughed out loud.

'No. Is the piano for sale or not?'

'As it happens, it is,' the man said as if he was upset.

'Right, then. Let's have a look and agree a price, then I can get it shifted.'

The effeminate fellow gave a shudder at Jack's brusque approach to business but he minced his way to a room further down the corridor where Jack was given a look at the upright piano, and one by one he tapped the keys gently, ensuring they were all working.

'You'll never be a pianist!' the man said with a girly giggle.

'You've got that right,' Jack replied.

Returning to the office and after ten minutes of haggling, Jack paid the money, received a receipt, and was in the cab rolling away to Hodges' yard. They were the only people he knew who would have a cart big enough to transport his new acquisition.

Feeling pleased with himself, he then thought ruefully, *Now I have to tell Dolly what I've spent her money on!*

31

While Jack was arranging for the piano to be transported to the Emporium, Ezra Moreton's two guards had returned.

'All we could find out was what we told you before, boss,' one said.

'All right, but I'm charging you two to keep your ears open and as soon as you hear anything more, you bring it to me.'

'Yes, boss,' they chorused.

'Right, get out!'

Alone again, Ezra wondered what the hell was going on. He had to find out what Dolly Perkins was up to.

Walking out onto the street, he whistled loudly. He waited and in a minute an urchin raced around the corner from Grosvenor Row. The boy was wearing worn-out boots which were too big for him, an old jacket with frayed cuffs and holes everywhere, and trousers which were too short and ended halfway down his calves. His face was smeared with dirt and his hair was a matted mess of tangles. His blue eyes were alert as he came puffing up to Ezra, who could hardly believe the lath-thin frame could hold the boy upright.

'Yes, boss?'

'I want to know if the rumour about Dolly Perkins is true. She's supposed to be looking to buy another pub. Find out what you can.'

'Yes, boss.'

Ezra pulled a shilling from his pocket and, handing it to the boy, added, 'Get some food in your belly.'

Pulling a forelock, the boy sped off, leaving Ezra shaking his head. *Poor little bugger!*

Ezra always paid the string of urchins for running his errands and the symbiotic relationship worked well. He couldn't help feeling sorry for them, knowing he was rich and they had nothing. As he walked back indoors he thought, *Good God, Ezra, you're in danger of becoming a good man!*

* * *

Back at Hodges' yard, Eli had sent his sons with the strongest cart they had along with a sturdy wooden ramp to collect the piano.

With an enormous amount of pushing and shoving and with the help of the theatre's porters, they managed to get it loaded.

Jack had told Eli he would be waiting at the Emporium when they arrived and had enlisted the help of his staff to unload and push the instrument indoors. He had decided to place it along one wall and although it would take up space, the large bar could accommodate it easily enough.

There was a lot of excitement as the piano was carefully slid down the ramp outside the Emporium. Crowds of people stood around giving advice as to how it should be done, but Eli's sons ignored them all.

'You ain't doing that right!' a man shouted.

'They are,' another said.

'If they get that thing on the ramp it'll tip over!'

'No, it won't. They've got all four castors on the ramp. Open yer bloody eyes, man!'

The argument raged on while two of Eli's boys stood on the ramp, their backs to the end of the piano. Slowly they moved forward with tiny steps. The heavy iron-framed piano inched its way down the ramp and did not, as some thought it might, roll down out of control.

They heaved it indoors, sweat dripping from their faces and pooling beneath their armpits, and eventually they man-handled it into place.

Applause sounded at the feat undertaken by the big burly builders, and Jack paid them well for their efforts.

'You gonna give us a tune then, Jack?' someone called out as Jack returned to the bar after seeing the Hodges boys on their way.

'Only if you want to go deaf as well as blind!' he answered as he motioned drinking from a glass. Laughter filled the room and then suddenly the keys began to tinkle.

The man who had entertained the customers with his trumpet a while ago began to play. By some miracle the piano was still in tune, and before long everyone was singing.

Jack's idea appeared to be a roaring success and he nodded, a big grin splitting his face. Bess and Gwen rushed into the bar to enjoy the music and clapped loudly as the refrain came to an end.

'Play another!' a woman yelled and the man duly obliged.

Jack was amazed at the sounds filling the bar, from modern songs to classical pieces, and he thought the man was wasted in a gin palace – he should be in a concert hall. He wondered what had brought the man so low that he spent his days trying to kill himself by drinking mother's ruin, and made a mental note to try and find out.

It was around tea-time when Jack got the opportunity to speak with the musician. The customers began to stagger out and go home to sleep off the effects of the gin and Jack took that time to speak with the man. The piano was quiet now and the man's long fingers caressed its keys affectionately.

'You can certainly play that!' Jack said as he neared the man sitting on the piano stool.

'I learned as a boy.' The man's voice held no regional accent and Jack guessed he had been well educated whilst growing up.

'Wyman York at your service.'

'Nice to meet you, Wyman.' The two men shook hands and Jack went on, 'You should be playing in a big fancy concert hall, not here in a gin palace.'

'I used to play with the orchestra at the Theatre Royal.'

'What happened?'

'I fell out with the musical director,' Wyman confessed.

'Don't tell me, you got the sack.'

Wyman nodded. 'He wanted to rearrange a time-honoured piece of genius and I told him to go to hell. I said I wouldn't bastardise such beautiful work because he wanted to make a name for himself.'

'Good on yer,' Jack said.

'Maybe, but it cost me my job doing what I love most in the world.'

'That's a crying shame. Could you not have gone to another theatre?'

Wyman shook his head. 'That one was my home as well as my workplace.'

'Where do you live now?'

'I lodge with an old woman over by the vinegar works when I can afford it, but...'

'Wyman, are you out on the street?'

Lowering his head, Wyman nodded.

'Come with me,' Jack demanded before leading the pianist to the kitchen.

Jack introduced him to Bess and Gwen then said, 'Would it be possible to include Wyman when we eat, please?'

'Most certainly,' Bess answered.

Hooking a finger, Jack beckoned Wyman to accompany him upstairs to a spare bedroom. 'It's not much but it's yours in exchange for keeping my customers happy. What do you think? Do we have ourselves a deal?'

Wyman looked around. 'Thank you, Jack, it's paradise compared to the street.'

'One thing, though, you have to stop drinking my gin.'

'Have you ever seen me drink gin?'

Jack shook his head and thought hard, then frowned. 'No, but...'

'I don't drink, Jack, I come in here to keep warm and blow a few notes on my trumpet.'

'Bloody hell! Well, good on yer. Come on, let's go and eat.'

Bess served tea and plates of hot food in relays so the bar was always manned, and while they ate Jack asked Gwen if she would make up the bed for Wyman.

'I'll do it now while you have your tea,' she said with a smile.

'Do you need to fetch your belongings?' Jack asked.

'No, all I have is my trumpet, which I left on the bed upstairs.'

Bess shook her head in sorrow at the man's plight and offered him more food, which he gratefully accepted.

'You brought that piano from the Theatre Royal, didn't you?' Wyman asked.

'Yes, I bought it today. How did you know?'

'I used to play it a lot. I recognised it.'

'Well, I got it from some bloke who was a bit airy-fairy,' Jack replied with a grin and a dainty wave.

'He must be new there. The one who gave me the push was a little overweight with piggy eyes and a flat nose. He also had an inflated opinion of himself.'

'May he rot in hell,' Bess mumbled.

'My sentiments exactly, dear lady.'

Jack listened to the chatter as he ate. A small seed of an idea began to germinate in his mind...

Well fed now and grateful to be given a room, Wyman York played joyfully that evening. He had folks singing and dancing, and copious amounts of alcohol were consumed.

At ten o'clock, Jack instructed him to quit and go to the kitchen for his supper.

Bess served plates of sausage sandwiches with fried onions and large pots of tea.

'I've made your bed up, Wyman,' Gwen said timidly.

'Thank you, sweet lady,' Wyman replied and saw the blush come to her cheeks.

Bess rolled her eyes and continued cooking, and as she did so, said, 'Frank has put the tin bath in the scullery and we have pans of hot water ready for you.'

'Angels, both of you.'

'Ar, well, this angel will be abed while you take your bath.'

Wyman laughed.

'Joey and Frank have both sorted some clean clothes and a razor out for you too,' Gwen added.

'I shall thank them for their kindness as I thank you for the care you are giving me.'

Gwen breathed a dreamy sigh at his elocution and Bess stifled a titter.

Once everyone had finished their suppers and the dishes were washed, Gwen and Bess retired for the night.

Jack helped Wyman fill the tin bath, then he provided soap and towels before leaving the man to bathe in privacy. Wyman emerged from the scullery looking like a different man. With wet hair combed and chin shaved, he felt better than he had in a long time.

When Jack locked up at midnight and everyone had gone home or to their beds upstairs, Jack and Wyman sat in the kitchen chatting.

'I can't thank you enough for what you've done for me, Jack,' Wyman said over yet more tea.

'You don't need to, you're earning a crust now.'

They talked on, Jack telling him about his fiancé Dolly who owned the Emporium, and Wyman enthusing about how much he loved music and the playing of it.

'Have you ever written any of your own?' Jack asked.

'Yes, a few pieces, but they're lost now.'

'That's a shame. You should write some more.'

'Go back to composing? It's a thought,' Wyman mused before he said goodnight and went to his new bed.

Jack turned off the lamps and went happily to his own bed.

It had been a good day.

* * *

The next morning, after breakfast, Jack took a cab to the Palace to see Dolly. He had some explaining to do and hoped she'd understand why he'd spent some money on a piano. He wanted to sound her out about paying Wyman a small wage in exchange for his services too. The man was proud and Jack guessed he'd accepted Jack's offer out of necessity, however, if he could be earning a little money, then any thought of being given charity could be forgotten.

Greeted warmly by the girl he was to wed, Jack again counted his lucky stars. He told her all about Wyman York and the piano and Dolly listened intently.

'Jack, what a marvellous idea!'

'We should get one for here,' Sadie put in.

They really would have to find somewhere private for their discussions, Dolly thought. Then again, weren't they one big family? And wasn't it said family should not have secrets from each other?

Dolly agreed to Wyman being paid for his efforts, leaving the amount for Jack to decide upon. Then Jack explained more about the pianist having been sacked.

'I know what you're thinking, Jack Larkin, and I'm not sure it's such a good idea,' Dolly said.

'Why not? Just think if we could get the theatre to employ him again.'

'How would Wyman feel about you interfering in his life? Have you thought about whether he would want to return there at all?'

'No, but I'm sure he'd love to at least have the choice.'

'Would it not be better to talk it over with him first?'

'I suppose. Yes, I think I'd better.' Jack's initial excitement waned a little.

Seeing this, Dolly ventured, 'Maybe it wouldn't hurt to have a word with the musical director and see what he says. After all, it wouldn't be a good idea to get Wyman's hopes up.'

'I knew you'd see it my way.' Jack beamed and, giving his beloved a quick kiss, he left her in peace. This time he had a man to see about a pianist.

The theatre door was opened by the same bent old man. 'Not you again!'

'Yes. I've come to see...'

'You know the way. Come in – bloody cold seeping in!' Closing the door, the porter waved a hand. 'Get along with you.' He shuffled away, muttering, 'Folk coming and going all the bloody time! Kids today, got no respect for their elders. I'm getting too old for all this running around!' Jack walked the length of the corridor with a grin on his face.

With a tap on the door, Jack walked in.

'What is it you want this time, a kettle drum?' the man asked.

Jack had no idea what that was and said, 'Mr...?'

'Renoit. Charles Renoit.'

Jack sniffed at what he felt sure was a made up name, then said, 'Mr Renoit, my name is Jack Larkin and I've come with a proposal.'

Intrigued, Renoit pointed to a seat with ladylike fingers, and listened carefully as Jack explained about Wyman York being dismissed from the theatre and the reason why.

'My God! I thought he'd died! My predecessor emphatically told me the man had passed on!'

'Well, he ain't, he's at my gin palace as we speak, banging out tunes on that old joanna I bought from you.'

Renoit grimaced then jumped to his feet and began to pace the room, his hands flapping around like fish out of water. 'We cannot allow that to continue. I'm sorry, Mr Larkin, but I must insist the maestro be returned to the Theatre Royal immediately!'

'I'm glad to hear you say that. That's what I had hoped you'd say. Now, may I suggest you come and ask him?'

Renoit and Jack hurried to the waiting cab, which set off directly for the Emporium. On the way, Jack was bombarded with questions he couldn't answer. Where had Wyman gone after he'd been sacked? How had he lived? Was he still at concert level with his playing?

Arriving, they climbed out of the cab and Renoit stared in horror. 'He lives here?'

'He does now,' Jack said. 'Let's go by way of the back, the bar will be packed with drunkards.'

As they made to move they heard Wyman begin to play.

'Chopin!' Renoit gushed. 'Exquisite!'

Following Jack into the kitchen and having been offered tea, which he accepted, Renoit sat and listened to the music with his eyes closed. Tunes came one after another and the man wept openly, apparently mesmerised by the beauty of the playing.

Bess and Gwen exchanged a look which said they agreed with the young man's sentiments.

Jack went through to the bar and asked Wyman to join him in the kitchen. He agreed and smiled at the groans from the punters, who called for more.

In the kitchen he was introduced to Renoit and Jack explained what he had done.

'You *must* come back to the theatre! I absolutely insist!' The man was flapping his hands around again and Wyman chanced a glance at Jack, who was doing his utmost not to laugh out loud.

'I simply cannot allow you to continue to waste your talents in this place!' Then turning to Jack said politely, 'No offence intended.'

'None taken, it's a good living for me,' Jack replied.

'Young Mr Larkin has been very good to me,' Wyman said.

'I'm sure, but Maestro, please – you *have* to come home!'

'Jack?' Wyman asked.

'I concur, that's why I approached Mr Renoit in the first place. You should be in that orchestra if not out there on the stage by yourself.'

'Then I agree, and Jack you will always have my thanks. May I ask a favour?'

Jack nodded.

'May I leave my trumpet here for safe-keeping and come back now and then to tickle the ivories in your bar?'

'Yes, of course. I'll get Frank to hang your trumpet over the counter for all to see and remember. You will always be welcome here.'

Shaking Jack's hand, Wyman left with Renoit, who was bubbling over with excitement.

'I wonder if we'll ever see him again,' Bess asked.

'Oh, I think so. It's my guess we'll be hearing a lot about Wyman York in the future.'

'Now you have to find someone else to play that piano,' Bess said and burst out laughing when Jack replied.

'Oh, bugger!'

33

It had been over a week since Dolly had seen Wilton Burton and she suspected he was keeping his distance because of his promise made to Jack. Then one morning he arrived at the Palace, but he was not his usual bright and breezy self. Dolly decided to spare him the anguish of having to tell her he was married and so dash any hopes she may have harboured regarding a relationship between them.

'Hello, Dolly,' he greeted her.

'Ah, Wilton, I believe congratulations are in order on the birth of your son!' Dolly said and she saw him visibly relax.

'Thank you, he's a bonny little thing.'

'Jack is home as I'm sure you know, and we are to be wed!'

'Congratulations to you also. I'm happy for you both.'

'Jack told me you found him and I'm so grateful,' Dolly continued.

'You're welcome, but I didn't exactly *find* him, more like I came across him. However, what is important is that he's home and – a wedding! How exciting.' Wilton was back to his old self again.

'Yes, we – or rather I – thought the spring, when it's warmer.'

They chatted for a while before Wilton went about his business, and Dolly headed behind the bar.

Aggie crooked a finger. 'I hear as Wyman York's been playing the joanna at the Emporium but he's now back at the theatre.'

So, Jack's plan had worked.

'Nothing gets past you, does it, Aggie?'

'Now Jack needs somebody else to lamp out a tune or two,' Aggie went on.

'I'm sure he'll sort it out.'

'Ar. I know summat else an' all.'

Dolly sighed and filled the old woman's glass. A few tots of free gin in exchange for information didn't hurt.

Taking a gulp, Aggie spoke quietly. 'Word is – you'm looking for another pub.'

Dolly was taken aback at that. 'Really?'

Aggie nodded, her grey hair bobbing on top of her head. 'Ar, an' it's got Ezra Moreton in a spin!'

'Why?'

Aggie coughed and drained her glass, which Dolly quickly refilled. 'Because he can't work out where you're getting the money from!'

Dolly laughed. 'I can't deny it's a pleasing prospect imagining expanding our business, but it will be some years yet before I can consider it.'

'Yes, but Ezra don't know that, do he? I, for one, am enjoying watching that bugger chasing his own arse!'

Dolly laughed again and moved away to serve another customer. As she worked, Aggie's words stayed in her mind. How had such a rumour started and why? Surely Ezra knew she was in debt to the bank and would be for a long time to come. The thought of owning a string of gin palaces in Birmingham and the surrounding towns was enticing, but it was just a beautiful dream for now.

Dismissing the idea, Dolly watched a young boy telling his mother he was hungry whilst tugging at her skirt. The woman clipped him round the ear and sent him off into the street, then continued to quaff her gin. Dolly shook her head. *Poor kid!*

Then her attention was drawn to a man who was singing loudly and badly. Another joined him and the cacophony assaulted her ears, making her wish she had a piano, too. At least it might keep the singers in tune. She worked on and smiled when Aggie put a stop to the man's caterwauling with a swift kick to his shin.

While Dolly was tending her bar, Jack was watching the Hodges family begin work in his dining room. The new gas lamps and chandeliers were being installed, leaving plenty of space for the large mirrors, which were to be delivered later.

Satisfied the work was progressing well, Jack returned to the bar and glanced at the piano. He missed Wyman's playing and sadly no one had touched it since the man had left. Jack wondered if the instrument was thought of with a kind of reverence and he smiled. There must be someone out there who could play, but finding them was another matter entirely.

'Have you heard the latest?' Frank said as Jack joined him behind the bar.

'What now?'

'Dolly is supposed to be looking for a couple of cheap pubs.'

Jack laughed. 'Good luck to her finding the money first.'

Frank grinned and nodded his agreement.

'I need to find somebody to play that now Wyman has gone,' Jack said, tilting his head towards the silent piano.

'Send the runners out,' Frank suggested.

'Good idea.' Jack pushed his way through the crowd and went

out of the front doors. He gave a loud whistle and shook his head at a waiting cabbie. A moment later a young girl came hurtling across the road from a triangle-shaped island of trees and bushes which divided the roads. About ten years old, the girl was wearing a shabby coat which hung off her skinny frame. She wore no socks or stockings, only a pair of tattered shoes on her bare feet. Her dark hair was long and matted and her face and hands were blue with cold beneath the dirt.

'I need a piano player to work long hours in my bar,' Jack said as he pulled a shilling from his pocket.

'Righto, guv.'

'When you've done that send a couple of boys to the kitchen where I'll be waiting.'

'Will do. Thanks, Jack!' the girl said as he passed over the shilling.

Going indoors via the back way rather than fight his way through the customers, he called out, 'Bess, I've a couple of runners coming shortly and I'd like some food put up for them to take back to their mates, please.'

Bess nodded and sent Gwen in search of a large basket from the scullery. Together they packed bread, cheese, ham, pickles, cake and biscuits as well as tea, sugar and milk.

Jack asked his staff if they had any old clothes that could be passed on to the runners. Frank and Joey said he could have those they had sorted out for Wyman. Jack ran upstairs to the room the pianist had occupied and found shirts, trousers and jackets hanging in the wardrobe. Gathering them into a bundle, he carried them to the kitchen.

A moment later a knock came to the door and Bess called, 'Come in.'

Two boys entered – covered in snowflakes.

Bess and Gwen had found some unused clothes which would help the girl runners out and Jack donated his old cloth cap.

The boys shivered and Bess threw open the range doors and told them to warm themselves while she poured hot tea and cut a slice of cake each for them.

'Ooh, ta!'

'There's a hamper there for you to share, though we'll need the basket back,' Jack said, 'and the staff have sorted out some clothes that might be useful.'

'Ta, Jack,' one said through a mouthful of cake.

'You're welcome.'

Having finished eating, the boys took the basket of food and the bundle of clothes and with more thanks they stepped into a world which by night-time would be white over.

'That was a lovely thing to do,' Bess commented.

'Those poor buggers have nothing. They rely on their message money and I'll bet not everyone tips them well.'

'How many of them are there, do you think?'

'God knows, but I'm willing to wager there are more joining every day.'

'It's a bloody shame. Somebody ought to take them in off the streets,' Bess said.

'Don't look at me! I can't have hundreds of urchins roaming around the place. Dolly would have a blue fit! I'll help out where I can, like today, but further than that I can't go.'

'You're right, of course, but I feel sorry in my heart for them, especially in this weather,' the cook said, closing the range doors again.

'Me too, Bess, me too.'

There was another knock on the door and Bess answered it, coming back with the basket, which had been returned as promised.

Jack smiled before heading out to the bar to serve while another barman took a break. He couldn't help but wish he could aid the runners a little more. His attention was diverted by a man in a fighting stance challenging his doormen. *I wouldn't do it if I were you, mate!* Jack thought with a smile.

He laughed when the burly doormen caught the man under the arms and carried him out of the doors into the snow. Then Jack went back to his work as his thoughts swirled around the rumour of Dolly chasing up another pub. Was there something Dolly wasn't telling him?

34

'Say that again!' Ezra Moreton boomed at the man standing before him.

'Dolly Perkins is after two pubs, boss, in Navigation Street by the market hall.'

'Somebody is having a laugh! She can't be! Are they up for sale?'

'Don't know, boss.'

'Then find out!'

'Yes, boss.' The man fled the office in terror.

'This is past a joke,' Ezra muttered to himself as he watched large fluffy snowflakes float lazily from the sky.

He scowled as his mind whirled. If it should be that those pubs are up for sale then they would soon belong to him!

It was mid-morning when the answer came back – the pubs were indeed up for sale.

Ezra lost no time. He and his two bodyguards caught a cab to Navigation Street and he was in no mood to argue. The landlords of both were *persuaded* to sell their premises to Moreton and by late afternoon, after visiting the bank, Ezra was the proud owner of two more drinking dens. The purchases had put a sizeable dent in his finances, but he was certain he could rectify that by putting good managers in place as he had with his other properties. Money was coming in from his assets situated all across the town so he was not unduly worried, but he would have to keep a close eye on things nevertheless.

In his office once more, Ezra whistled a little tune as he built up the fire. He wondered how Dolly would react when she found out Ezra Moreton had bested her yet again.

Whilst Ezra was gloating, Dolly was being informed about his new acquisitions.

'How do you get to know these things?' she asked.

Aggie gave a toothless grin and tapped the side of her nose. 'You know me, wench, I've got spies everywhere.'

'Why on Earth is Ezra buying all these places?'

'Because, and it's only a guess mind, he thinks you're after them and he won't be outdone by a woman!'

'But I'm not after them. What on Earth gives him that idea?'

'He's convinced you are so you can have another palace.'

'If that's what he believes, then he's pretty stupid.'

Aggie grinned again as her glass was filled. 'Ta, sweet'eart.'

Dolly shook her head in mock indignation and work behind the bar went on.

Meanwhile, in the dining room at the Emporium, the lighting was all in place and the mirrors were being hung, beneath which sturdy shelves were fitted. Jack had been to the cooperage works on Loveday Street and ordered miniature casks which would adorn the shelves.

All that was left to do was wait for the diners. Jack fretted that his venture might prove fruitless and people wouldn't come. He would have wasted Dolly's money and he couldn't bear the thought of letting her down.

'That's it, Jack, all done.'

'Thanks, Eli, you've all done a sterling job.'

'Jack, can I ask... are your fancy diners going to enter by way of the bar?'

Jack's mouth fell open. 'Bloody bugger! I never thought of that! Christ, Eli, what am I going to do? Dolly will kill me!' He dragged his hands through his hair as he paced the floor.

'My lads can put a door in the wall just there,' Eli pointed, 'but we'll have to put a lintel in to strengthen the structure. We can paint the door to match the others and you can hang a sign to tell folks it's the dining room.'

'Why didn't you tell me this before?'

'Because it ain't my place to tell you what to do. Besides, I didn't want you to think I was after getting more money out of you.'

Jack nodded at the man's honesty. 'How quick can you do it?'

'We'll get on to it straight away. We ain't got anything else on the books at the minute.'

'Thanks, Eli, you're a life saver.'

Eli grinned and yelled for his sons to give them their instructions. To Jack he said, 'There will be a lot of dust, I warn you.'

'I'm not bothered as long as it's done before Dolly pays us another visit!' Jack felt badly about spending Dolly's money but was sure once the dining hall was up and running they would recoup the expense in no time.

Eli laughed, then the Hodges family returned to their yard to collect the necessary things to knock a large hole in a wall.

Jack informed Bess and Gwen of his oversight and apologised for the cleaning that lay ahead of them.

'Better to have it done now,' Bess said philosophically.

'True. I'm off to the sign-writer. Just pray Dolly is too busy to visit for a while.'

Gwen giggled as Jack rushed out of the back door.

'He's doing his level best to get this project underway,' Bess said.

'I think it could be a great success, especially once folks know what you've cooked up.'

Bess beamed her pleasure at the compliment. 'We'll need to get the menus printed up, though.'

'Why? I can write them out,' Gwen said.

'Do you reckon? Give it a go then and we'll see how they look.'

By the time Jack returned, a menu in beautiful copperplate writing was waiting for his approval. Having written 'Emporium of Dreams Dining Room' on the top, Gwen had listed neatly the foods on offer, each with a price by its side. At the bottom in smaller script she'd put:

Thank you for your visit and we hope to see you again soon.

'Gwen, this is amazing!' Jack gushed. 'I had no idea you could write like this!'

'I love to do it,' she responded simply.

'Would you be in charge of them, please?'

'Certainly.'

'Ladies, I don't know where I'd be without you. Thank you both.'

'We're happy to be of service, let's just hope it takes off,' Bess answered.

'It will, I feel it in my bones,' Jack said. He just wished he felt as confident as he sounded.

The following day saw the Hodges arrive at six o'clock and soon they were hard at work installing the door. Jack grimaced as each hammer blow was struck, hoping the mirrors on the adjacent walls were safe. He needn't have worried, the builders were professionals and in no time at all the lintel and door were fitted, the rubble swept up and transferred to their cart, and a coat of paint finished it off.

Eli and his sons had toiled throughout the day in an effort to get the job done in one go. They had not stopped for their usual breaks but had eaten while they worked and only slipped away to use the privy.

Jack was delighted at how swiftly the work was completed and couldn't thank them enough. The sign arrived and Jack hung it himself. Standing back to look at his handiwork, he smiled proudly.

Going inside through the new door, being careful of the wet paint, he was happy to see Bess and Gwen already hard at work cleaning away the dust. By the end of the day they would be ready for their first customers.

Please God let this work, he thought as he went to make the ladies a cup of tea.

At Jack's instruction, Joey had lit a fire in the dining room to take the chill off after it had been exposed to the weather all day. Jack knew there would be an icy blast each time the door was opened, but he could not do anything about that other than keep the fire stoked.

The ladies sat, grateful for the tea he'd made, and Bess reiterated Jack's worries. 'You'll need a porch of some sort over that door.'

'I know, I was thinking the same thing but I daren't spend any more of Dolly's money.'

'Put it to her, see what she says.'

'I will,' Jack said.

It was a couple of days later when Dolly visited and she was thrilled by the work done.

Jack breathed a sigh of relief when she suggested adding a porch to the door.

'I'll see if Eli is available,' Jack said.

He was, and along with his sons, Eli worked on building a

portico, moaning all the time that the cold was murder on his old bones.

Nellie and Nancy were invited to see the changes made, as were Sadie and Alice from the Palace. The women sat around the kitchen table, exchanging gossip over pots of tea and home-made cake and biscuits.

'Have you thought any more about your wedding, Dolly?' Nellie asked.

'No, we've been so busy I haven't had time.'

'You'll need to book in with the vicar and get a frock,' Nancy added.

'A gown, Nance,' Nellie corrected.

'Gown, frock, it don't matter as long as she doesn't go in her birthday suit!' Laughter filled the kitchen and talk of the wedding petered out as it was a way off yet. It was replaced by the swapping of recipes and cooking tips, ready for the new dining room to receive its first guests.

Dolly joined Jack in the bar when an urchin runner pushed his way to the counter. After speaking with Jack, the boy was given a shilling and ran off happily.

'He's found us a pianist,' Jack said and Dolly grinned. 'A fella is coming round shortly.'

An hour later, the man arrived by cab and sought his way through the crowd with the aid of a white stick.

'Randall Green is my name and I'm seeking Jack Larkin.'

'That's me,' Jack said, a look of bewilderment on his face.

'Ah, good to meet you, Jack. I believe you are looking for a pianist?'

'Erm yes, but forgive me saying...'

'I'm blind? Yes, I know,' Randall gave a little titter, 'but I can play. Show me to your piano and I'll prove it.'

Jack headed around the bar and grabbed Randall's arm.

'Not like that, Jack, may I rest a hand on your shoulder?'

Jack nodded, before remembering that Randall couldn't see him, so he said, 'Yes, sorry.'

At the piano, Randall rested his cane against his leg and made himself comfortable on the stool, before running a fingernail along the keys. 'Not bad, but it needs a tweak.' Pulling out a small roll of tools from his pocket, he lifted the lid. After a moment he tried again with the keys. 'Much better. It sounds very busy in here, Jack.'

'Always is, Randall, folk love their gin,' Jack said and shrugged at Dolly, watching from behind the bar.

Adjusting the stool, Randall began to play and beautiful music filled the room once more. Jack smiled and a hope rose in him that Randall would stay and entertain his customers regularly.

Applause rang around the room and Randall grinned. 'So Jack, will you give me the job?'

'Yes, indeed, but why aren't you in a concert hall?' Memories of asking Wyman the same question rose in Jack's mind.

'I choose not to be. I live alone quite happily but sometimes I crave company. I am requested to tune instruments which I enjoy, but now I'd like a job playing as well.'

'Then welcome, Randall. Come to the kitchen and meet everyone. Bess, our cook, will fill you with tea and cake and then you can start work whenever you would like to.'

'Thank you kindly, Jack.' Placing a hand on Jack's shoulder again, Randall went to meet the team, the cheer the customers gave on seeing him causing him to laugh loudly.

After refreshments, Randall returned to the piano, choosing to walk alone so he could get used to the layout of the place and learn where everything was situated. He was in his element when loud singing broke out, and as Jack watched he smiled broadly. Later, Nellie and Nancy returned to the Crown Saloon, singing as they went, and Dolly went home to the Palace.

That evening, everyone was amazed when the dining room began to fill with well-to-do couples. Men in top hats and tail-coats with silver-topped canes brought their ladies in fine dresses dripping with jewels.

Gwen was volunteered as waitress and Bess's hot food went down a storm.

Liver paste spread on buttered bread was on offer as a starter, then kidney pudding made with suet and seasoned with nutmeg, salt, pepper and garnished with chopped parsley. Chitterlings, the small intestines of a pig which were plaited into a chain, were served hot with onions and swede. Pidgeon was cooked with bacon and served with mashed potatoes and French beans. Grey maple peas, known locally as 'grey pays', and fried bacon came with chunks of fresh bread. Lardy cake, made from basic bread dough and containing currants, spices and sugar, was baked until brown and offered hot or cold.

Naturally the toffs were fascinated by the tale of the body in the wall, which Gwen regaled them with enthusiastically.

Jack was elated at how well the evening had gone, and once the diners had left he sat in the kitchen with Bess and Gwen, showering them with his thanks.

'What a night!' Bess said, pushing her hair off her face.

'Tell me about it,' Gwen added as she rubbed her aching feet.

'Tomorrow I'll get a couple of waitresses and an assistant for you, Bess, from the Servants' Registry.'

'Thanks, Jack, because if tonight is anything to go by, we're going to need them,' Bess replied.

'The food was a great success as well,' Gwen added.

'I thought we'd keep this menu for a month, then swap it around with some other dishes,' Bess volunteered.

'Excellent idea. You two are bloody marvels!' Jack praised the ladies who had worked so hard. Their ears ringing with compliments, he sent them off to have a well-earned rest before heading to bed himself.

Early the following morning, Jack's visit to the Registry bore fruit and by mid-morning two waitresses and a cook's assistant were hired by Bess. Jack had given her leave to interview and hire whoever she felt would be best suited for the positions and the woman glowed at being given so much responsibility.

Gwen asked if she might be given a couple of hours off as she had something she needed to do. The time was granted without question from Jack, and the maid hurried over to the printers, having first wrapped herself warmly against the biting cold. She purchased some paper and rushed home. In her room, she folded a sheet of paper in half and then she began to write. On the front page she sketched a picture of the Emporium and inside she related the story of the body in the wall, the theories about her murder, and the details of how the corpse was discovered. Pleased with her first booklet, she took it to the kitchen for Jack to see.

'This is fantastic, Gwen!' Jack gushed. 'Dolly will love it!'

'I thought – one on each table with the menu. They could be a real talking point and maybe attract new customers too,' Gwen suggested.

'Yes!' Jack replied.

'You know folks will pinch them,' Bess put in.

'I didn't think of that,' Gwen said a little sadly. 'It would take up a lot of my time to keep doing replacements.'

'We should get this printed up so we can have a box full,' Jack mumbled. Then as he looked at it again, he added, 'Put your name on the bottom so everyone will know who wrote it.'

Gwen beamed.

'Then take it to the printers and see how much it would cost and how many they'll do for us.'

Gwen donned her coat and set off immediately, thrilled at Jack's response to her efforts and desperate to see her name in print.

An hour later she was back, invoice in hand.

'That's a good price for five hundred,' Jack said.

'They will deliver in a couple of days so it will need to be paid then.'

'I'll see to it. Well done, Gwen!'

The kitchen was a hive of activity and Jack joined Joey and Frank behind the bar. All those opinionated women in one room could be a disaster but Jack trusted Bess to keep order. Wonderful aromas drifted through to them as the day wore on and mouths watered in anticipation of lunch.

One of the revellers yelled over the music, 'Hey, Jack, you selling food now an' all?' And Jack had an idea. Going to the kitchen, he ran it past Bess.

'Bloody hell! Evening dinners, cooking for you lot and now this?' Bess boomed out.

'I was only asking your opinion, maybe it's a step too far,' Jack replied sheepishly.

'I suppose I could make up a bloody great pan of stew. With a chunk of bread...'

'That's a great idea, Bess!' Jack's excitement rose.

'All right, you work out a price and leave the rest to us.' Bess shook her head at the extra work Jack's idea entailed.

'Thanks, Bess. A raise in wages is called for, I think.'

'I should damn well think so!' the cook said but her smile belied her frustration. 'We're going to need a bigger order from the grocer an' all.'

Jack nodded his agreement and wandered back to the bar. He was enjoying being the manager and hoped his ideas wouldn't land him in hot water with Dolly.

A moment later he was back, for it was then that Ezra Moreton and his bodyguards walked in.

36

'Ezra.'

'Jack. Music now, is it?'

'What can I do for you, Ezra?' Jack asked, ignoring the question.

'I hear Dolly was interested in the two public houses over in Navigation Street which, I might add, now belong to me.'

'What has that got to do with me?' Jack asked.

'I thought you might pass that information along to her.'

'Well, you thought wrong. Anything you want my fiancée to know, you tell her yourself.'

'Fiancée? Congratulations, Jack. A wedding to pay for as well as searching for more premises. Dolly must be doing extremely well.'

'Are you drinking?' Jack asked pointedly.

'Good God, no!' Moreton replied as he cast a glance around.

'Then make room for those who are.' Jack saw Joey and Frank move to his side in a show of strength.

'I see you have opened a dining room,' Moreton said with a curl of his lip.

'Ezra, you'll get nothing from me, so I suggest you go about your business. As you can see, we're very busy and I don't have time to chat, not that I'd want to.'

Ezra's goons took a step forward, but Ezra held up a hand to forestall them. 'I was just passing the time of day with you, Jack.'

'No, Ezra, you were poking your nose where it's not wanted and doesn't belong. Now, if you'll excuse me...' Jack turned away and he and his barmen resumed their work.

Ezra stamped from the Emporium in a foul temper at being dismissed by this boy. In the cab on his way back to the brewery, he didn't speak a word and his men clamped their jaws tight enough to make their teeth ache.

Back in his office, Ezra knew he would get nothing more from Jack. He wanted to know how Dolly Perkins could afford all the changes that were being made. Maybe it was time to send out the runners again.

For his part, Jack was worried, and once Ezra had left, he hailed a cab. It was time to let Dolly know about Moreton's interest in her affairs. While he was at it, Jack took one of Gwen's little story books with him so Dolly could see what he was spending her money on. He would need to request the petty cash be replenished too but felt sure Dolly would agree once she heard his ideas.

He was right, of course. Dolly was thrilled with how Jack's endless ideas were bringing in more money, and said it was time for him to have access to the business account at the bank. It made perfect sense that he could draw what was needed rather than have to come to her each time. Dolly trusted he would not abuse the privilege, especially as they were soon to be husband and wife.

Then Jack filled Dolly in about Ezra's visit.

'What's he up to, I wonder?' Dolly asked, looking puzzled.

'I don't know, but he's mighty interested in you and your businesses, that's for sure.'

'Aggie told me about him buying the pubs on Navigation Street because he thought I wanted them.'

'Surely he knows you ain't in a position as yet to be on the market for another place,' Jack said.

'That's why I can't work all this out,' Dolly said with a frown.

A banging on the kitchen door interrupted their conversation, and Sadie let in a scruffy urchin out of the cold.

'Dolly, we thought as you should know, Moreton's got us all out trying to find out which pub you'll go for next,' the lad said.

'Thank you,' Dolly said, then to Sadie, 'Tea and cake for Jimmy, please.'

'Ooh, ta! I'm glad I came now!'

Dolly smiled and watched as the boy wolfed down the cake and slurped his tea. She gave him a sixpence and he shot off with a whoop.

'What do you make of that?' Dolly asked.

'I haven't got a clue,' Jack replied.

'It's all very mysterious, isn't it, but as long as he doesn't interfere with our businesses I think it's safe to ignore him.'

'I agree, but we need to keep an ear to the ground in the meantime,' Jack responded. 'Dolly, I've been thinking, I know you said we should be married in the spring but...'

'But you'd like it to be sooner?' Dolly asked.

'Yes. As soon as possible as far as I'm concerned.' Jack's eyes sparkled as he spoke. 'I love you, Dolly, and I want to be with you day and night.'

Dolly blushed at his forthright manner.

'How about as soon as you can arrange it with the vicar?' she asked.

Jack grinned. 'I'd love that!'

Applause sounded and eyes teared up before they celebrated with tea.

'You'll need to draw up a guest list,' Sadie said, and Alice's ears pricked up. 'I'm guessing you'll need food preparing an' all.'

'Yes, please, and I'm going to need some help with all this organising, Sadie,' Dolly said.

'We can do that,' Alice put in eagerly.

Jack and Dolly shared a kiss before they parted company, Jack saying he was off to see the vicar straight away.

The three women sat at the table with pencil and paper, eager to begin preparations without delay.

'First thing to decide is where to have the wedding breakfast,' Sadie said.

'Oh, I don't know!' Dolly admitted she had thought little about the wedding and all that went into it. 'I need your advice, ladies. I have to confess, I'm clueless about this sort of thing.'

'The Emporium is bigger and the kitchen is as well, so maybe that would be the best location?' Sadie suggested.

'All right, that makes sense.'

'Alice and I can help Bess and Gwen do the food so you've no need to worry about that.'

'Maybe Gwen would write out some invitations,' Dolly mused.

'I'm sure she will,' Alice agreed.

'Right, now, who will be coming?' Sadie asked.

'Nellie, Nancy and Fred, the staff at the Crown, the staff at the Emporium and everyone from here.'

Alice clapped her hands, thrilled at being included.

'You'll need a wedding dress but there's lots of places to look for that. Just don't leave it too long in case it has to be made and fitted,' Sadie advised.

'Oh, goodness, there's so much to think about!'

'You'll also need somebody to give you away. Any ideas?'

'I had thought about that, and I think Fred is the perfect choice. He's always looked out for me, and I think he'll agree, don't you?'

Every decision they made was noted down, lest something be forgotten, and Dolly could feel her excitement grow as more plans were made.

'She'll need a posy to carry,' Alice said.

Sadie nodded. 'Anything else?'

The others shook their heads, happy that they'd thought of everything.

'There is, you know,' Sadie said after a moment's pause.

Dolly and Alice exchanged a questioning glance.

'You and Jack have to decide where you'll be living once you're wed.'

Dolly blew out her cheeks, then said, 'Oh Lord!' How on Earth were they going to choose?

37

Jack's visit with the vicar went well and they agreed a date for three weeks hence. In an ebullient mood, Jack hot-footed it back to the Palace to tell Dolly the good news.

'Three weeks! That's so soon.'

'Yes, so you need to get cracking!'

'So do you. You'll need new clothes.'

'Oh crikey, yes! I hadn't thought about that.'

'Jack, Sadie brought up an important issue that needs addressing too.' Dolly looked at her betrothed's frown and went on seriously, 'Where will we be living after the wedding?'

'Where would you like to live?' he asked simply.

'I love it here but...'

'Then here it will be, but you'll have to get a bigger bed!'

Dolly flushed scarlet and Sadie and Alice burst out laughing.

'You wouldn't mind moving from the Emporium?'

'No, not at all. I can still work there. I can go in the mornings and come back at a reasonable hour to spend time with you. Joey and Frank can lock up. Just think, I'll have lived in all three gin houses then.'

'Oh yes, you will. Thank you, Jack. I would have been sad to leave my home, to be honest.'

'I tell you what, Mum will be over the moon when she knows she has a wedding to look forward to so soon, and that you'll be living so near to her.'

'Shall I tell them over at the Crown and you can sort out your end?'

'Yes, that's the best idea.'

'Oh, and Jack, would you ask Gwen if she'd be good enough to write out the invitations?'

'Will do. I'll ask her to pop and see you and you can thrash it out between you.'

With another kiss, Jack left for home and Dolly wandered across the road to the Crown.

She explained to Nellie and Nancy what had been discussed and arranged and, to her surprise, panic took hold of the women.

'We'll need new frocks!' Nellie said frantically.

'And new hats!' Nancy put in. 'Fred will have to have a new suit, but how he'll get one to fit I don't know!'

'We'll have to close up for the day,' Nellie said.

'What about the customers?' Nancy asked.

'Bugger them! This is the kids' wedding, Nance!' Nellie boomed.

Dolly grinned at the happiness of the two women she loved most in the world.

'Nancy, do you think that, if I asked, Fred would give me away?'

'Oh, bab! He'd love it, I'm sure,' Nancy replied with a tear in her eye.

They both jumped as Nellie yelled, 'Fred! I need you a minute!'

'Coming Nellie,' came the reply.

Fred joined them in the kitchen and Dolly asked her question shyly. 'The wedding has been arranged for three weeks' time and I wondered, would you give me away?'

'I'd be honoured, sweet'eart,' the big man answered, pulling the girl into a hug.

'Thank you. Now that's all settled, I'd better get back to work.' Dolly left Nellie and Nancy discussing her wedding eagerly, and as she walked back to the Palace, she found herself counting her blessings once more. She had found a wonderful man who would shortly become her husband. Her business was doing well and she was surrounded by good people and dear friends.

Walking into the kitchen, she said to Sadie, 'Could you add Wilton and his family to the guest list, please?'

Sadie nodded, twitching her eyebrows at Alice who just grinned.

It was later that day when Dolly sent a runner asking Gwen to come to the Palace. When she arrived, she was very excited at being asked to write out the invitations. With the list and some money from Dolly, she headed off to buy some good quality paper suitable for the task.

Jack had said she could write them during the evenings because in the daytime she would be needed in the kitchen.

Bess had reminded Jack he would need a best man and, as Fred was spoken for, he feared he would have to choose between Joey and Frank, so to save any arguments he decided to make a trip to the theatre to ask Wyman.

Knocking on the theatre door, he was let in by the old man who said, 'I'll get a bed moved in 'ere for you shall I?'

Jack laughed. 'I've come to see...'

The man waved a hand towards the corridor.

'Wyman York,' Jack finished.

'Down to the bottom and through the door on the right.'

'Thank you.'

'You're a bloody menace!' the old man said, but then he chuckled. 'I heard what you did for Mr York. Bless you, lad!'

Jack patted the man gently on his bent shoulder and strode down the corridor.

'Jack! How lovely to see you!' Wyman enthused as Jack walked into the large room. It housed a small piano, which was where Wyman sat now, his shirt sleeves rolled up above his elbows and a pencil tucked behind his ear.

'How are you, Wyman?'

'Good, my boy, very good.'

Jack told the pianist why he had come and Wyman clasped his hands together.

'A wedding! I'd be delighted to be your best man, Jack. Many thanks for thinking of me.'

The two chatted a while, catching up on each other's news, and Jack told him about the blind man playing at the Emporium now.

'Randall Green. I know him well, he tunes pianos everywhere and is a brilliant pianist,' Wyman said.

'The crowd love him, but I think they still miss you.'

'You're too kind, Jack, but I'm sure they don't. Give everyone my regards.'

Jack nodded and left him to his work. He had noticed the paper Wyman was writing on and Jack surmised it was a new piano composition. He hoped he was right and that Wyman had begun to compose once more.

It was snowing heavily again when Jack climbed into the cab. The horse struggled to find purchase on the icy roadway and the cab slewed from side to side. He could hear the cabbie calling reassuringly to the horse as they proceeded carefully towards their destination.

Once indoors, Jack warmed himself by the range. 'If this weather keeps up, folks won't be able to get here for their gin.'

'Oh, they'll come, even if they have to break out the sledges,' Bess said with a laugh.

'If we get snowed in, I won't be getting wed.'

'You will. We'll send a sledge for the vicar and he can marry you two in the bar.'

Jack moved to stare out of the kitchen window, praying for more clement weather.

But, as if in defiance, the snow kept falling, thicker and thicker.

38

'That bloody roof is leaking again!' the man snapped, making Ezra look up from his accounts.

'Put a bucket under it.'

'We've got buckets everywhere. That roof is like a colander! It needs fixing!'

'I ain't spending money on it yet. When the snow's gone I'll get a roofer to have a look. Meanwhile you'll just have to manage.'

The worker walked out of Ezra's office in a huff.

Ezra sighed. He'd known about the leaky roof for a while and had intended to get it repaired, but he'd been too busy. It would have to last until the spring and then he would get a builder in. He thought his workers were making mountains out of molehills and, shaking his head, he returned his attention to the figures before him.

He was at his financial limit now, so if he wanted to buy more property it would have to be on a mortgage facility. He chided himself for being rash in buying the pubs on Navigation Street as it had taken up all his capital. However, they now belonged to him which meant that at least Dolly Perkins couldn't get her hands on them. The satisfaction he was feeling was worth it.

Ezra looked up again at the ceiling. No one in their right mind would climb up there to inspect his brewery roof while the snow was still falling. Building up the fire, he stared out at the street where everything had turned white.

The whole of the following week it snowed day and night and the snow lay inches thick everywhere. Folk were out with shovels clearing pathways but the next day it was just as bad again. Businesses suffered as people stayed indoors, not daring to venture out for fear of catching their death of cold.

Pubs and gin palaces alike saw a drop in custom, but as Bess had predicted, some still braved the weather for their alcohol.

The next week saw no let-up in the weather, although the snow only came at night. The snow drifts were measured in feet rather than inches. The streets were empty of carts and cabs, the owners unwilling to risk their horses on the ice.

It was as the week drew to a close that the catastrophe happened.

One night there was an enormous crash and, although people heard it, they refused to get out of their warm beds to investigate. They could find out what had happened when they rose in the morning.

Ezra Moreton arrived at the brewery early, having had to trudge through the snow, which was falling yet again, to find his workers out on the road.

'What's going on?' he asked from beneath his snow-covered umbrella.

'The roof's caved in! I warned you but you wouldn't listen!' It was the same man who had reported the leak who spoke.

'Christ almighty!' Ezra exclaimed as he tried to get a look at the damage.

'All the stock is smashed to pieces,' the man said.

'Bloody hell!'

'Well, we can't work in that lot,' the man spoke again.

'Isn't there anything we can salvage?' Ezra asked impatiently.

'No, not a thing.'

'We have to do something!' Ezra uttered truculently as he saw the beer had spread across the snow from the wrecked barrels.

'Such as?' the worker asked.

Ezra shook his head. For once he was at a loss for words. He was devastated. His brewery couldn't function like this, which meant no beer could be brewed or delivered. That in turn meant no money coming in. He *had* to get a builder in now to repair the damage, and that would cost. Having examined his finances closely, he knew he could not stretch to that without approaching the bank for a loan. Besides which, work could not commence until the snow stopped falling.

The grumbling of his workers snapped his attention back and he shouted, 'Go home! Come back when I can get this lot sorted out.'

'What about our wages?' one called out.

'We need to work!' another yelled.

'What do you want me to do? You can't work in that, you just said so yourself!' Ezra said belligerently.

'My missus will skin my hide when I tell her!' yet another mumbled.

'It's not my fault!' Ezra railed.

'Beggin' your pardon, boss, but it is,' one of the braver men muttered.

'Just bugger off, all of you!' Ezra turned and fought his way through the snow heading for home. His brewery looked like a building site and he could do nothing about it. He slipped on the ice and fell on his back, which only blackened his mood further. Infuriated and with a sore backside, he trudged on.

* * *

In contrast, over at the Palace it was warm and full of customers. Dolly marvelled at how they had managed to get there but was glad they had.

Aggie arrived cold and wet, puffing and panting.

'You should have stayed at home,' Dolly said.

'You'm kidding, ain't yer? The weather was worse than this when I was a youngster. Snowed in for weeks we were; almost starved to death 'cos mother couldn't get to the market!'

Dolly filled a glass and pushed it across the counter.

'Here, that's for your efforts.'

Aggie nodded her thanks as she removed her two pairs of woollen mittens. Taking a gulp, she then said, 'Ezra Moreton is spitting fire!'

'Why? What's wrong with him now?' Dolly frowned.

'The roof of his brewery has only gone and collapsed under the weight of the snow!'

'Good grief!' Dolly exclaimed.

'Ar, and all his beer had piddled away 'cos the barrels was all bosted!'

'Did any of the barrels survive?'

'Not a one!'

'Poor man.'

'Poor man, my arse! Moreton's had this coming to him for a long time,' Aggie remonstrated.

'Even so, it's hard luck,' Dolly returned.

'It ain't! He should have had it seen to afore this. Now his customers will be going somewhere else,' Aggie said.

'What about his new pubs on Navigation Street?' Dolly asked.

'If he wants to keep them open, he'll have to buy beer in.'

Dolly replenished Aggie's glass and the old woman went on. 'He'll have to buy beer for all his pubs, although I don't rightly know how many he has now.'

Dolly was surprised. There was actually something Aggie *didn't* know!

Aggie took her glass to stand by the roaring fire, where she could spread the news of Ezra's bad fortune.

Dolly's customers settled in for the day and outside the snow still fell from the heavens.

39

Jack and Dolly's wedding day drew nearer, and the weather gave no signs of letting up. Shovels were still being dragged across pathways in an effort to keep foot traffic flowing, but it was a thankless task.

The young couple, in their separate establishments, fretted that their special day might have to be cancelled, or at the very least postponed.

Dolly had been unable to go hunting for a wedding dress and so Sadie had managed to get some material from the market and sat sewing until her eyes ached. The cream silk slowly came together and Dolly was delighted, although she wondered if she would ever get to wear it.

The invitations had gone out before the snow prevented them, but the idea of a posy went out of the window. However, Alice said Dolly could borrow her small prayer book to carry if she'd like to.

Jack also had been unable, as had Fred, to purchase new clothes, so they brushed up what they had in the hope the wedding could still go ahead.

Jack, Dolly and Nellie were glad they had stocked the cellars and had ordered extra supplies at the onset of the bad weather, for no carts were able to get through now.

Jack dressed warmly and he and Frank trudged through the thick white layers to the vicarage. He needed to ask the vicar if he would perform the service at the Palace. They had planned on the Emporium as it was bigger for the after party, but Jack didn't want Dolly traversing the lethally icy streets, and he doubted anyone would get to the church.

Invited in, Jack explained why they were there.

'Hold a service in a gin palace?' the vicar gasped.

'It's the only way,' Jack said, rubbing his cold hands together.

'The place would have to be blessed first and your guests may not be able to travel,' the vicar said. He was trying his best to dissuade Jack so he would not have to go out himself in the dreadful weather.

'Please vicar, we *have* to get wed – it's all arranged!' Jack pleaded.

The vicar narrowed his eyes. 'Your intended isn't expecting a child, is she?' he asked with a frown.

'No, of course not!'

'Then what's the hurry? You could rearrange for a time when this awful weather improves.'

Jack explained how he had almost lost Dolly once before and how desperate they were to get married, and finally the vicar relented.

'Very well. The Palace it will be.'

Thanking the man profusely, Jack and Frank set off to tell Dolly about the new arrangements. They had gone together in case one slipped on the ice and broke a bone.

They were frozen by the time they reached the Palace and gratefully accepted hot food and drinks.

'Oh, Jack, we could have waited. You didn't need to go out in this!' Dolly said.

'I did. I'm not letting you get away from me. On Saturday next you and I will become man and wife, and I'll be the happiest I've ever been. Snow be damned!'

'What about our guests? They won't want to risk it.' Dolly waved a hand towards the kitchen window where they could see the white flakes still falling heavily.

'It won't matter. Mum and the others only have to cross the road so that's not a problem. As for everyone else, it will be up to them. The vicar is coming here to bless the place before the ceremony.'

'Well, if you think it's a good idea...' Dolly began.

'It's the only way if we want to be married,' Jack said.

'All right, let's do it,' Dolly conceded with a beaming smile.

Then she filled Jack in on the news of Ezra's roof collapsing.

'Blimey! That's gonna cost to get that fixed!' Then to his friend he said, 'Righto, Frank, are you ready to go?' Frank nodded and Jack kissed Dolly before they set off once more, eager to get home as soon as possible.

'I'm not coming out again until Saturday,' Jack said as they pushed on through the ever-increasing snowfall.

'Nor me! I'm soaked to the skin and I can't feel my toes!' Frank replied.

'Let's hurry up then, otherwise we'll have frostbite.'

Eventually they reached the Emporium and both men went to change into warm dry clothes.

Jack then filled the whole team in on the changes they were having to make to the wedding, saying he would understand if they felt they could not attend.

'What, and miss it? There's no way on God's green – or rather white – Earth I wouldn't be there!' Bess said and was pleased to see the nods of agreement from all of her colleagues.

'Good. Well, let's hope God stops sending this white stuff, then, and everything goes according to plan,' Jack said with a grin.

As the day progressed, Jack's customers left to brave the cold on their way home. It was early evening by the time the bar was empty. Jack locked up and turned off the lamps, retiring to the kitchen, where it was warm and cosy. He had sent his staff home too, saying they should stay away until the weather improved.

Jack, Bess, Gwen, Frank and Joey enjoyed a hot meal of stew and dumplings with freshly baked bread.

It was dark outside but the gas lamps in the kitchen threw out a rosy glow. The range doors were left open to heat the room and it was then Jack and Frank finally had the time to fill their friends in on Ezra's misfortune.

The same tale was being related in the Crown Saloon by Aggie at that very moment. In exchange for free gin, she was describing the devastation over at the brewery site to Nellie.

'Dear God! Was anybody hurt?' Nellie asked.

'No, fortunately it went overnight otherwise the blokes would have been crushed to death.'

'Nance! Come and hear this!' Nellie called out and, again for a free tot, Aggie revelled in the telling of what had befallen Ezra Moreton.

Later, Nellie closed up earlier than usual, so folk could get home through the snow.

The following morning Birmingham breathed a collective sigh of relief to see the snow had stopped, and again shovels and spades were brought out to clear walkways. Everyone prayed for a thaw but it didn't seem likely for a while. Those businesses that could had opened up, but custom was sparse so many closed again and owners struggled homeward.

The kitchen at the Palace was busy as Sadie, Alice and Dolly cooked the food needed for after the wedding ceremony. Rolling out pastry for pies, Dolly's nerves jangled.

This time tomorrow she would be a married lady. She wondered if she would feel any different. She flushed as she thought about her wedding night and pushed the hair off her face with the back of her forearm.

Pull yourself together, girl, there's a lot to be done if we are to be ready on time!

Humming a little tune, she tried to concentrate on the baking, but again the flush came as her mind strayed to finally being alone at night with Jack.

40

Whilst wedding preparations were underway at the Palace, Ezra had walked solemnly to his brewery to assess the damage further. The office was still standing and a crowd of people were gathered around discussing Ezra's plight. Conversations were halted abruptly when they saw him coming, and as he neared they saw the scowl on his face.

'Did anyone see what happened?' he called out.

Heads shook and a woman said, 'We heard the crash.'

'Did you investigate it?'

'No.'

'Why not?'

'Because it was the middle of the bloody night!'

Ezra huffed. Clearly no one had been prepared to leave their warm beds to discover what had caused the roof to finally give way.

Unlocking the gate and walking through the yard, he saw the snow had turned a pale golden colour where the beer had escaped the smashed barrels. Going into the office, he collected his accounts ledger and the money he had hidden away in the safe. Then he walked through to the works. He gasped as he saw the rubble, which had once been the roof, piled on the floor. Looking up, he could see the sky and he heard the creak of remaining timbers.

'You shouldn't be in here, sir,' a voice said. 'It's far too dangerous.'

Ezra turned to see a policeman standing in the doorway.

'Come away now, there's a good man,' the bobby said kindly.

Ezra took a last look at what had been his livelihood and the constable spoke again.

'It's not safe, sir, the rest could come down at any minute.'

Ezra nodded and walked towards the other man. Suddenly there was a loud crack, a rumble and both men fled as an almighty crash brought down another portion of the roof. Timber and tiles flew everywhere and huge clumps of snow splatted onto the concrete floor.

Outside, the crowd of people ran for cover, slipping and sliding on the icy ground.

'Are you all right, sir?'

'Yes, thank you constable,' Ezra replied, but he was shaking with fright.

'You need to get this place locked up until a builder can have a look at it for you.'

Ezra nodded and they left the unstable building. The constable then turned to the crowd who were gathering once more. 'There's nothing more to see here, folks, so go on about your business.' Spreading his arms wide, the policeman herded the gawping people away from the scene.

With another look at the building, Ezra then locked the gates and walked away. Would that be the last time he would do that? Would he ever get the brewery up and running again? As he trudged towards the bank, he saw nothing of nature's white beauty. To him the snow was a curse that had ruined his business.

At the bank on Temple Row West, Ezra was surprised to see it was open and he was pleased to be ushered into the manager's office.

Jonah Blessep pointed to a seat and said, 'I'm sorry to hear about what happened to your brewery, Mr Moreton.'

'Yes, well, that's why I'm here. I'm in need of a loan to cover the expense of the repairs.'

'I see. Will your insurance not cover that?'

'No. Unfortunately it ran out last month and I never got around to renewing it.'

'Oh dear, how very unlucky.' Jonah pulled out a file from a cabinet which stood close to his desk. Retaking his seat, he flipped the file open and scanned the contents. 'How much were you looking to borrow?'

'I've no idea how much I'll need, but there won't be a problem paying it back. The money from my pubs will cover that.'

Jonah's fingers brushed over his white whiskers as he listened, his grey eyes watching the discomfort of the man in front of him. Looking again at the papers, Jonah shook his head slightly. He felt rather than saw Ezra squirm at having to come cap in hand for aid.

'The problem is, Mr Moreton, your public houses are not really pulling in enough to cover your costs. Your main income, as I'm sure you are aware, came from the brewery. Now that is out of action, I'm not sure I am able to help.'

'Once the roof is fixed, I'll pay off the loan in no time!' Ezra began to sweat as he saw the possibility of borrowing money slip away.

'Mr Moreton, you must see this from my perspective. For the

bank to enter into a loan facility with you at present would be a bad risk.'

'I need the money! I can't get the roof mended without it!' Ezra snapped.

'Calm down, Mr Moreton, yelling won't help anyone. Now, let's see what we can do for you,' Blessep said. Picking up his pen he scribbled some figures on a note pad and rubbed his whiskers again. Jonah was enjoying making the town bully shuffle on his seat. He liked the idea of Moreton being beholden to him. Moreton had ruled the roost for many years and now he was down to his cake and milk. Jonah Blessep had every intention of making Moreton beg.

'I'm not sure...' Jonah began.

'Please, Mr Blessep, you're the only one I can turn to.'

Jonah smiled benevolently and went back to his figures. Scratching out his previous numbers, he worked the maths again. Once more he shook his head.

'You *have* to help me Mr Blessep! Please, I'm begging you!'

There it was. Jonah's sigh was one of pure pleasure, although Moreton would think it one of concentration.

'This amount is the best I can do,' Jonah said as he pushed the paper across the desk to Moreton.

'I'll take it!' Ezra said.

The loan papers were drawn up, signed by both and witnessed by a bank teller, then Moreton said, 'Thank you. I'll get the builders on to it as soon as possible.'

'Your repayments will begin next week, Mr Moreton. Be advised that if you do not pay and fall into arrears then your businesses could become forfeit.'

Ezra nodded. The two men shook hands and Moreton left, a satisfied man.

Jonah Blessep wiped his hand on his handkerchief, which he

dropped into the waste bin. He was also a satisfied man, for he knew Ezra Moreton was unlikely to find a builder who would work in this weather. Furthermore, he doubted there would be a man in the town who would come to Ezra's aid, no matter how much he promised to pay.

Glancing out of the window, he saw weak sunshine light up the tiny ice crystals in the snow. They looked like diamonds embedded in ermine.

Jonah smiled and whistled a little tune as he thought, *Ezra Moreton is on borrowed time at last!*

Leaving the bank, Ezra went immediately to Hodges' yard. Unable to work because of the snow, Eli and his sons were clearing a pathway to the road.

'Now then, Mr Moreton, what can I be doing for you?' Eli asked, knowing full well why Ezra was at his premises.

'Good day to you, Eli. I need the brewery roof fixed. I'm sure you will have heard about it collapsing?'

'Ah, yes, I did hear summat. A shame, that is.'

Ezra nodded. 'So I want to know when you can make a start.'

Eli blew out his cheeks. 'The problem is all this stuff,' he said as he pointed at the snow with his shovel. 'We can't do bugger all until this has gone. It ain't safe, see?'

'Come on, man, this can't wait. I have just arranged a mortgage with the bank so you will be paid by them if that's your concern!' Ezra could have bitten his tongue off at revealing his private business but his temper was getting the better of him.

'It ain't that, Mr Moreton. I can't risk my boys up on what's left of that roof. It's more than likely the rest will come down yet.'

'Nonsense. Then I'll find someone else to do it!'

'Good luck in the trying but I tell you now, there ain't a man in the town would take that job on until after the thaw.'

Ezra stamped away in a mood blacker than coal dust. He knew Eli was right, of course, but he'd hoped the man needed the money badly enough to accept the work.

All Ezra could do now was wait for the thaw and hope the income from his pubs would cover his new mortgage. It galled him to have to pay out money to the bank whilst nothing was being done about repairs to his building, but if he was to get his business up and running again then it was the only way.

Ezra returned home cursing heaven, hell, Jonah Blessep and Eli Hodges.

While Moreton was fighting his way through the snow drifts, Jack had opened the Emporium and was surprised that there were any customers at all. The bar was nowhere near as crowded as usual, but custom was there.

Bess and Gwen were busy cooking food to take to the Palace the following day for the wedding. The waitresses and cook's assistant had been told not to risk coming to work in such awful weather, so Bess and Gwen were up to their armpits in pastry without any help.

Jack kept the ladies, as well as Frank and Joey, supplied with tea. He was sad not to hear the piano playing but Randall would never have safely negotiated the icy roads on foot. The cabs were still out of action and even the dray carts were struggling to get through. One person who always managed, however, was Aggie, and today she had news to share.

'I've got summat to tell you, Jack,' she said.

Jack grinned and poured her a gin.

'Ezra Moreton's had to get a mortgage to mend the brewery roof.'

'How on Earth would you know that?' Jack asked.

'Don't ask, but nobody will take the work on 'cos of the snow.'

'He's in trouble, then.'

'Ar, an' about time too!' Aggie replied with a chuckle. Emptying her glass and guessing rightly that she would get no more handouts, Aggie left. She was on her way to the Palace and then the Crown Saloon where she would divulge the same information for more free gin.

Tottering along, her thin frame covered in layers of clothing, Aggie returned the greetings of people out shovelling snow. She smiled at the children rolling large balls to be made into snowmen, while others slid down sheets of ice on the road and fell over at the end. The shouts of delight as snowballs were thrown made her laugh as she went. *What it is to be so young and full of fun*, she thought.

Coming at last to the Palace, she stepped indoors, having stamped the snow from her boots beforehand.

'Hello, Aggie, I didn't expect to see you today,' Dolly said.

'Ar, well, I've summat to share with you.'

Here we go! Dolly thought as the gin was poured and passed across the counter.

Aggie explained again about Ezra and cackled loudly at the finish.

'I can't help but feel sorry for Ezra,' Dolly said.

'Well, don't, because he's had this coming for many a year,' Aggie snapped. 'So, what's all the hustle and bustle about? Jack's place is the same.'

'Jack and I are to be married tomorrow. I'm surprised you missed that snippet of information,' Dolly said with a grin.

'I didn't miss it, I just can't believe it's come round so quickly.'

'Neither can I, to be honest. The weeks have fled past,' Dolly said wistfully.

'So, this time tomorrow you'll be Mrs Larkin.'

'I suppose I will, I hadn't thought of it like that.'

'Well, I think we should have a toast to the happy couple,' Aggie called out then said, 'Oh dear, my glass appears to be empty!'

Dolly refilled it yet again with a warm smile.

A while later Aggie moved to the Crown, where she informed Nellie and Nancy of Moreton's business.

'Christ, Aggie! You must have eyes and ears everywhere!' Nellie exclaimed.

'Too bloody right!' Aggie confirmed as she enjoyed yet another free gin.

'You're on to a good thing here, Aggie,' Nellie said, nodding to the glass on the counter.

'I know. Grand, innit?' Aggie said and then cackled like a witch.

The day wore on and by bedtime everyone was exhausted, both in the Crown and in the Palace.

Dolly and Sadie sat up with tea when all was locked up for the night and everyone had gone to their beds or homes.

'Tomorrow's the day, then,' Sadie said.

'Yes. I'm so nervous,' Dolly confessed.

'No need to be, gel, all will be well.'

'I hope so.'

'Jack would never let anything spoil your day, lovey, not even the weather. He's a good man.'

'The best,' Dolly acknowledged.

The two women went to their beds shortly afterwards, unaware that outside the snow had begun to fall silently from the heavens once more.

42

The morning dawned and Dolly was in a panic. 'It's snowing again! How will anyone get here now?'

'They will come, Dolly, don't you fret. Now eat your breakfast, we don't want you passing out from hunger,' Sadie said sternly.

A banging on the front door prompted Alice to run to answer it. A moment later, she led the vicar through to the kitchen where he was given tea and a chair by the range.

A notice had been put up on the door saying the Palace was closed for the day, and Nellie had done the same at the Crown. Dolly hoped Jack had remembered to do his also.

After tea and hot food, which the vicar accepted gratefully, he went about his business of blessing the building.

Dolly left him to it and helped carry plates of food to be placed on the long counter in the bar. People would help themselves once the ceremony was over. Plates, napkins and cutlery were set at one end and slowly folks began to arrive. Bess and Gwen came bearing gifts of pies and cakes, sandwiches and other tasty treats. Frank had managed to discover where Randall lived, with help from Aggie, and had brought him along. Joey was helping with a large box which he'd carried all the way carefully. He'd been told if he dropped it, it would cost him his life, for inside was a wedding cake made and decorated by Bess.

Sadie ushered Dolly upstairs to her room to get changed into her wedding dress just as Nellie and Nancy arrived, also carrying food. Fred, in a nice suit, was helping too. One by one the guests arrived and even Wyman had managed to get there. Wilton Burton and family unfortunately did not come. It was thought the journey with a new baby would have been out of the question for them, and so no one was surprised.

Jack was among the last to get there and was made welcome by all.

'Do you have the ring?' the vicar asked and Jack gaped.

'Bloody hell, I forgot! I didn't get one!' He began to panic until Nellie came to his rescue.

'I suspected you would, so I went instead. Here,' she said as she passed a small box to Jack.

Opening the box, Jack drew in a breath. A gold wedding band sat on a tiny cushion of silk. Giving it to Wyman, Jack threw his arms around his mother.

'Thanks, Mum.'

Jack folded her in his arms even tighter and whispered, 'I love you, Mum.'

'I love you too, son,' Nellie whispered back.

A moment later, Sadie came to the bar looking for Nellie and Nancy. 'Come on, Dolly's upstairs.'

The two followed Sadie to Dolly's room and they both gasped when they saw the girl who had been transformed into a woman.

'Oh, Dolly!' Nellie said as her tears fell.

Nancy was blubbering too and was quite unable to say a word.

'Do you like it?' Dolly asked as she did a twirl so they could see her from all angles.

'It's beautiful!' Nellie sobbed.

'Sadie made it,' Dolly divulged, 'I just told her what I wanted and she did it! I didn't want anything too fancy; I don't like all those frills.'

'Bloody hell! You're handy with a needle,' Nellie said. 'Dolly, you look gorgeous, sweetheart.'

Sadie beamed at the praise and cast her eye over the cream silk gown once more.

Dolly's dark hair was piled up in curls and little cream silk roses were pinned here and there. The dress had a fitted bodice which flared gradually to Dolly's feet. It had long sleeves and a high neck. Simple but classy.

Nellie, Nancy and Sadie went downstairs and sent Fred up.

'Dolly!' Fred said on a dry sob. 'You look beautiful!' He noticed she was wearing the little necklace he had bought her for her fourteenth birthday and a tear escaped his eye.

'You ready?' he sniffed.

Dolly nodded. With Alice's prayer book in one hand, Dolly followed Fred down the stairs then, taking his arm, they walked slowly through to the bar where everyone was waiting.

Delighted so many of their friends had made it to her special day, Dolly returned the smiles directed at her as she was led to stand next to Jack. Dolly saw the grin which split his face and she gave a little nervous titter.

The vicar cleared his throat and the service began. Nellie, Nancy and all the other women cried tears of joy. Wyman stood next to Jack and produced the ring as requested by the vicar.

Applause broke out when Jack and Dolly shared a kiss, denoting the service was complete. Jack picked Dolly up and swung her round, then placed her back on her feet gently. Fred passed Dolly her cane which he'd been carrying, and then the couple were congratulated by one and all.

Fred and a couple of others disappeared and came back with a barrel of beer, which had been swapped for a cask of gin on Nellie's instruction.

Then the merriment began.

'I had hoped to play for you both,' Wyman said.

'So had I,' Randall added and they laughed.

'Well, I hope you don't mind but I brought this with me,' Jack said as he went behind the bar and held up an instrument.

'My trumpet! Excellent!' Wyman blew a few notes then launched into a haunting melody which brought everyone to tears yet again. Then he went straight into an uplifting bouncy tune which had everyone singing along. Randall played the spoons to accompany him, much to Wyman's delight.

The vicar said he would forego the ale but accepted a gin, and another until he was dancing with his robes held up over his knees.

Jack grinned. 'Somebody is going to have to get him home,' he said to Dolly.

'Not you, I hope,' she replied, a mischievous twinkle in her eye.

'Oh no, not me!' Jack said as he kissed the tip of her nose. 'I love you, Dolly Larkin.'

It was the first time she'd heard her new name and she felt a warm glow wash over her at the thought that they were finally husband and wife.

'And I love you too, Jack Larkin,' she said, and she meant it, with all her heart.

By late afternoon, the guests drifted away, wanting to be home before darkness fell. Dolly and Jack, Nellie and Nancy, Fred,

Sadie and Alice sat in the warm kitchen enjoying hot tea and chatting about how special the day had been.

'Frank and Joey took the vicar home,' Jack said. 'He was too pis... drunk to stand.'

Laughter filled the kitchen and Dolly asked, 'What about Randall?'

'Wyman saw him back, I believe they were going to play Randall's pianos for a couple of hours,' Fred put in.

'How many does he have?' Nancy asked.

'I dunno, but they were excited about it,' Fred answered.

Eventually Fred escorted Nellie and Nancy back to the Crown, and Sadie and Alice retired, leaving the newlyweds alone in the kitchen.

Both felt as nervous as each other, and they seemed to be putting off going to bed until Jack said, 'Come on.' Taking Dolly's hand, he led her to the stairs. 'You go on up, I'll see to the lights.'

Dolly smiled and Jack's heart almost burst with happiness.

43

It was the end of the week before the thaw finally began, resulting in dirty brown slush everywhere. Shops and market stalls opened again and some sort of normality returned to Birmingham at last.

Ezra Moreton had spent his time chewing his nails down to the quick in utter frustration at not being able to get his brewery roof repaired.

Naturally, news of the disaster had spread like wildfire and landlords tied to him were forced to find their ale elsewhere. From necessity sprang pleasure at no longer having to only sell Ezra's beer, so giving their customers a wider choice.

Money continued to drip into Ezra's account from the public houses he owned but it was not nearly enough, and he worried he would not be able to pay off his loan. He *had* to get the brewery up and running again as soon as possible.

Taking a cab, Ezra journeyed once more to Hodges' yard.

'I can't take the job on I'm afraid, Mr Moreton, I'm too busy. Maybe in a few months I'll have time to spare,' Eli informed him, silently delighted to be able to turn the man down.

'That will be too late! That roof needs doing now!' Moreton exploded.

'Sorry and all that, but I can't help you.' Eli hitched his horse to the cart which he then began to load up with house bricks.

Moreton hissed a curse and climbed back into the cab.

Once he was sure Ezra was gone, Eli unloaded the cart again and freed the horse from its traces. There was no way Eli Hodges would undertake work for that man, and he doubted anyone else would either.

Moreton tried every builder, roofer, carpenter and handyman he could think of, only to be given the same answer. They were far too busy to take on any more work at the moment. He returned home, sure there was a conspiracy; surely not everyone was *that* busy.

He swore again and kicked the fire guard when he saw the fire had gone out. As he built another, he thought the world was against him. He muttered a string of curses which would have made a sailor blush as he watched the flames lick around the coal nuggets.

If he couldn't get the roof fixed then there was nothing he could do to save his brewery – the business he had built up over the years. If only he hadn't bought those premises on Navigation Street. He would then have had some money in his pocket. He could sell them, of course, but who would be interested in a couple of run-down pubs? He wasn't desperate enough yet to offer them to Dolly Perkins. He would see that woman in hell before he'd sell to her!

He should have had the roof mended as soon as his workers had complained it was leaking, but he hadn't, and now the brewery was standing idle. He was losing money hand over fist and could do nothing but sit at home and mope.

Was there a chance he could cancel the agreement made with

the bank? It was unlikely because he'd signed the documents and saw them witnessed. It was a binding contract.

Ezra Moreton was in the mire up to his neck and felt himself being dragged further down with each passing day. Was he destined to die a lonely old man with nothing to show for his life's work?

No matter how much he thought about his predicament, he could see no way out. He was stuck between the devil and the deep blue sea, and it was all of his own making. With no money coming in from the brewery, and stubbornly unwilling to sell his pubs, thereby giving Dolly a chance to buy them, he was unsure of what to do next. He just had to hope his small income would cover his bank loan and then he must tighten his belt.

Never once giving a thought to the men laid off from the brewery work, Moreton cared only for himself. How would *he* manage? What was to become of *him*?

Going to the kitchen to make tea, Ezra fed the range but then realised it too had gone cold. He kicked the cast iron doors and howled as pain shot through his toes. Hopping around on one foot he yelled, 'Bugger it! Bloody, bloody bugger it!' It did not, however, make him feel any better.

* * *

While Ezra was nursing his injury, Jack and Dolly were still getting used to being a married couple with Jack living at the Palace. He'd brought his belongings over and found it strange to be going out to work every day. He left the Emporium each night at nine o'clock, secure in the knowledge that Frank and Joey would lock up at midnight. The following morning Jack would head over to the Emporium and cash up before opening the doors to the thirsty public.

Dolly would stop work when Jack got home so they could spend time together and exchange news.

At nine on the dot one morning, Aggie was first in at the Palace.

'Blimey, Aggie, you're in early!' Dolly said as she pushed the door closed to keep out the cold.

'Oh, have I got summat to tell you!' the old woman said, her mouth stretching into a wide toothless grin.

'Come on, then,' Dolly said as she limped to her place behind the counter. She grimaced as she watched Aggie gulp the gin poured for her. How could anyone drink alcohol at this time of the day?

'Have you eaten yet?'

Aggie shook her head. 'This is my breakfast and lovely it is,' emptying her glass she corrected herself, 'was an' all.'

Dolly refilled the glass and asked, 'So, what have you to tell me today that's got you here so early?'

'What? Oh, ar, Ezra Moreton is in the do-do! He can't get a builder anywhere to fix his roof!'

Dolly listened and again couldn't help but feel a little sorry for the man.

'Nobody will work for him. They've all said they'm too busy!'

'They're conspiring against him?'

Aggie nodded.

'Why?'

''Cos he's a murdering bastard!' Aggie snapped.

'Aggie, nothing has ever been proved as far as I know.'

'Maybe not, but it don't change the fact that everybody knows he's guilty!'

'That's slander, so you just be careful he doesn't hear of it,' Dolly warned.

'I don't care a bugger if he does! I'm too old to be worrying about that varmint!'

'Just remember I warned you,' Dolly said again, seriously.

Aggie took her drink over to the fireside as the bar began to fill up and work in the Palace started in earnest.

Dolly thought over what Aggie had said as she served her customers. Was Moreton a murderer? If so, why had he never been arrested? Did he have the police on his payroll? Dolly shook her head, dismissing the idea as ridiculous. The police were honest, hard-working men who kept the town safe. But the thought of Moreton killing people lingered and Dolly shivered involuntarily.

It was then that Wilton arrived, looking haggard. Clearly his young son was keeping him up at night, but Dolly was surprised to realise that she envied him.

44

'Congratulations, Mrs Larkin,' Wilton said quietly and, nodding his thanks for the offered tea, went on, 'I'm sorry we couldn't get to your wedding.'

'I'm not surprised, with the weather as it was,' Dolly replied with a forgiving smile. She noted Wilton didn't give her a smile of his own. His complexion was pallid and he had dark circles beneath his eyes. His hair was a mess and his hands shook. Was he ill?

'Wilton, what's wrong?' Dolly asked gently.

'My son died,' he said in hardly more than a whisper.

'Oh my God! Wilton, I'm so very sorry!' Dolly exclaimed.

Sadie and Alice gasped as they looked at each other in shock.

Silent tears rolled down his pale cheeks and dripped off his chin. Suddenly he drew in a great breath and, throwing back his head, he roared his grief and pain and anger at the heavens.

Alice dropped a cup and Sadie almost jumped out of her skin.

Dolly watched her friend's anguish pour from him and wondered if this was the first time he'd been able to grieve. It was her guess he had been supporting his wife and staying strong for her. Now all of his emotions were bursting forth in a torrent of fury and utter misery.

Wilton sobbed for a long time and Dolly allowed him his grieving time in her kitchen. Her tears fell too as she watched him shake his head, still trying to come to terms with why this had happened to his family.

No one spoke as Wilton's heart was breaking; there was nothing to say that could ease his sorrow. Eventually he dried his eyes and looked at Dolly. The usual sparkle had gone and she wondered if it would ever return.

Wilton sipped his tea then said, 'My little boy went to sleep as usual, but he just never woke up.' He sniffed. 'The doctor said it happens like that sometimes and they don't know why.'

'Oh, Wilton! How is your wife?' Dolly knew it was a stupid question the moment it left her lips, but she didn't know what else to say.

'Devastated. She won't eat and she can't sleep. The doctor gave her a sleeping draught and it helped a little.'

'Should you be working? I mean...' Dolly began.

'I had to get out of the house. I couldn't bear it any longer, seeing her so distressed.'

And needing to grieve yourself, away from her, Dolly thought but kept her counsel.

'We buried him in the little churchyard. He had a lovely little white coffin which I carried myself,' Wilton said almost to himself.

Sadie was undone and wept into her apron. Alice put an arm around the older woman, her own tears falling fast.

'He is safe in the arms of the Lord now,' Wilton said and tried to force a smile.

'He is,' Dolly agreed.

'Oh, my poor boy! My little Cedric!' Wilton sobbed.

'Wilton, you know you will always be welcome here, but I really think you should be at home with your wife. You need to be together at a time like this.'

'You're right, of course. I just wanted to...'

'I know, and we appreciate it,' Dolly cut across to save him the explanation.

Wilton stood to leave and Dolly threw her arms around him. He held her tightly for a moment then left as quietly as he'd come.

'Cellar's full again now, Dolly,' Danny Whitehouse yelled and Dolly called out her thanks.

'That poor man,' Sadie said as she dropped onto a chair.

'Life is so unfair at times,' Dolly replied.

'To the good ones it is,' Sadie agreed.

Dolly sighed and tried to imagine how she would feel if it happened to her. She prayed she would never truly understand.

That night Dolly told Jack about Wilton's sad news. Jack felt wretched for the man and also at how he had treated Wilton before he'd taken the time to get to know him.

'He howled like a wounded animal, it was awful,' Dolly said.

'I can't imagine how he must be feeling,' Jack responded.

'Neither can I, but he made the journey to let us know and, I think, to cry it out, which he couldn't do in front of his wife. My heart goes out to them both.'

Jack nodded.

Later, in bed, Jack and Dolly clung to each other for comfort, their thoughts with the Burtons.

Over the next few days, the thaw continued, leaving dirty puddles in its wake. People ventured out despite it still being cold, but life slowly began to return to normal. This winter was one they would remember for a long time to come.

The gin palaces were full again and shops of all kinds and the market were doing a roaring trade.

Dolly's mind turned to Christmas and how they would celebrate. She decided to put to Jack a notion she had about having a party for the staff of all three gin houses. They could close early for one day and invite the staff to join them, where they could be praised and rewarded for all their hard work throughout the year. They could have mulled wine and Christmas foods and, if it was held at the Emporium, music too. They could sing carols around the piano. She wanted to give Jack a special gift but had no idea what, so she would have to think on that some more.

When Dolly mentioned it to her husband he was in full agreement, so it was left up to Dolly to arrange the party.

Going across to the Crown, Dolly told them about her idea. Everyone was excited at the prospect but Dolly noticed Nellie was not her usual cheery self.

'Are you all right, Nellie?' she asked.

'Yes, lovey, I'm just tired,' Nellie replied.

Dolly, however, feared it was more than tiredness. Nellie was clearly unwell but wouldn't admit to feeling ill.

'You should take it easy. You have enough staff to cope without you needing to run yourself ragged,' Dolly said. It was only now that she saw Nellie had lost weight too. Her face was drawn and pale and she walked with a stoop. Nellie Larkin was getting old and no one had seen it coming.

'I suppose you're right,' Nellie said but Dolly knew the woman would take no notice of her advice. She would go on running her bar until she dropped.

Dolly would let Jack know what she thought when he got home that evening. Maybe he could persuade his mother to let the doctor check her out. She doubted it, for Nellie was a headstrong woman, but it was worth a try.

Nellie stayed on Dolly's mind for the rest of the day and no sooner had Jack arrived home than Dolly told him her worries.

'I'll go across in the morning before I go to work, I'm too tired just now,' he said.

Dolly nodded, seeing her husband yawn.

They retired early, leaving Danny Whitehouse to lock up before he left for home. Jack was asleep within minutes of getting into bed and Dolly found herself worrying about him too. Was he working too hard as well?

Dolly drifted into a fitful sleep. She had a feeling the fates had not finished with her yet.

45

The next day, Dolly and Jack ambled over to the Crown Saloon before the doors were thrown open to the public.

Nancy greeted them with hot tea.

'Dolly said Mum was looking a bit peaked,' Jack said by way of explanation for their early visit.

'She ain't herself and that's a fact. She's still in bed,' Nancy replied.

Jack and Dolly exchanged a worried glance. Nellie Larkin was never the last to rise. All his life, Jack knew she was usually the first to be up in the mornings.

'Go on up, lad, and take her this,' Nancy said, handing over a cup of tea.

Jack nodded and headed for the stairs.

'It's not like Nellie to lay abed,' Dolly said once he'd gone.

'I know, sweet'eart, and I'm worried too,' Nancy replied.

'I think the doctor should be called,' Dolly suggested.

'I agree. I'll send a runner shall I?' Nancy asked.

'Yes, it would be for the best. It would set our minds to rest if nothing else.'

'Nellie won't be happy, you know that don't you?'

'I do know that but I'm afraid I don't care. Her health is too important, Nancy.'

Nancy called for her husband Fred and instructed him to whistle for a runner. 'Send the kid for the doctor to come and see to Nellie,' she explained.

Fred did as he was bid, concern written all over his face. Outside he whistled loudly and watched as a scruffy urchin skidded to a halt in front of him.

Handing over a sixpence he said, 'Fetch the doctor for Nellie, would you, lad?'

'Will do, guv'nor,' the boy said, tucking the tanner in his pocket before he sped off.

Fred returned to the kitchen to wait.

Jack was upstairs a long time and Dolly became even more anxious. A while later the doctor arrived and was shown upstairs.

Jack came down, saying, 'Who sent for the doctor?'

'I did,' Dolly said.

'Thanks, that was the right thing to do. Mum ain't at all well.'

They waited and shortly the doctor came down to the kitchen where he was given tea and Nancy paid his fee.

'Nellie is tired to the bone,' he said. 'She needs rest to recuperate. I'll leave a medicine for her which will help to build up her strength again. You must insist she undertakes no more work for the present; I cannot stress this enough.'

Tipping his hat in farewell, the doctor left.

'It's going to be hell here when Mum knows she can't work,' Jack said.

'We'll manage,' Nancy replied.

'I don't envy you trying to keep her out of the bar,' Dolly said sympathetically.

'For once, Nellie Larkin will have to do as she's told!' Nancy replied sternly.

'Good luck with that,' Jack muttered.

'Nancy, if you need help, just yell and I'll come over,' Dolly added.

'Thanks, lovey.'

'Keep us informed as to her progress,' Dolly said as she and Jack stood to leave.

'I will.' Nancy watched them go and wondered how on Earth she would be able to ensure Nellie rested.

'I'll help, my love,' Fred said.

Nancy beamed. 'I know you will. It's gonna take some doing, believe me!'

It was mid-morning when Nellie came down to the kitchen, a dressing gown draped over her nightie. She sat at the table looking worn out and nodded her thanks for the tea Nancy provided.

'The doctor said you have to rest, Nellie,' and she watched her friend nod. 'You ain't to work in the bar until you feel stronger.' Another nod had Nancy really worried at Nellie's easy acquiescence. 'So, have something to eat, then get yourself back to bed.'

'I will. God, Nance, I'm so tired!'

'You've worked yourself half to death in this place, Nellie, and look where it's got you!'

'I know, Nance. It's time to be a boss rather than a worker,' Nellie replied with some effort. Even talking was tiring her out.

Nancy cooked some scrambled eggs and when Nellie had eaten she insisted her friend retire back to bed.

Nellie went without complaint.

Later, Nancy took up a cup of tea. Nellie was sleeping peacefully so she left it on the bedside cabinet and tiptoed out of the room. On her way back to the kitchen, she decided Nellie would be having her meals in her bed for the time being, and tried to think of something to tempt Nellie's appetite.

The day passed in its usual fashion, the bar packed to the gunnels. Its patrons sang and danced and the staff coped admirably without Nellie.

Nancy took her friend a bowl of beef broth for her lunch and Nellie ate sparingly.

'How's the bar doing?' Nellie asked.

'It's full again so you've no need to worry,' Nancy replied.

'Nance, I've been thinking…'

Nancy shuddered. Was Nellie worried she might die?

'You should be resting, not thinking!' Nancy remonstrated.

'No, listen. I've arranged with Mr Sharpe to leave my half of the Palace to Dolly and Jack when I've gone.'

'I'd forgotten it was co-owned,' Nancy said.

'I hadn't. My worry is for you and Fred.'

'Why? We wouldn't be turned out if that's what you're thinking.' Nancy guessed what Nellie was fretting about.

'I know, that's why I've put in my will that they can have the Crown provided you and Fred can live and work here until…'

'Bless you, Nellie. I'm grateful for that, but I think now is the time for more sleep.'

Nellie nodded and snuggled down. 'You know what, Nance? I don't half love you.' Then Nellie's eyes closed and she fell into a deep sleep.

'I love you an' all, you old bugger!' Nancy whispered before she returned to the kitchen, her eyes glittering with tears.

During the afternoon, Dolly called in to see how Nellie was doing.

'She had some eggs for breakfast and some broth for her dinner, and now she's sleeping soundly,' Nancy informed her.

'Good. Sleep is a good healer.'

'Tell Jack not to worry, she's doing fine. If I need anything I'll send for one of you.'

'Thanks, Nancy,' Dolly said. Leaving the cook in peace, she wandered back across the road but she was still worried. She loved Nellie and Nancy with all her heart, and the thought of either of them not being around tortured her. Trying to shake off the feeling, Dolly returned to work, sure that would keep her mind off her worries.

Over the next couple of weeks, Nellie's strength returned and she looked and felt much better. To everyone's surprise, she had heeded the doctor's words and left the staff to man the bar.

Dolly called round as she had every day since Nellie took ill. 'The last payment to the bank for the Palace has been made! It's ours now, yours and mine,' Dolly said excitedly.

'That's good news. We've worked hard enough for it though, ain't we?'

'We have, but it was worth it.'

Nellie glanced at Nancy who shook her head very slightly as if to say, *don't tell Dolly what you've put in your will because it will only worry her.*

'Something else to celebrate at Christmas,' Nellie said instead.

'Absolutely. By the way, I want to get Jack a special gift but I don't know what, any ideas?' Dolly said.

'Whatever you give him, he'll love it,' Nancy put in, and Nellie agreed.

'You could always buy him a new cap. You know how much he thinks of that one he has. I wonder he doesn't sleep in it!' Nellie said with a laugh.

'It's a thought.' Dolly was pleased to hear Nellie laughing again, her illness had had them all frightened for a while.

Dolly returned to the Palace to see a new delivery being made.

Expecting to see Wilton, she hurried indoors, but was sad to see he was not there.

'All done,' the drayman said with a knock to the back door.

'Thank you. How is Mr Burton, do you know?'

The man took off his cap and shook his head. Dolly's heart lurched.

'I'm sorry to say, missus, Mr Burton passed on.'

'Oh no! How? When?'

'Last week, the doctor said it was his heart.'

'Wilton had heart trouble?'

'Oh no, missus, not young Mr Burton. It was senior who died.'

'Oh! I'm sorry to hear that. Please pass on my condolences.'

'Will do,' the drayman said as he left the kitchen.

'Blimey, that gave me a scare, I thought he meant Wilton,' Sadie said.

'Me too,' Dolly confessed as she sighed, feeling a little relieved although of course she was sad that old Mr Burton had gone from this world, especially as it added to Wilton's burdens. Poor Wilton, he had lost his son and now his father. He and his wife were in mourning again and Dolly wondered how Wilton would cope.

Later that day, an official-looking letter arrived from Burton's Brewery and Distillers informing their clients of Ned Burton's demise. It assured that there would be no disruption to business or deliveries.

Dolly knew it would upset Nellie when she received her letter. Mr Burton senior and Nellie had formed a tight working relationship over the years. She hoped it would not impact on Nellie's health, hearing of her friend's death.

* * *

While Dolly was worrying about Nellie's reaction to Burton senior's demise, Ezra Moreton was staring in horror at the pile of letters he had received from the bank about his debt to them, and the mounting warnings that if the arrears owed were not paid immediately then the bank would have no choice but to take further action.

What action? What could they do? He didn't have the money so how could he pay it? Should he visit Jonah Blessep and try to explain? Or should he ignore the letters and see what would happen? Was he desperate enough to put his pubs up for sale? Would the bank take them if he didn't pay what was owed?

The thought of Dolly getting her hands on his properties stuck in his craw, but he was fast reaching the point where he would have to do something.

Donning hat and coat, Ezra whistled for a cab. Swallowing his pride, he had decided to approach Dolly who, he was informed, was still seeking new premises. He spat on the road before climbing into the cab.

The cabbie shook his head. 'Dirty sod!' he muttered before flicking the reins and moving his horse forward.

Inside, Ezra was furious with himself for sinking so low that he would have to go cap in hand again.

46

'Out of my way!' Ezra snapped as he pushed through the throng at the Palace. 'Miss Perkins!' he called out.

Dolly turned and said, 'I'm Mrs Larkin now. I'm surprised you didn't know.'

'He ain't got anybody to tell him now, has he?' Aggie put in with a chuckle.

'Mind your own business, old woman!' Ezra growled.

'Or what? You don't scare me, Ezra Moreton!' Aggie said as she fronted up to the man.

Realising people were staring now, he turned away and addressed Dolly once more. 'I wonder if you could spare me a moment of your time, Mrs Larkin.'

'Why, of course. Come through,' Dolly said, indicating to one of the staff to allow him entry through the little gate at the end of the counter.

Offered tea in the kitchen, Ezra nodded.

'Take a seat and tell me what's on your mind, Mr Moreton,' Dolly said.

Sadie and Alice continued to work but with ears on high alert.

'I find myself in somewhat of a predicament,' Ezra began.

Although Dolly guessed at the reason for his visit, she kept quiet and listened.

'You see, with the brewery unable to function and all of the builders too busy to attend to its repairs *as yet*,' he emphasised the last two words, 'I am in need of capital to meet expenses.'

Dolly nodded. So, he couldn't pay his mortgage.

'Therefore, I wish to put one of my properties up for sale.'

Again, Dolly nodded. *Here it comes!*

'I was wondering if you might be interested in purchasing one of my properties.'

Dolly looked over at Sadie, who had pushed her tongue into her cheek to stop a grin forming.

'I'm sorry to hear of your misfortune, Mr Moreton, but I'm afraid I am unable to help,' Dolly said with a shrug of her shoulders.

'Why ever not? I was informed you were in the market for another property to convert. Was this information incorrect?'

'I'm always on the lookout, Mr Moreton, but not to the detriment of my business and overstretching my finances.'

Sadie snorted which she instantly covered with a pretend sneeze.

Ezra ignored the cook and went on. 'Let me be honest with you, Dolly. May I call you Dolly?' Seeing her nod, he continued. 'I have an – expense – I must pay very shortly, which one of my public houses will more than adequately cover. However, it has to be sold first as I'm sure you understand.'

'Mr Moreton, I understand perfectly, but as I said, I'm not willing to take on a further building at present. Unless it was given as a gift, that is.' Dolly smiled at her little joke.

Ezra's smile was more of a grimace. 'Ha ha.' His laugh was

forced before he said, 'Most unlikely, of course. Then I take it you are not interested?'

'No, Mr Moreton, I'm not interested, but I thank you for the offer.'

With nothing left to discuss, Dolly saw Moreton out of the back door.

'Would you credit it?' Sadie asked.

'Moreton's definitely in the do-do, as Aggie puts it,' Dolly answered. Then she, Sadie and Alice all burst out laughing.

Dolly knew somehow word would get out about the meeting with Moreton because Aggie had witnessed his arrival. It would not then take long for the astute old woman to deduce the reason, then the whole town would be privy to the knowledge.

Ezra walked back to the cab waiting for him in Gin Barrel Lane, his face a mask of thunder.

Bitch! I know your game! You're waiting for me to drop the price to almost nothing before you dive in and steal it from under my nose! Well, it ain't happening, Dolly bloody Larkin!

'Take me home!' Ezra boomed out as he scrambled into the already moving cab. 'Damn you, cabbie!' he yelled as he was thrown into his seat.

The cabbie grinned and clucked to his horse.

As predicted, the news of Ezra's calling into the Palace travelled quickly, thanks to Aggie. She knew exactly why he had come and had no qualms about telling anyone who would listen. Ezra Moreton was in trouble.

The following day, Ezra received another letter from the bank informing him of their intent to repossess the public houses on Navigation Street. Notice to quit had also been forwarded to the managers.

Ezra screwed up the letter and threw it on the floor of his living room in disgust. Well, at least he would not owe the bank anything now. But Ezra Moreton could not have been more wrong.

* * *

In the kitchen of the Crown Saloon, Dolly was relating the tale of Ezra's visit.

'So, he's really up the Swanee!' Nancy said.

'He is most certainly in great difficulty,' Dolly replied.

'Yoohoo!' Aggie's voice screeched out and Nellie and Dolly moved to the bar.

'Back again, Aggie?' Nellie asked.

'Of course. Here, you'll never guess what!'

Nellie motioned for Aggie to be given her tot.

'Them two pubs on Navigation Street...' she paused to take a gulp, 'now belong to the bank!'

Nellie and Dolly exchanged a quick glance and, responding to a nod from Nellie, Aggie was given more gin.

'The landlords have had notice to quit and are packing to leave as we speak!'

'Oh dear, what a shame,' Nellie said sarcastically. Aggie cackled and Nellie said, 'Thanks Aggie.'

Returning to the kitchen, they told Nancy what they'd heard.

'How the hell does she find these things out?' Nancy asked.

'I suspect the runners tell her,' Nellie replied, 'besides which, she ain't daft. She puts things together and usually comes up with the right answer.'

'The bank didn't waste any time in taking those pubs. I wonder what they'll do with them,' Dolly put in.

'Put them up for sale to cover Ezra's debt. Why, are you thinking...?' Nellie asked.

'No. I can't afford it, but it would be nice, though.' Dolly rolled

her eyes dreamily. Then added, 'I'm going to the Emporium, are
there any messages?'

'No, just give our love to Jack,' Nellie said.

Bidding them farewell, Dolly donned her hat and coat and
went outside to hail a cab. It was time to see how the Christmas
preparations were doing.

Arriving at the Emporium after a perilous journey on the icy
roads, she saw that holly and ivy adorned the welcome rings
above the door as she entered. The two metal hoops were looped
and tied together in the shape of a ball and were there to
welcome all who entered. More holly and mistletoe hung around
the room and Randall was at the piano, playing carols.

In the kitchen, Bess and her helpers were busy cooking, not
only for the staff, but also for the dining room, which was proving
a great success. The little booklets Gwen had designed about the
body in the wall helped a great deal to draw in curious customers.

The staff gathering had been planned for Christmas Eve,
which was the following day, and Dolly had promised food would
be arriving from the Palace and the Crown so as to lighten Bess's
load.

All three gin houses would close at lunchtime and not re-
open until Boxing Day to enable all to spend Christmas with
their families or friends.

Happy that everything was well underway, Dolly kissed her
husband and laughed at the shouts and whistles that came her
way. Then she set off in the cab once more. She had gifts to buy
and she knew exactly what she wanted to get. A set of embroi-
dered handkerchiefs for Fred. A silk scarf for Nancy. A new cap
for Jack, and for Nellie a locket with a lock of Jack's hair inside.
She patted her bag which held the hair she had snipped off
whilst Jack was asleep one night. For the staff she decided an
envelope containing a financial bonus would be more appreci-

ated. It would eat into her profits, of course, but every worker in all three gin palaces had worked their hands to the bone this last year so, in her mind, they all deserved it.

As she found each present in turn, shop assistants carried her purchases to the cab, eager to be of help when they saw her walking stick, and Dolly thanked them for their kindness.

On her way home, the swaying of the cab had Dolly feeling a little queasy and she dared to wonder... could she be pregnant? She had missed her monthlies but hadn't wanted to get too excited. Would it be too early to tell? Would the doctor know? Banging her stick on the roof, she felt the cab draw to a halt.

'You all right, missus?' the cabbie asked as he jumped down.

'Yes, thank you. I wonder if we might stop by the doctor's house first,' she asked with a smile to allay the cabbie's fears. 'I'm feeling a tad sick.' Dolly patted her stomach.

'Ahh! Right away,' he said with a smile, tipping his hat as he caught her meaning.

Before she climbed back into the cab a little while later, she said, 'I wonder if you could do me a favour.'

The cabbie nodded as he listened to her request.

On arriving back at the Palace, the cabbie carried her boxes and bags indoors and laid them on the table. Dolly paid him and added a large tip, which he accepted gratefully. Wishing all a merry Christmas, he left.

Alice took a couple of journeys transporting everything to Dolly's room whilst Dolly sat and enjoyed tea and cake, and she was relieved that it helped settle her stomach.

'You've been busy, I see,' Sadie said.

'Yes, now all my shopping is done I can enjoy our party.'

'I'm really looking forward to it,' Sadie agreed excitely.

'So am I,' Dolly concurred with a huge smile.

Dolly locked up at lunchtime the following day, much to the disgust of her customers. She knew Nellie and Jack would be doing the same. The request she'd made to the cabbie who took her shopping the previous day had been honoured, and out in Gin Barrel Lane six cabs were waiting for all of her friends. Sadie and Alice carried Dolly's gifts and the food was brought out by everyone else and piled on the cabs where luggage would normally be stored, held in place by the rail which ran around the roof.

Nellie, Nancy and Fred joined Dolly in one cab along with Sadie and Alice. It was a squash but they made room, laughing when Nancy sat on Fred's knee. Filled to capacity, the cabs rolled away in convoy towards the Emporium. They would be back for the return journey at ten o'clock that evening.

Randall was playing as they all trooped indoors, and Dolly was delighted to see Wyman had joined them too. Luckily she had bought a spare box of handkerchiefs just in case that could be given as a gift for him. The food was brought in and taken to the kitchen and laid out on the huge table.

A large roasted goose with sage and onion dressing was placed as the centrepiece on the table. Ribs of beef and Yorkshire puddings were set to the left and a huge ham to the right. Tureens of rabbit stew, dishes of potatoes and vegetables were dotted about and at one end sat plates of cranberry and mince pies and plum pudding.

A small Christmas tree stood in the bar and was decorated with tiny candles and sweet treats. Discussions were taking place about which games might be played once the feasting was done.

There was excitement as mulled wine was passed out and food consumed. Everyone was in high spirits and the piano sat silent whilst the pianists ate.

Eventually Dolly called for silence. 'This gathering is to honour all of you, and to say thank you for all of your hard work over the last year. I have a gift for everyone, so let's make a start.' One by one the gifts, cleverly wrapped as snowballs or crackers, were given and opened, and Dolly's heart soared with happiness as each person loved their present. Nellie cried a little over her locket.

Then Dolly came to Jack. 'For my husband – a new cap.' Cheers sounded and Dolly held up a hand. 'I have one more gift for you, Jack...'

Everyone waited with bated breath to see what it was.

'Although I can't give it to you until the summer.'

Groans sounded loud in the room, but Nellie and Nancy stared at each other, each thinking the same thing.

'Jack, your special gift will be a son or a daughter!'

Jack's mouth dropped open as the room erupted. He was patted on the back and had his hand shaken by every single one of their friends, and he watched with pride as Dolly was hugged by them all in turn. Then, as soon as he could get near to Dolly, he wrapped his wife in his arms.

'Thank you, Dolly, that's the best present I could ever wish for, I love you so much.'

Applause sounded again then they all went silent as Wyman hit one key on the piano.

'I have a gift for Dolly and Jack and I'd like to play it now. I have named my new composition "Larkin's Dream".'

No one spoke as Wyman sat at the piano. Pulling a sheet of music from his pocket, he propped it on the stand and then he began to play. There was absolute silence until he finished. With a flourish he pulled the sheet music from the stand and with a bow he presented it to Jack.

The applause was deafening. Then pulling Jack aside he said, 'The copyright for "Larkin's Dream" belongs to you, Jack, but I would ask permission to play it in London in the New Year.'

'Of course! Thanks, Wyman, I've never had such an unusual gift! What an honour.'

'I am touring the great concert halls and would love for my audiences to hear it.'

'They'll love it, I'm sure. Wyman – what is copyright?'

'I have registered it as belonging to you with myself as the composer. This means under the law, anyone wishing to play it must pay a fee, some of which will come to you and some to me. It won't be a huge amount, but it all adds up.'

'Surely folk will play it without paying a fee?' Jack asked.

'They could but they would be breaking the law.'

'Thank you, Wyman,' Jack said as he took the sheet music offered to him, 'this is a very special gift.'

'It's my way of thanking you, Jack,' Wyman said, then as Randall began tinkling, he winked. 'Watch this.'

Joining Randall, they each took an end of the piano keys and after a whisper from Wyman, the music flowed forth. Jack found

Wyman a chair and the two pianists entertained the gathering for an hour or more, playing together and separately.

Nellie was still sobbing at the news she was to be a grandmother, until Dolly said, 'Nellie, you'll have to get your knitting needles out now.'

'Oh, blimey, that child will have so much stuff it will last until he's ninety years old!' Nancy said with a grin.

Dolly laughed and thought how strange it was that people always thought an unborn child would be a boy. Perhaps she would have a daughter instead and surprise them all.

At ten o'clock the cabs arrived to take everyone home and Dolly paid them well.

Exhausted but happy, Dolly and Jack returned to the Palace to enjoy a good night's sleep.

* * *

Whilst the noise of the party was shaking the rafters at the Emporium, Ezra Moreton was sitting alone, feeling very sorry for himself. He had always spent Christmas alone, but this year was different. In previous years he'd been wealthy, now he was not and he was having difficulty coming to terms with the fact. He decided he would put two of his other pubs on the property market come the New Year. Could he wait that long? Should he do it just after Christmas? Maybe that would be a better idea, because the quicker it was known they were up for sale, the quicker he would be rid of them.

Christmas came and went quietly for Ezra and on the first day of trading he went to find an estate agent.

'I can put your pubs on my books, of course, but how soon they will sell is another matter entirely,' the man behind the desk said.

'Just do your best!' Ezra snapped and walked out.

The man grinned. *You'll be lucky!*

On his way home, Ezra felt a little better. The Navigation Street public houses now belonged to the bank and two more were on the market, which would give him some much-needed cash. That would leave him only two to bring in drips and drabs of coin for his personal use.

Ezra was looking forward to the day his brewery would be functioning again. Then he would be back on top once more.

* * *

In the meantime, Aggie was in the Palace, bustling her way to the counter.

'Dolly! I have...'

'I know, something to tell me,' Dolly said with a laugh.

'Ar, Moreton's got two pubs up for sale!'

'I thought the bank owned them,' Dolly said with a frown.

'Two of 'em yes, but the Old Guy on Mill Lane and the Royal George on Alison Street are now in the hands of the property seller!'

'Goodness,' Dolly said.

'That only leaves him with the Three Tuns on Upper Mill Lane and the Old Red Lion at the Bull Ring!'

'Do you think he'll have to sell those too?'

Aggie gave a curt nod in thanks for her drink. 'My guess? Yes.'

'What will happen then?'

'Moreton will be bankrupt!'

Dolly shook her head and moved to serve other customers. It was a shame anyone could fall so low, but Ezra's tumble had been by his own hand. Greed and spite had brought him to this point and now he was suffering the consequences. He only had himself to blame.

As Aggie went from one gin palace to another, the news went with her and more than one person rejoiced at Moreton's prospective downfall. The brewery giant was suffering and many thought it was not before time.

A lot of people over the years had had dealings with Moreton. His lending of money and charging exorbitant interest rates had seen many at the gates of the workhouse. Now the thought that he could be facing that prospect himself was making countless people happy.

The folk of Birmingham watched and waited to see how Moreton would fare. His private business was touted everywhere thanks to Aggie, although he had no idea it was she who was spreading the gossip.

One day soon, Ezra Moreton might be penniless and that day couldn't come soon enough for a great many people.

48

The weeks passed with no movement on the property market and Ezra was forced to try to sell his two remaining public houses as well. He was told by the estate agent there was little money around for people to buy property and that the market was deathly quiet, and Ezra despaired, but he put them up for sale nevertheless. He really had no other choice.

Then, one day, he received another letter from the bank. His two ale houses repossessed by them had been valued and the resulting figure was insufficient to cover his loan. Therefore, they would be taking possession of the others held on the estate agent's books.

Ezra, in a fury, took a cab to the bank to see what on Earth Jonah Blessep was playing at.

'You have to understand Mr, Moreton, the valuations have been made and are low due to there being no interest from possible purchasers.'

'But that's ridiculous! I didn't borrow that much in the first place!' Ezra slapped his copy of the mortgage facility on the desk. 'I haven't seen a penny of this either!'

'You are forgetting the interest on the loan, Mr Moreton. Plus, the agreement was, and you'll note it is written there,' Jonah tapped a finger on the paper, 'that monies would be paid by us to any builder who undertook the repairs to your brewery roof. Now, as I understand it, that has not come to pass.'

'Not yet, but...'

'I would also point out that you signed said agreement whereby your property or properties would become forfeit should you fail to honour your repayments.'

Ezra sighed loudly. 'Mr Blessep, be reasonable. I just need more time!'

Blessep shook his head. 'Mr Moreton, I'm afraid you are all out of time. Notices to quit and notification to the estate agent have already gone out.'

'You can't do this!'

'Oh, but I can. It's done, Mr Moreton. All of your property save the brewery now belongs to this bank. Therefore, our transaction is complete, the public houses have been received in full and final settlement.'

'Mr Blessep, please...!'

'Good day, Mr Moreton.'

Jonah rang the hand bell on his desk and a teller came running. 'Would you be kind enough to see Mr Moreton out, please?'

'Certainly, sir,' the teller answered with a grin.

In the cab on the way home, Ezra's melange of feelings fought each other for prominence. He was furious at Jonah Blessep for taking part of his livelihood and at himself for being so greedy and not wanting to spend money to save the brewery roof. He was angry at Dolly for not buying one of his properties in order to help him out. He was worried about having very little money coming in now to sustain his extravagant lifestyle. All that he earned now was the interest on a few loans he had agreed with folk who could not afford to repay him. He had no workers for he had no work to give them, and the builders were still unwilling to do his bidding.

Ezra Moreton was at rock bottom as he sat by an empty fire grate in his living room. He knew everyone would know his misfortune in double-quick time, and his reputation would sink to that of a beggar.

Not even able to summon the strength to kick the fire guard, Ezra fell into a deep depression.

* * *

Whilst Ezra could not summon the will to move out of his chair, Aggie was dancing at the Emporium, her skirts up over her knees showing her bloomers to all and sundry. She could not have been happier. Ezra Moreton had got his comeuppance at last! He was on his knees financially and Aggie was revelling in his misery. She had known a lot of people who had been beholden to him, and she had seen the misery he put them through to get his money back from loans he had given. Now it was his turn to suffer.

Aggie had told Jack the news and when the music ended she made her way out of the door. Now to tell Nellie and Dolly.

Walking through the town, Aggie's face was lit up by her grin, one which would last a long time.

Entering the Palace, she pushed through to the counter.

Dolly saw her coming and beat her to it. 'You have something to tell me.'

'Oh, I have! But first, congrat'lations on having a babby.'

Cheers and applause sounded as the crowd overheard her words and Dolly laughed.

Once the noise had died down, Aggie related the sorry update to the tale of Moreton and his lost pubs. Silence descended as she spoke, everyone eager to hear what Aggie had to say.

'It's strange, though, nobody has seen hide nor hair of him for weeks. Even I can't find out what's happened to him!'

The shocked hiss of indrawn breath sounded loud in the quiet of the bar before Aggie continued. 'He ain't been to the bank, he ain't been to see the property developer, Eli Hodges ain't seen nothin' of him neither!'

'What about the runners, ain't they discovered anything?' someone asked.

Aggie shook her head. 'No. It's a bloody mystery! I'll tell you summat else an' all, it's a mystery I intend to solve one way or another!'

When she had finished, a buzz of conversation ran round the bar.

Slurping her free drink, Aggie's cackle was loud as she clapped her hands.

Dolly couldn't help but smile at Aggie's antics, although she did feel a little sorry for Ezra. She knew the rumours about his bully-boy tactics but she also knew nothing was ever proved. People were too afraid to inform the police evidently.

She wondered then what the bank would do with six empty public houses. Would they be able to sell them on now Ezra was no longer involved? For a moment she wished she had the funds to buy at least one of them, but quickly pushed the thought away. Hadn't it been greed that was the cause of Ezra being where he was now?

Dolly had enough on her plate for the time being. Being the proud owner of the Emporium and co-owner of the Palace with Nellie, as well as being pregnant, would keep her busy for years to come.

According to Aggie, Moreton's brewery still lay untouched and Dolly wondered what would happen to it. Time would tell. It would be a shame to watch it crumble into dust.

Dolly ambled into the kitchen where she sat to rest and convey the gossip to Sadie and Alice.

* * *

The weather began to improve and the puddles dried up. The wind was still fresh, but a weak sun threw out its much-needed rays, lifting everyone's spirits. Spring was on its way and snowdrops wilted as crocuses began to bloom in tiny gardens. The trees and bushes formed buds and birds chirped loudly. The winter was receding and businesses everywhere began to flourish. The weeks seemed to fly past and Dolly found herself feeling more tired at the end of each day. She needed to take things easy as her birthing time was not so very far away.

One pleasant morning, Aggie rushed into the Palace, yelling for Dolly.

'Important news!' she called out.

Dolly sighed and left her seat by the range.

'What is it, Aggie? I was having a rest.'

'Ezra Moreton has been found dead!' Aggie's words stopped all conversation in the bar.

'Ezra's dead? Are you sure? Oh dear! How? When?'

Aggie took a breath then let it out slowly.

Dolly filled a glass and waited while Aggie slurped. She noted all ears in the room were attuned to the old woman now.

'I told you I'd find out, d'aint I? Well, it seems there was a ghastly smell coming from his house over in Drury Lane and the neighbours reported it to the council.' Aggie paused to empty her glass, which Dolly then refilled. She was known to enjoy dragging out a tale and the crowd began to shuffle impatiently. 'Any road up, the council went to investigate, and they found him in his chair, dead as a doornail.'

Dolly instantly recalled the odour emanating from the wall in the Emporium on discovery of the body and her stomach roiled.

Chatter began in the room at this news, and after yet another refill Aggie continued. 'They fetched the police in and my sources tell me he had started to melt into his armchair.'

Dolly gagged. 'Enough with the details, Aggie,' she said as she grimaced at the thought of the grisly scene.

'The coroner scooped him up...'

'Aggie!' Dolly snapped.

'Sorry,' the old woman said sheepishly.

Dolly gave her a last free gin and as Aggie went to the fireplace to divulge the details to an eager audience, Dolly returned to the kitchen, where she shared the news rather more sparingly.

'He must have just sat there and died,' Sadie said.

'It's so very sad,' Dolly said quietly.

'You're one of the few who believe that,' Sadie said.

'I know he was not well liked but...' Dolly began.

'Dolly, he was hated!' Sadie snapped.

Dolly nodded, knowing it to be the truth. 'Even so, to die alone and not be found for weeks...' A shudder overcame her as she spoke.

'The fates can be a bitch,' Alice said and the others nodded. Dolly wondered what else they might have in store for them all.

49

That evening, Jack and Dolly discussed the demise of Ezra Moreton and the fate of the public houses held by the bank.

'It's a damned shame we can't afford to buy one of them,' Jack said.

'I thought the same, but I need to clear our mortgage first and that will take years,' Dolly replied.

'He was a nasty piece of work, was Ezra, but I wouldn't wish that sort of death on anyone.'

'Nor me,' Dolly said with a shudder. Then suddenly she said, 'Jack, feel this!'

Jack laid a hand on her stomach and was startled to feel the baby move.

'Bloody hell! Don't that hurt?'

Shaking her head, Dolly said, 'No, it feels wonderful!'

'I'm glad you're taking more rest, Mommy.'

Dolly laughed and said, 'I am, Daddy.'

Jack beamed. 'I still can't believe it. We're having a baby!'

'*I'm* having a baby,' Dolly corrected him and they burst out laughing. All was well with their world and they went to bed hand in hand.

The following week, Ezra Moreton was buried in a pauper's grave and only the vicar was in attendance, although the burial drew a crowd who stood on the road to watch. The brewery and his house stood empty as he had no family to leave them to. It was not long, however, before the house was looted and all his remaining possessions were stolen.

The six public houses were still owned by the bank and, despite being put on the market, they had not sold. Although the asking price was very low, there were few who could afford to take them on, and those who could didn't want to.

Aggie trundled into the Palace one afternoon with yet more news.

'It's about Ezra,' she said to Dolly after accepting the customary free gin. 'As you know, nobody saw him for weeks before he croaked...' Seeing Dolly's frown she corrected herself. 'Before he passed on, so no one knew he'd gone. Anyway, the word is summat in his brain went wrong.' She halted for a quick slurp. 'When they found him, he was slumped down in his chair as if the whole of the left side of his body had died first.' Aggie took another sip then emptied the glass. She gave her usual dry cough.

Dolly sighed and filled the glass yet again.

'His face was sagging down on the one side an' all.'

'How awful, I wonder what caused it,' Dolly said.

'Apoplexy, the doctor called it.'

'When my time comes, I'd like it go in my sleep,' Dolly said with a shudder.

'Wouldn't we all?' Aggie picked up her glass and wandered into the crowd to re-tell her gossip to eager listeners.

Dolly knew this piece of gossip would be talked about for a very long time.

* * *

Over time, the gin palaces continued to conduct a strong trade and with each passing week Dolly's stomach swelled. She was a picture of good health but her back ached and she grew tired quickly. Each afternoon she took a nap and every evening she retired early. This having a baby lark was taking its toll on her. Only having a tiny frame herself and with her crippled leg, she was finding it difficult to get around, but she persevered.

The doors of the Palace were propped open as the weather improved and spring became the summer. The sun shone down full and strong, and trees and bushes were heavy with leaves. Birds called and swooped, some enjoying riding the thermals as the heat increased. Children ran around barefoot with barely a stitch of clothing on as their mothers sat on chairs outside their front doors, passing the time by sharing gossip.

Over the past months, Nellie and Nancy had knitted scores of baby clothes and Dolly had drawers full of little jackets and caps, cardigans, shawls, mittens and bootees.

Sadie had bought some absorbent material from which she made piles of napkins to wrap the baby's bottom in. Baby toys and banana shaped bottles poured in from their many friends and were stored in a spare room.

Eli Hodges gave her a gift of a wooden rocking cradle made by one of his sons and Jack bought blankets and sheets and a baby carriage. Everything was ready for the day Dolly's baby decided to arrive.

In the early hours of a summer morning, a feeling of discomfort woke Dolly up. Then she realised the sheet was wet. Jack stirred as she climbed out of bed, then as she gasped, he was fully awake.

'Dolly?'

'Jack! The baby – I think it's coming!'

'Shit, shit, bloody cack!' Jack mumbled as he began to throw on his clothes.

'Owww!' Dolly moaned as she leaned forward, clutching her stomach.

'Wait! Not yet, I ain't dressed!' Jack yelled.

'I don't think the baby cares, Jack!' she yelled back.

'I know, I'm sorry. Oh, hell, what do I do?'

'Fetch Sadie!'

Jack hobbled down the hallway to Sadie's room with one leg in his trousers. The other leg went in after he banged on the cook's door. 'Sadie! Come quick! Dolly's in labour!'

The door opened and Sadie, looking like an apparition in a flowing white nightgown, rushed through. 'Out of my way!' she said as she ran to Dolly's side.

Jack followed but was prevented entry. 'Put the kettle to boil and fetch towels,' Sadie instructed before closing the door. Then opening it again she yelled, 'And fetch Alice!'

Jack banged on Alice's door, yelling that Dolly had started her labour. Then he went to the airing cupboard, pulling out a bundle of towels. As he made to take them to Sadie, he saw Alice come from her bedroom.

Alice took the towels from him saying gently, 'A cup of tea would be nice.'

Jack went to the kitchen like an automaton. He made tea in a daze and carried it upstairs on a tray. Kicking the bedroom door, he was relieved of the tray when it opened. 'Hot water,' said Alice.

'What?'

'A bowl of hot water now, please,' Alice repeated firmly.

Jack nodded, then hearing a groan from Dolly he grimaced and fled.

A little while later he took the hot water to the bedroom. 'How is she?' he asked.

'All's well, don't worry,' Alice said, taking the bowl from him before kicking the door shut.

Jack paced the landing, shuddering each time Dolly yelled out. *Please, God, look after my wife and child.* Over and over Jack prayed as he wore a groove in the strip of carpet.

A scream rent the air and Jack's hand raked through his hair. This was his fault. If he'd been more careful then Dolly wouldn't be suffering now.

Sitting on the top step, Jack cried into his hands. He couldn't bear to think of his beloved wife in so much pain. Each time she yelled, he drew his shoulders up to his ears. *Let it be finished, for both our sakes!*

At the other side of the bedroom door, Dolly groaned. Beads of sweat formed on her brow before pooling and running down her face.

'You're doing fine, it won't be long now,' Sadie said encouragingly.

'Oh God! Please let it be over soon! Aghhh!' Dolly wailed as another wave of pain rolled over her. She gripped the bedclothes, waiting for the agony to pass.

'All right, take a deep breath and push,' Sadie instructed.

Sucking in air, Dolly raised her head from the pillow. Holding the breath, she pushed down with all her might.

'That's it. Now rest a minute and when the pain comes again give another push.'

Over and over Dolly strained hard until she felt her strength fading. 'I can't...'

'You have to, gel, you can't leave the little mite half in and half out. One more go should see it finished. Come on now, let's get this child into the world.'

With a final effort, Dolly felt the baby slide from her body and she lay back panting.

'Well done, Dolly. It's a boy!' Sadie said excitedly.

'Is he all right?' Dolly asked on a whisper, feeling tired to the bone.

'He's perfect.'

Dolly heard the slap and then the baby wail and she cried with relief. A moment later, the swaddled bundle was in her arms.

'Right, we just have to expel the afterbirth now so, Alice, place your hands there on Dolly's lower belly and when I say, you press down hard.'

Alice did as she was bid.

'Dolly, we need you to give one last push, then it's all over.'

Dolly nodded but was intent on staring at the beautiful baby in her arms.

'Ready, Alice?' Seeing the nod Sadie went on, 'Ready, Dolly?' Another nod. 'Now!'

Dolly winced at the pressure on her lower abdomen but felt something slick slip away from her.

The towel beneath Dolly's bottom caught the sticky mess and Sadie bundled it up and threw it into the bowl. That would be taken downstairs to be burned in the yard.

'Congratulations,' Alice said as she peeped over at the tiny infant.

Dolly smiled, too tired to reply.

Jack had also heard the slap then the wail of an infant. A little while later, the door opened and he was allowed in. 'Come and see your wife and son,' Sadie said.

Jack rushed to Dolly who held the baby in her arms, a tired smile on her face.

'Oh, Dolly! Thank God you're all right!'

'Jack, meet your son,' Dolly said as she held out the child.

'Oh, I ain't sure...'

'Just hold him firmly,' Dolly said.

So Jack did. He looked down at the little pink face and muttered, 'He's perfect.'

Sadie and Alice slipped quietly from the room and went to the kitchen. They would all be needing more tea. Alice set the kettle to boil while Sadie took the bowl outside where she burned the afterbirth in a corner of the yard.

A few hours later, Jack was banging on the back door of the Crown Saloon.

Nellie's voice carried to him as she yelled, 'Wait a bloody minute!'

Unlocking and opening the door, she was surprised to see Jack standing there.

'It's a boy! Mum, I have a son!'

Nellie hugged him tightly. 'Congratulations, lad, I'm so pleased for you. Are they both all right?'

'Yes, they're champion. Mum, you have to come and see him. Bring Nancy,' he said impatiently.

'Just as soon as we're dressed, we'll be over,' Nellie said and smiled as Jack raced away. There was still so much of her little boy in him.

Nancy came down bleary eyed. 'If that's Aggie I'll bloody kill her for disrupting my sleep!'

'Nance, Dolly's had a baby boy, and they're both fine.'

'Oh, Nell, thank the good Lord.'

The two women hugged and shed tears of joy. Then they went

to dress as fast as they could so they could visit Dolly and the baby.

Dolly was snoozing when her friends arrived. The baby was sleeping soundly in the cradle Eli's son had made and Jack had placed next to their bed. Jack was dozing in a chair. The new parents woke when Nellie and Nancy entered quietly.

'Come in,' Dolly beckoned.

They went instantly to the cradle and again happy tears fell silently down their faces.

'Oh, Dolly, he's beautiful!' Nellie said on a breath.

'Bloody gorgeous,' Nancy said. 'What are you going to call him?'

Dolly glanced at Jack who shrugged. 'I like the name Joseph,' she said, her eyes still on her husband.

Jack nodded. 'Joseph it is, then,' he said.

'Hello, Joseph,' Nellie whispered and the baby wrinkled his nose in his sleep.

'Oh look, Nance, he knows his name already.'

'You can pick him up, Grandma,' Dolly said and saw Nellie beam with pleasure at the name. Holding the child, Nellie rocked him gently, talking to him all the time.

'Give us a hold,' Nancy said and Nellie passed the boy to her friend, reluctantly.

The two women couldn't take their eyes off the tiny bundle and when Joseph snuffled then let out a whimper, they all knew he was hungry. Passing the little one to his mother, they all left her to feed him in peace and quiet.

Over tea in the kitchen, Jack yawned and before long they were all doing it.

'You'd best be prepared, lad, now the baby is here you won't be getting much sleep,' Nellie warned.

'Why not?' he asked innocently.

'Crikey, you've a lot to learn about babies,' Sadie said.

Jack nodded, realising the truth of it. 'Mum, Sadie and Alice were amazing. I couldn't have... you know, helped Dolly.'

Nellie thanked the women for bringing her grandson into the world safely then asked, 'How long was she in labour?'

'About four hours all told?' Sadie's question was directed at Jack who nodded.

'Bloody hell! Usually the first takes an age. I bet she'll be one of these girls who can have kiddies like shelling peas,' Nancy said.

The women laughed loudly at Jack's shocked expression.

'I ain't sure I could go through that again!' he muttered much to their amusement.

'It won't be up to you, lad. If Dolly wants more children then you'll just have to step up to the mark,' Nellie said.

'Oh, blimey. Maybe I should move back to the Emporium!'

The women burst out laughing as Jack dropped his head into his hands.

50

On the pretext of having the accounts audited, Nellie went to visit Mr Sharpe, her solicitor.

'Come in, Nellie, how very nice to see you.'

'And you. Mr Sharpe, I've come to change my will.'

'Take a seat, dear lady, and tell me what needs altering.'

'Dolly had a baby boy this morning, so I want to include him.'

'Congratulations! I trust mother and baby are both well?'

Nellie nodded.

Picking up a pen, Mr Sharpe made notes as Nellie spoke. Then at the finish, she asked, 'What do you think?'

'My opinion is you have been very fair. I'll get this drawn up immediately and, if I may, I will bring it to you for signature.'

'Thanks, Mr Sharpe, I'd appreciate that.'

'And are you quite well, Nellie?' he asked with a worried expression.

'Yes, thank you for asking. It's just with Joseph being born – I'm feeling my years a bit that's all.'

'Ah, you and me both,' Andrew Sharpe said.

'I'll away now, I have some shopping to do. Thanks for your help,' Nellie said as she rose to leave.

'Give my regards to everyone.'

'I will,' Nellie said and with a wave she was gone. She had little in the way of savings, but what there was she had left to Joseph to be held in trust until he was of an age to make it useful.

At the jeweller's, Nellie bought a silver money box for Joseph then flowers for Dolly from the market before heading home.

Everyone dropped a coin into the money box and Nellie took it and the flowers across the road.

Dolly was thrilled with the thoughtful gifts and she and Nellie chatted quietly, Joseph sleeping comfortably in Nellie's arms as she sat in the chair by the bed.

'I think Aggie's missing having something to tell us all now Ezra's gone,' Nellie said.

'It was so sad. I wish I could have helped him out,' Dolly replied.

'Ezra was a law unto himself, Dolly, he would have ended up the same way no matter what. Anyway, you just concentrate on yourself and this little man.'

'Jack's been so good, Nellie, he adores his boy.'

'That he does. A word of advice, if you don't mind me saying. Joseph will keep you busy all the time, feeding, washing his clothes and later colic most likely. So remember you have a husband as well. You'll both be tired and short-tempered but keep the love between you.'

'Thanks, Nellie, I'll do my best.'

After an hour or so, Nellie left Dolly to sleep while the going was good.

Dolly's laying-in period was ten days and for the first week of his baby son's life Jack stayed home to help out. He quickly learned to change napkins and spent more than enough time rocking the child in his arms. For the second time in his life, Jack was in love – with his newborn son. With all his help, Dolly was able to sleep and recover from the trauma of childbirth. Sadie and Alice were happy to do what they could and so give the young couple plenty of rest.

Frank and Joey managed the running of the Emporium perfectly well whilst Jack spent time with his wife and new baby.

Nellie and Nancy visited every day, if only for an hour, and Dolly welcomed their advice. Soon Dolly was well enough to take Joseph out in his baby carriage. Life was sweet for the Larkins.

* * *

One morning, around eight o'clock, Aggie walked into the Palace and the staff, who were busy cleaning and restocking the bar, noticed she was not her exuberant self.

'I wonder, can I have a private word with Dolly?' she asked.

Danny Whitehouse trotted off to the kitchen, where Dolly sat chatting with her cook and maid. A moment later he led Aggie through.

'What's on your mind, Aggie?' Dolly asked.

'I've brought this for the babby first off,' the old woman said, handing over a beautifully knitted shawl.

'It's beautiful, Aggie, thank you. I have to ask, how could you afford it?'

'I begged the wool from the market and made it myself,' Aggie said proudly.

'Then I thank you again, that makes it extra special,' Dolly said.

Aggie sat at the table and accepted tea and cake from Sadie.

'I've been making enquiries and Ezra's brewery is still empty.

It don't belong to anyone now, so why don't you stake your claim with the council?'

'What would I do with it?' Dolly asked, but already her mind was considering the idea.

'You could store extra gin there, or even have your own distillery!'

'My finances wouldn't stretch to getting the repairs done, let alone setting it up as a going concern.'

'Not yet, maybe, but if you don't put your name on that building, some other bugger will.'

'Aggie has a point,' Sadie put in.

'All you need is a name plate telling folks it belongs to you and you're good to go – when you have the money, that is.'

'Would it be that simple?' Dolly asked.

'Yes! Get yourself to the council and tell them what you're doing, then all you need is a sign with your name on it, which could be hung on the gates,' Aggie said.

'I'm not sure what Jack would say about it,' Dolly said tentatively.

'If I know Jack, he'll be pleased. You ain't got time to dilly-dally, my wench, if you want it then take it while you have the chance! It won't be long before the kids start bostin' the winders then it'll be more expense to put it right.'

Dolly looked at Sadie and Alice who both nodded their agreement.

'You'll never get another opportunity like this, Dolly,' Sadie said. 'Remember when you told Ezra you could only take on another building if it was a free gift? Well, this is it!'

'I'm not sure the council will allow it,' Dolly proffered.

'It ain't up to them. Ezra Moreton owned the land and the building and had no one to leave it to,' Aggie went on.

'I could ask Mr Sharpe to come with me. He's my solicitor so he'd know the law.'

'Even better!' Aggie enthused.

'Why don't you go now? Alice and I can look after Joseph for a couple of hours,' Sadie offered.

'He'll need a feed...' Dolly began a little reluctantly.

'He can have a bottle just this once if he wakes,' Alice said.

'I'll go and have a word with Mr Sharpe, then,' Dolly said as she got to her feet. 'Thank you, Aggie.'

'My pleasure.' Aggie grinned as she followed Dolly through the bar to the main room.

'Danny, Aggie has earned herself half a dozen free tots today. I'm just popping out, I shouldn't be too long,' Dolly called as she grabbed her purse and bag before leaving.

'What have you done to deserve this, then?' Danny asked as he poured her first drink.

'Wouldn't you like to know?' Aggie chuckled.

Dolly alighted from the cab at Mr Sharpe's office and was greeted warmly.

'Many congratulations on the birth of your baby,' Andrew said.

'Thank you, Mr Sharpe,' Dolly replied, wondering how he knew, then chided herself. Aggie most likely. 'I'm in need of your expertise on a certain matter.'

'Take a seat, my dear, and explain.'

Dolly did as she was bid. When she had finished speaking, Mr Sharpe said, 'I see no reason why you can't claim ownership, although we should check first with the council. As far as I know there are no living relatives so it belongs to no one at present, but may I suggest – a little financial remuneration to the council may go a long way in helping your cause.'

'A bribe, you mean?'

'Of sorts, although I prefer my words to yours,' Mr Sharpe said with a little laugh.

'Wouldn't I need the deeds to the property?'

'It would be my guess they will be in the safe in the office. If you are to visit the council, would you like me to accompany you?'

'Yes please, Mr Sharpe. They might ask questions I can't answer.'

'Then let us be off,' he said, grabbing his hat. 'There is nothing here that can't wait a while.'

Dolly was nervous as they arrived at the council office, but Mr Sharpe assured her all would be well. It was he who spoke to the council representative in his best authoritative solicitor's voice.

After checking the files, the officer said, 'There's no reason that I'm aware of that would prevent you having the building. No one has come forward to claim the land and building so...' The man left the sentence hanging before adding, 'There would be a small administrative charge, of course, for us to amend our records.'

'How much?' Dolly asked pointedly.

'Oh, say ten pounds? I think that would cover it.'

Dolly nodded and, digging into her purse, she handed over the money and received a receipt in return.

'Nice doing business with you,' the man said, tucking the money into his pocket.

'Likewise,' Dolly said as she shook her head at his brazen actions.

In the cab on their way back to Mr Sharpe's office, Dolly laughed. 'It's unbelievable! That man pocketed the money right in front of us!'

'There's corruption everywhere, Dolly, you just have to keep your wits about you.'

Thanking him for his help, Dolly then went to see the sign-writer. Explaining what she wanted, she was pleased when he said he would accept the job. In the meantime, he would put a temporary sign up on the gates. Once the work was complete he would invoice her.

Dolly returned home a happy woman and the owner of a large building with a broken roof. The thought made her laugh, and she hoped Jack would approve of her rash decision and actions.

51

Later that evening, Dolly explained to Jack about her visit to the council with Mr Sharpe. She laid out her plans to eventually get the roof fixed and get the brewery up and running again. She enthused about possibly having their own distillery for the gin as well as brewing beer as Ezra had.

Jack did thoroughly approve, although his words tempered Dolly's excitement somewhat.

'Good thinking, my love, but I ain't sure how we can get that roof mended, though,' he said.

'I know. I'm worried we are now in the same position Ezra was.'

'We'll think of something. At least it's yours now and no one else can lay claim to it.'

'It's ours, Jack,' Dolly corrected. 'All we have to do now is find the money to fix it up.'

'Have a word with Mum, she might know.'

'Good idea. I'll take Joseph with me tomorrow, she always loves to see him.'

After his mid-morning feed the next day, Dolly pushed

Joseph in his carriage across to the Crown. She explained everything and asked Nellie and Nancy for any ideas they might have.

'I don't know, lovey,' Nellie said as she rocked the carriage.

'Could the bank help, do you think?' Nancy asked.

'That's a good thought, Nance! Maybe Mr Blessep could increase your mortgage on the Emporium,' Nellie said.

'Possibly, but I don't want to over-extend myself. I need to be sure I can cover the costs.'

'Have a word with him and see what he says,' Nellie encouraged.

'It wouldn't hurt, I suppose.'

'You gonna take little man with you?' Nancy asked.

'It would probably be best if I don't. Would you mind looking after him for an hour?'

'Mind? We'd love it, wouldn't we, Nance?'

'Definitely.'

'I always keep a fresh bottle with me when I go out and there's a napkin in the carriage too.'

'We'll see to him if he wakes up,' Nellie replied.

Dolly left them, happy in the knowledge her son would be well taken care of for a short while.

Arriving at the bank, Dolly was soon shown into the manager's office.

'Mrs Larkin! How lovely to see you. Come in. Do sit down,' Jonah Blessep said with a beaming smile. 'How can I be of service today?'

Dolly explained about taking over the brewery building, and her tentative plans for the business.

'I heard your name plate was on the gate,' he said. 'It's a very brave thing you are doing, especially with the roof as it is. However, you would firstly need to get an estimate for the work to be undertaken. We could then add that amount to your existing mortgage facility if the costs were reasonable.'

'I don't want to end up like Ezra, being unable to make repayments and losing everything I've worked so hard for.'

'Naturally, therefore my advice would be to get that estimation of repair costs then work out whether you can afford it,' Jonah said.

'Thank you. That seems the best course of action for now.'

Dolly left, feeling a little better, and on the way home asked the cabbie to stop at Hodges' yard.

Eli readily agreed to look over the property. 'I'll have to smash the lock off the gate first though, but don't worry, I'll fit a new one and give you the keys.'

'Would you do me another favour, please, and check the safe for the deeds? They might be better in my keeping than left there.'

'I will. If I find them I'll drop them into the Palace with my estimate.'

'Thank you, Eli. Oh, by the way, Joseph is very happy in his cradle your son made.'

'I'm glad to hear it, and my lads will be as well. They was very proud of that there cradle!'

The cabbie drove Dolly home and thanked her for her tip. Going to the Crown to collect her son, Dolly shared her news with Nellie and Nancy.

'This little 'un has been golden while you were out,' Nellie said with a sigh.

'I hope that doesn't mean he'll have me up all night,' Dolly said with a smile.

'If he still grizzles after his feed, give him a little drink of sugar water, that should settle him right down,' Nellie suggested.

'Thank you, I will.'

That night, Jack was praising Dolly's efforts saying, 'I'm so glad you're getting out and about. It's nice for Mum and Nancy to have Joseph an' all. You don't mind that, do you?'

'Goodness, no! I love that they're so interested in him. I want them to be part of his life as he grows up.'

Then, right on cue the little one let out a wail. He was hungry – again!

* * *

A few days later, Eli arrived with his estimate. 'I found these too. You were right, they were in the safe. It's a good job I looked an' all cos the safe wasn't locked.' Eli handed over the deeds to the property.

'Thank you, Eli,' Dolly said.

'Righto, let me know what you decide,' he said and bade her farewell.

Dolly looked over his figures quickly. She and Jack could go over them more fully when he got home.

'It's a lot ain't it?' Jack asked.

'It is. We would have to put the building to good use to justify spending so much on it,' Dolly replied.

'How? Other than storage, what could we do with it?'

'We could open it as a brewery again.'

'What?'

'Hear me out first, then tell me what you think,' Dolly said and laid out her plan. 'We could hire the original workers who would know how to get the place going again. If we contacted the same suppliers we could agree a contract with them. I'm sure the foreman would know all these things.'

'Dolly, we don't know anything about brewing beer!'

'Not as yet, but we could learn. Besides, the workers will do all that. What we would need to do is find some buyers for the beer.'

'Oh, that easy, eh?' Jack laughed.

'No, but it would be a start. If we kept our prices down I know we could do it.'

'What about transport?'

'The draymen will probably be keeping the horses, but we'd need to find out.'

'Dolly, this could cost a fortune! There would be fixing the roof for starters, then employing workers and draymen, buying in supplies of hops and the like!' Jack ticked off the list on his fingers.

'I wonder where Ezra kept his account book,' Dolly mused.

'At home would be my guess,' Jack said. Then seeing her look he gasped, 'Oh no! You can't, it would be trespassing!'

'The house is empty, Jack, and it has been ransacked and looted already, but people wouldn't want a book full of numbers.'

'I'm *not* having you go over there, it could be dangerous! You don't know who could be hanging around!' Jack was adamant.

'But Jack, we would need to know prices and costs!' Dolly pleaded.

'No, Dolly!' Seeing her face fall he added, 'I'll go instead.'

Dolly flung her arms around him. 'I love you, Jack Larkin. Take someone with you, just in case.'

So it was that in the early hours while the town slept, Jack and Danny Whitehouse stole through the empty streets to Drury Lane. There was no one around but they still kept a wary eye out. Going around to the back of Ezra's abandoned house, Jack tried the back door and to his relief it opened. They went in quickly and closed the door behind them. Everything must appear the same to anyone glancing out of a window.

'Bloody hell! It's been stripped bare!' Jack whispered.

'It's no wonder with the amount of poverty,' Danny whispered back.

'Right, where would this damned book be?'

'I'll look upstairs,' Danny said, then added, 'Jack, stay away from the windows, else you might be seen.'

Jack nodded and began his search. He found nothing. Hearing Danny's light tread on the stairs, he asked, 'Any luck?'

'Is this it?' Danny handed over the ledger.

A quick look inside told Jack it was and he nodded with a grin. 'Let's get home before we're caught and hauled off to jail!'

They slipped out quietly and stepped along smartly, nodding to passing miners who were on early shift at the coal pits.

Indoors at last, both men sighed with relief.

'Thanks, Danny.'

'No problem. I wasn't about to let you go on your own.'

'What were you doing up so early anyway? Jack asked.

'Needed to pee! Then when you said what you were about, I thought I'd tag along.'

'Well, I appreciate it and Dolly will too.'

'It's a good job I took Dolly's advice and moved in so I could let out my house,' Danny said. 'The money is useful and I've rented it to a family who were desperate.' He put the kettle to boil and prepared the cups.

'I'm glad for you,' Jack said. 'It makes sense you being here.'

'Jack, can I ask what you want with that book?'

Over tea Jack explained, in confidence, what they had in mind.

'I won't breathe a word, I swear,' Danny said.

'Good man.'

After breakfast, Jack kissed his wife and son and left for work and Dolly spent the morning poring over Ezra's ledger. She was surprised at what she discovered.

52

Aggie was kicking her heels up in the bar when Dolly called her through to the kitchen.

'I'm glad you got the brewery,' Aggie said as she took the seat offered.

'Thanks to you, Aggie. I would never have thought of it otherwise, but there's something I want to ask you.'

'Oh, ar, and what would that be?' the old woman asked as she accepted tea from Alice with a nod.

'Was it you who started the rumours about me looking for another pub?'

Aggie sighed and nodded again.

'Why?'

Taking a breath, Aggie began her story. 'Do you remember years ago, an old fella by the name of Pickles?'

'Yes, I recall Nellie saying about him.'

'Right, well, Jed Pickles was in his eighties and he gathered wood which he sold in bundles. He borrowed some money from Moreton and paid it back a penny a week.'

Sadie and Alice sat down to listen too.

'He needed it for his daughter's wedding, I believe,' Dolly said.

'He did. She moved away with her new husband and old Jed took ill so he couldn't collect his wood.'

'So he couldn't pay Ezra back!' Sadie put in.

'That's right. Now, when he told Ezra this, that bugger cut off his little finger with his cigar cutter!'

'Oh my God!' Sadie said, her hand going to her mouth.

'But I thought that was never proved,' Dolly said.

'No, but the doctor found it in his lap when he found his dead body. Ezra Moreton left Jed to die for all he cared, but his heart gave out first.'

'How do you know all this?' Dolly asked.

'Because one of my spies saw it all!'

'How?'

'Through the window. He was about to visit old Jed to see how he was doing, but when he saw Ezra and his goons, he hid.'

'Why weren't the police brought in?'

'An urchin's word against a pillar of the community? Who would the coppers have believed?'

'She's right,' Sadie said.

'What has this to do with anything?' Dolly asked.

'Jed Pickles was my cousin and I swore then I would see Moreton pay!'

'Oh, Aggie! I'm so sorry.' Dolly could hardly believe her ears.

'The only way I could see to do it was with the rumours. I knew he wouldn't be able to resist buying those pubs. I'm sorry it had to involve you, lovey, but I knew he wouldn't be bested by a woman again, not after Nellie did for him by getting her gin elsewhere after she paid him off.'

'What would have happened if a builder had taken on the job?'

'I made sure none of them would.'

'But the bank lent him money!'

'Yes, but Jonah Blessep was wise enough to word the agreement so, no matter what, Ezra would lose out.'

'How did you find that out?'

'The bank teller was in on it an' all, so that's how I got to know.'

Dolly blew through her teeth and shook her head. 'I had no idea.'

'It had to be that way in case Ezra got wind of it,' Aggie said. 'Now, when my time comes, I can die a happy woman.'

'Poor Mr Pickles,' Alice said quietly.

'All for a tanner,' Aggie replied. Seeing the puzzled looks she explained. 'Sixpence was all that was left to pay on Jed's loan.'

'God almighty!' Sadie whispered.

'Well, that's one bloke Ezra won't be seeing, he's going downstairs where he'll burn for all eternity,' Aggie said with a toothless grin.

'No more than he deserves,' Sadie muttered.

'Thank you for being honest, Aggie,' Dolly said, 'and be assured your secret is safe with us.'

Sadie and Alice nodded in agreement.

Dolly requested a tiny cask be filled with gin for Aggie to take home with her.

'You have a good heart, Dolly Larkin,' Aggie said, 'I just want you to know how much I admire you, gel. It's a rare thing to have a true friend such as you, but I've been lucky enough to have three. You, Jack and Nellie.' She smiled as she returned to the fireplace in the bar.

Dolly frowned as she watched the old woman begin conversation with those around her. What was all that about? Was Aggie trying to tell her something? She didn't realise Aggie thought of her as a friend and was surprised by the revelation. It did, however, give her a warm feeling to be told as much.

'Well, I'll go to the foot of our stairs!' Sadie said.

'I'm not sure it's all true, but we have to keep our word to Aggie and *say nothing*,' Dolly emphasised.

'Cross my heart and hope to die,' Alice said and Dolly shuddered at the oath.

That night she had a lot to tell her husband and Jack gaped in disbelief as the tale of Jed Pickles was told. Then Dolly brought out Ezra's ledger.

'Look at these figures, Jack! No wonder he was wealthy!'

'How did he get away with it? Next to nothing going out and all this coming in!' Jack pointed to the columns of figures.

'Clearly he had a hold over a lot of people,' Dolly answered.

'How does this help us, though?'

'Well, now we know what he paid for supplies and what he charged for his beer.'

'And?'

'We have to work out how much we could do it for.'

'That's your area, I'm no good with sums.'

'I'll need to visit Mr Blessep again. He'll help me to see if it's worth trying.'

'Fair enough. I'll leave it in your capable hands.'

As they climbed the stairs to bed, Dolly felt the excitement build in her. This pipedream might actually come to fruition after all.

The next day, before Jack went to work, he whistled for a runner. The bedraggled boy stood in the kitchen of the Palace, listening carefully.

'Have you got all that?' Dolly asked.

'Find brewery foreman and workers. Tell them to come and see you tomorrow at nine in the morning,' the boy repeated.

'Good lad.' Dolly handed over a shilling and off the lad went, the coin clutched tightly in his hand.

Dolly took Joseph across to the Crown, asking Nellie if she would look after him for an hour. 'I have an errand to run.'

Nellie agreed enthusiastically.

Dolly called to a cabbie to take her to the bank. In her bag were the deeds to the brewery site, Ezra's ledger and Eli's estimate. As the cab rolled away, Dolly hoped and prayed Mr Blessep could help her work out how much it would cost to set up business once the roof was repaired. She didn't particularly want to borrow more money, but at least she'd have an idea of what would be needed when she could afford it.

Jonah Blessep and Dolly spent a couple of hours over their discussions and poring over the figures and when Dolly left she had mixed feelings. She wasn't able to procure another mortgage, and to extend her present one would see her just beyond her limit. She was sad about the delay, but she also had a better idea of what she needed to save. She was sure Jack would be pleased but relieved she had not agreed to sign anything that might jeopardise their livelihood.

After spending an hour with Nellie and Nancy, she took her baby son home in order to rest her aching leg. She was right, of course. Jack simply said it would be a good project for the future.

The next day, the brewery workers turned up on Dolly's doorstep on the dot of nine. Over tea and cake, she explained what she was trying to do but that she could not afford it as yet.

'What I want to know is whether you would take up your posts again once I can get up and running.'

Each man gave her an emphatic, 'Yes!'

'We've been out of work for months,' one said wearily.

'Since the roof went,' another put in.

'I'm sorry to hear it, and I can't say how long it will be before I can fix it either.'

'So why bother calling us here today?' the man she took to be foreman asked sharply.

'I know nothing about brewing beer, so your expertise would be needed. I'm sorry if you think I'm giving you false hope, but it *is* my intention to see that place working again.'

'But you don't know when.'

'No, I'm afraid not.' Dolly should have realised the men would be cross and frustrated with her for raising their hopes, and she felt wretched for them.

'Just send a runner when you need us,' the foreman said off-handedly before they all trooped out to go home, grumbling about it being a waste of time their coming in the first place.

'I'm thinking that was a mistake,' Sadie mumbled.

'It's all so maddening!' Dolly said.

'There's no point in getting upset. You feared you couldn't afford it when you went into it first off,' Sadie reprimanded.

'I know,' Dolly said feeling deflated.

'Something will turn up, you'll see,' Sadie said, trying to comfort Dolly.

The fates had interfered again and Dolly was left wanting.

A couple of days later, a man arrived asking for Mrs Dolly Larkin. Shown to the kitchen, he removed his hat, saying, 'Good day to you, Mrs Larkin. My name is George Grindle and I am a solicitor.'

'Take a seat, Mr Grindle. Will you have tea?'

'Thank you, yes.' Putting his hat on the table, the man opened his briefcase balanced on his knee.

Dolly exchanged a brief glance with her staff who shrugged their shoulders.

'I am acting on behalf of the late Miss Agnes Dewey.'

'I'm sorry, I don't know who that is,' Dolly interrupted.

'Ah, my apologies. You would probably know her better as Aggie.'

'Did you say *the late*...?'

'Yes. Again, I must apologise. I take it you did not know that my client had passed away?'

'No,' Dolly said quietly, her eyes instantly brimming with tears.

'Oh, my dear lady, I thought you would have heard.'

'No, I thought, as we hadn't seen her for a while, she must have been dancing in the Emporium.'

'Alas, that was not the case. A runner informed me of her demise this very morning. She passed away peacefully in her sleep. Would that we could all be so fortunate.'

Dolly's mind recalled her conversation with Aggie not so very long ago about that very same thing. Her tears still fell as she muttered, 'Poor Aggie. I will organise her funeral. I'm supposing that's the reason you are here?'

'Not at all. Aggie's funeral is organised and paid for, she made sure of it some time ago.'

'Then why...?'

'Aggie left her will with me.'

'She made a will? How? I mean, Aggie had nothing to leave but her house and clothes.'

'On the contrary, Aggie was an extremely wealthy woman and she's bequeathed it all to you.'

'To me?'

Grindle nodded and pushed the will over to Dolly to see.

'Good grief! Is this amount right?' Dolly gasped.

'It is and every last penny will be transferred to your account, which is held by Mr Blessep, I'm reliably informed.'

Dolly nodded, too much in a daze to ask how he knew. She had inherited a fortune from a little old woman she thought to be penniless.

'Where did she get all this from?' Dolly asked at last.

'Saved it, inherited it herself? Who knows?' Grindle said, shrugging his shoulders.

'The sly old bugger!' Sadie said.

'She was that,' Grindle said with a chuckle, then added, 'I'm sorry for your loss and I'll be in touch with your bank as soon as possible.' Picking up his hat, he took his leave.

Dolly, Sadie and Alice sat in silence for a long time once the man had left, their thoughts centring on Aggie and her antics.

Their quiet time was interrupted by Nellie and Nancy bustling in.

'I've just had a runner pop in, old Aggie has passed on!' Nellie said, feeling out of breath through rushing.

'We know,' Dolly said sadly.

'Oh, you had a runner an' all?'

'No, a lawyer.' Dolly explained about the inheritance and pushed the copy of the will to Nellie to see.

'Bloody hellfire!' Nancy gasped as she peeped over Nellie's shoulder.

'Not quite my words, Nancy, but perfect under the circumstances,' Dolly said.

* * *

After much discussion about Aggie and her will, Nancy returned to the Crown and Nellie and Dolly took a cab to the Emporium. Nellie carried Joseph in her arms, knowing that Bess and Gwen would enjoy seeing him again.

While Nellie was busy showing off her grandson, Dolly pulled Jack into the empty dining room and told him the news whilst showing him the will.

'Well, damn my eyes! Old Aggie had money all this time and still sponged drinks off us for years?' Then Jack burst out laughing. 'You know what this means? You can get the brewery sorted out now!'

'Do you think she knew it would come to this?'

'How could she? But Dolly, you know she thought the world of you and this was her way of ensuring her money wasn't wasted,' Jack said. He wrapped her in his arms as Dolly's tears fell again. 'I tell you what, once we're up and running you can name a beer after her.'

'That's a nice idea, but I think a gin would be more appropriate.'

'Right then, one cask will always be called after Aggie, both in the Palace and the Emporium, how's that?'

'Wonderful, thank you, Jack,' Dolly said before they returned to their son, who was being fawned over by everyone.

Over the next couple of days, the runners were out in force. The message was sent that Aggie's funeral was at ten in the morning on Friday at St Peter's Church, Dale End.

Black clothes were aired out and brushed down and Nellie, Nancy, Jack and Dolly each bought flowers for the grave. Sadie and Alice were happy to take care of Joseph while they went to the funeral.

When they arrived, they stood by the church door waiting for the coffin to appear and were amazed to see the runners lining both sides of the street. They seemed to stretch for miles and Dolly heard their sobs as the horse-drawn hearse passed them by. Then they fell in behind to walk in an orderly fashion into the graveyard. She saw the backs of dirty hands slide beneath runny noses and heard the sniffs as they followed the casket, now carried by four coffin bearers, to the graveside.

Dolly, Jack, Nellie and Nancy joined them, as did many people from the town. The cemetery filled to capacity and folk stood on the roadway to pay their respects. Men lifted their caps and laid them on their chests and women dabbed at watery eyes. Aggie was clearly loved by a great many people.

The service began with the vicar standing at one end of Aggie's final resting place. Then the casket was lowered into the ground.

The emotion was too much for them now and the children

began to cry out loud. Dolly's heart went out to them. These boys and girls had so little in their lives, and the person they loved most in the world had left them. Dolly had no idea where or how they lived but she knew their lives would be harder now Aggie had gone.

She watched as the older children tried, even though their own distress and grief was heart-breaking, to comfort the younger ones. Dolly's own tears fell as she silently said her last goodbye to Aggie. The Palace would not be the same without her.

Mopping away her tears on the handkerchief Jack had passed to her, she turned to him, saying quietly, 'I know what I want to do with some of the money Aggie left to me.' She tilted her head towards the sobbing children.

'What?' he asked in a whisper.

'A home for those children. Somewhere they can go back to after a day's running, for I don't think for a minute they would give it up.'

'Aggie would definitely approve,' he said as he held her hand, 'and so do I.'

54

The following day, when Jack had gone off to his work at the Emporium, Dolly asked Danny Whitehouse to whistle for a runner. It took a few moments before he came into the kitchen with a lad of about twelve years old.

'I need you to find the foreman of the brewery and ask him to call on me at his earliest convenience please. Then can you get the same message to Eli Hodges, please.'

'Righto, Dolly.' The boy nodded and thanked Dolly for the tanner, which he shoved in his boot. A slice of cake from Sadie and he was gone.

A couple of hours later, the foreman arrived with a knock to the back door. He was allowed entry by Alice, then Dolly welcomed him and indicated he should take a seat.

'Nice to see you again, Mr...?'

'John Jeffries.'

'If you remember, John, I said I would call on you when I was in a position to get the brewery roof repaired. Well, I am now in that position.'

'That's good news.'

'However, I need your help,' Dolly said.

'Anything I can do, I will.'

'Firstly, I need you to round up the workers and see if they will help with the work. If they agree, you can have them report to Eli Hodges at the site. He will instruct them as to what can be done about aiding him – shifting rubble, maybe.'

'I'm sure they'd be glad of something to do, especially if it means getting the brewery going again,' John said.

'Good, because that's where you come in. I need you to write down some things for me.'

'What things?' John asked with a puzzled frown.

'I've made a little list.' Dolly pushed the paper across the table to him and, while he read it, she asked Sadie if they might have some tea.

'I can do this, well, most of it, anyway.'

'Excellent.'

Sadie made the tea while John filled in answers by the questions Dolly had written down. How much did the men earn whilst working for Ezra? Who and where were the suppliers? What goods were damaged in the cave-in? Was there anything else which would need replacing? Who did Ezra supply to? Who was taking care of the dray horses now? Would the men entertain having a woman for their boss?

John smiled at the last and wrote, 'Yes, ma'am!'

Dolly read John's answers as he was given tea and cake by Alice.

'Thanks, chick,' he said.

'This is very helpful, John.'

'I'm sorry I don't know what Ezra paid for the hops and things, though,' he said.

'That's all right, I do. Now I'm willing to pay the men the same amount as Ezra did whilst they work for Eli.'

'Thank you Dolly, they'll be so glad of that.'

Dolly held up a hand and went on. 'When the roof is repaired and all the mess is cleared away I'll need the men back in their original jobs, for which I will increase their wages.'

Dolly saw John swallow the lump in his throat as he nodded.

'Now we come to you. How did you find it being a foreman?'

'Well enough. I was accepted as such by the other blokes; we made a good team.'

'Well, I'm offering you the job of manager of the works with a salary to reflect the status of the position.'

John bowed his head and covered his eyes with a hand, his shoulders heaving quietly.

Dolly looked at Sadie, who wiped away a tear of her own. She heard the man's sniffs and eventually the heels of John's hands rubbed his eyes. 'I'm sorry about that. Thank you, from the bottom of my heart, I thank you.'

Dolly glanced at the freshly baked cake and Sadie held up a tea cloth in question. Dolly nodded and Sadie wrapped the cake in the cloth.

'Go and tell your family you'll be working for Dolly Larkin as from today, then get those men to the brewery site to wait for Eli.'

John stood and looked at the cook, who passed over the wrapped cake.

Unable to speak, lest his emotions overwhelm him again, John gave the three women a casual salute and left the kitchen briskly.

'Oh, I hate to see a grown man cry,' Sadie said.

'Me too, it reminds me of Wilton that day,' Dolly replied.

'We ain't seen much of him lately,' Alice said.

'I expect he's extremely busy now that he's taken over from his late father,' Dolly answered. 'I do miss his little jokes, though.'

'I suppose he has to stay in the office more now he's the boss,'

Sadie added. 'Right, I'll get on and make some more cake as you keep giving them away!'

Dolly smiled and it was then she heard Eli's voice as he called out before walking through the back door. 'It's only me, Dolly.'

'Come in, Eli.'

'Tea?' Sadie asked.

'Ooh, ar! That would be lovely.'

'I'd offer you cake but Dolly's just given it away to somebody else,' Sadie said with a big grin on her face.

Dolly rolled her eyes then said, 'I hope you are well, Eli. And I'd like, if you can, for you and your team to repair the brewery roof, please.'

Eli clapped his hands together. 'Wonderful! All I have in the way of work at the moment is to replace a broken window in the chapel.'

Dolly explained how she had requested the brewery workers to lend a hand, under his supervision of course, and that she would pay them a small wage for their efforts. 'They are being asked to meet you at the site.'

'I'd best get over there, then,' Eli said before slurping the last of his tea. 'Thanks, Dolly.'

Joseph niggled in his carriage and Dolly smiled. He would be waking for a feed shortly.

'Shall I carry him upstairs for you, Dolly?' Alice asked.

'Yes please, Alice. It's at times like these that I wish I didn't have to use my stick.'

'I'm a little glad you do,' Alice said quietly as she lifted the baby.

Sadie sucked in a breath and flashed a look at Dolly.

Alice rushed on, 'Oh, I mean only because I get to cuddle Joseph!'

Dolly laughed and Alice breathed with relief that her friend and employer had not taken offence at her remark.

'Go on before he starts wailing,' Dolly said.

Sadie tittered as she set about her baking. Dolly hitched up her long skirt with one hand and held her cane in the other as she made her way precariously up the stairs behind Alice.

Once Joseph was fed and changed, Dolly called Alice to fetch him down to his carriage once more.

'I'm going out for a while, so I'll ask Nellie to mind this one,' Dolly said, tilting her head to the perambulator, 'that will give you ladies a bit of peace.'

Laying her stick across the carriage, Dolly manoeuvred it through the back door. Watching for traffic coming her way, she strode across the road to the Crown.

'Oh here he is, my sunshine!' Nellie said as Dolly arrived.

'Would you have him while I run some errands?' Dolly asked.

'Of course, we'd be delighted wouldn't we, Nance?'

Nancy nodded as she peeped at the sleeping babe. 'He's growing so fast!'

'Where you off to?' Nellie asked.

'I'll explain when I get back,' Dolly answered with a grin.

'All right, lovey, take your time, there's no rush,' Nellie said as she placed the baby carriage next to the table.

Outside, Dolly took a cab to the bank first to see Mr Blessep. On the journey, she glanced out of the windows at the soot-blackened buildings and people ambling about. Many of the pedestrians didn't appear to have a destination in mind and Dolly presumed a lot were out of work.

Arriving at the bank, the cabbie nodded when asked to wait.

'Come in, Dolly, please have a seat,' Jonah Blessep said as she entered his office.

'Thank you. I've come to see how my account stands.'

'In the pink, my dear,' Jonah said. He pulled her file from the cabinet and set it in front of her.

Dolly nodded happily. Aggie's money had been transferred as Mr Grindle promised it would be.

'You are a very fortunate young woman,' Jonah said. 'Do you have any plans for that?' He nodded towards the open file.

Dolly explained about the brewery roof being fixed with the help of the brewers and what she would do with it once that was done.

'Another string to your bow,' Jonah said.

'Yes, but there's something else I want to do also,' Dolly said and told him her ideas about providing a home for the urchin runners.

'It's a noble sentiment. You will of course need women to care for them once you find a building large enough to house them all.'

'I know, and I thought maybe a teacher too.'

'They would certainly benefit from an education.'

'I'm going to visit the estate agent now to seek his help in finding a suitable place.'

'Good luck, Dolly, if anyone deserves it, you do.'

Giving her thanks shyly, Dolly set off for the property seller's office.

Squashed between two shops, the building had one window with notices stuck on and a door over which a bell tinkled. A desk and chair took prominence in the room with two chairs opposite. Gas lamps on the walls shed a yellow pool of light, giving the whole a dingy look and feel. A coat stand stood by the door with only one garment hanging from a hook.

Having taken the seat offered, she began, 'I need somewhere large enough to house the runners.'

The man behind the desk could not prevent his mouth from falling open at her request.

'Do you have any idea how many urchins are running the streets?' he asked, astonished at her plan.

'No. Do you?'

He shook his head as her answer took him by surprise.

'Well, then. Do you have anything on your books that might suffice?'

'Erm, actually...' The man searched through a pile of papers on his desk and, finally locating the one he was looking for, he pulled it out and passed it to her.

Dolly read the details. On its own land, the house had a sitting room, parlour, living room, kitchen, scullery, music room and butler's pantry on the ground floor. Upstairs there were eight bedrooms and a back staircase leading to another eight servants' rooms. Two double privy blocks were at the back of the property next to stables, wash-house and various other outbuildings.

'This would be ideal, certainly to begin with anyway for as you say – we have no idea how many runners there are,' Dolly said, passing the paper back.

'You have seen the price?' the man asked.

'Yes. Now I want to see the house.'

'Well, I'm sure the present owners would be delighted to arrange a viewing time to suit you.'

'Mr...?'

'Phillips.'

'Mr Phillips, I have a young baby who is at home with his grandma and will be requiring a feed before too long,' Dolly said, and seeing his blush she went on, 'I have the cash in the bank so I will not be needing to negotiate a mortgage should I decide to purchase the house. Therefore, I wish to see the property immediately. I have a cab waiting.'

The man flushed scarlet again at her forthright manner but realised he couldn't risk losing this sale. 'I see. Then I will accompany you.' Grabbing his hat and coat he held the door open for Dolly. 'After you, Mrs...?'

'Larkin.'

Dolly looked out of the window as the cab bounced over the cobbles and she tittered. Phillips gave her a puzzled look and followed the direction of her nod.

Out in the street, women were standing with the hems of their cotton dresses pulled up and tucked into the legs of their bloomers.

'Oh my word!' Phillips said, a blush coming to his face yet again.

Where else in the world would you see a sight like that?

The house was situated on the corner of Corporation Street and New Street and stood well back from the busy highways. A long gravel drive led to the grand stone building. Pillars flanked the front door on which Mr Phillips hammered once he had helped her from the cab.

A maid invited them into a massive hallway and Dolly was immediately impressed.

'Mrs Larkin wishes to view the property,' Phillips explained.

'Yes, sir. The master and mistress are not at home at present but have left instructions to allow any viewings to go ahead. I'll be in the kitchen when you've finished.'

'Thank you,' Dolly said and smiled as the maid bobbed a curtsy before disappearing.

'We'll start here, then work our way up. Can you manage stairs?' Phillips asked, nodding at her walking stick.

'Yes, thank you, I can.'

Dolly followed along, listening to Phillips enthusing about the house's size and prominent position. They looked in every room, cupboard and outbuilding until finally Dolly had seen it all.

'What do you think? Magnificent, isn't it?' Phillips asked eventually as they went to the kitchen to inform the maid they were leaving.

'It is indeed,' Dolly concurred.

In the cab Dolly said, 'What is the lowest they will accept for it?'

'The figure you saw on the paper.'

Nothing more was said until they reached Phillips's office.

As he stepped down onto the road Dolly said, 'Thank you. Would you be so kind as to draw up the paperwork, Mr Phillips, please? I would hope to be able to organise staff and bedrooms as soon as possible.'

'I will indeed! Thank you, Mrs Larkin, thank you most sincerely.'

Dolly gritted her teeth at the man's grovelling then said, 'I will be at the Daydream Palace on Gin Barrel Lane when the papers are ready for signature, and Mr Phillips – time is of the essence.'

'Very good. I'll get on to it straight away.'

'Thank you. Good day to you.' Dolly banged her stick and the cab moved off.

Once it was rolling, Dolly blew through pursed lips, before the questions began to form in her mind. Had she done the right thing spending so much money all in one go? Would the urchin runners even want to live there? How many would the house accommodate? What would happen to any she couldn't fit in? Would she be able to find staff? How much could she afford to pay them?

More importantly, what would Jack say about her extravagant purchase when he knew?

55

Somehow Dolly knew Jack would be pleased for her, and that night he merely smiled as she told him about the house.

'I'm glad you found somewhere, and so soon!' he said.

'Fortuitous indeed, but Jack, whatever will I do if the runners take against the idea?' Dolly asked, clearly perplexed.

'They won't. Come on, Dolly, would you if you were a runner? You've seen those kids. They're half-starved and dressed in rags. God only knows where they sleep! They're ingrained with dirt and in the winter are blue with cold.'

'I know all that but...' Dolly started to say.

'Look, stop fretting. Once the documents are signed you can gather the runners there then you'll have a better idea of numbers. They'll soon let you know how they feel and it's my guess they'll love the idea. And Aggie would be delighted to know you have used her money so wisely.'

'I'll need beds and linen, furniture and food... Oh, Jack, there's so much to think about!'

'Yes there is and you have plenty of time to do it. I'm so proud of you, Dolly.'

'As I am of you,' she responded.

'On that note, I suggest we head for bed before Joseph starts screaming for his supper,' Jack said and, taking her hand, they climbed the stairs.

It was two days later that Mr Phillips arrived to seek Dolly's signature on the papers that had already been signed by the sellers. He said he would contact the bank for payment and Dolly was left with her copy of the agreement and deeds. He would let her know, he said, when the property was empty and she could take possession. He thought it likely a few weeks should do it.

Once the man had gone, Sadie asked, 'Is that something we should know about?'

'I've just bought a massive house,' Dolly said as if in a daze.

Sadie and Alice looked at each other then back at Dolly.

'Why? You're not moving, are you?' Sadie asked, looking worried.

'No, it's to house the runners.'

'Good God above!' Sadie exclaimed.

'Yes indeed, and I'm going to be needing His help if I'm to pull this off.'

'I ain't seen anything beat you yet,' the cook replied.

'Taking on the brewery and this house could well do it.'

'No it won't. There's lots of us to give a hand if needed,' Alice said.

'Thanks, ladies, just pray everything goes according to plan.'

Over the next few days, Dolly was kept informed about the work being done by Eli and his gang of workers. The repairs to the brewery roof were well underway and the rubble had been cleared. Work was progressing and Dolly was pleased.

The gin palaces continued to do a roaring trade and each proudly displayed an Aggie cask as was promised by Jack.

320   LINDSEY HUTCHINSON

At the end of the week Dolly received a packet from Mr Phillips containing a letter and a set of keys.

Dear Mrs Larkin,

I write to inform you that Lord and Lady Dorchester, along with their staff, all goods and chattels have vacated the property known as Dorchester Manor. I am pleased to enclose the keys to said property which you are now at liberty to do with as you will.

Many congratulations.

Sincerely yours,

A. Phillips Esq.

Dolly picked up the keys and clutched them tightly. She needed to tell Jack the good news and she asked Sadie to watch over Joseph while she went on her errand.

'I'd love to, Dolly, any time you like.'

Dolly hailed a cab and with the keys and letter in her bag, she set off for the Emporium.

Stepping down from the cab at the end of the short journey, she asked the cabbie to please wait. Music could be heard as Randall played popular songs and she heard the cabbie humming along to the tunes.

Dolly entered through the back door and was welcomed warmly as always. She showed Jack the letter and his eyebrows rose with excitement.

'Will you come with me and see the house?' Dolly asked.

'Yes, I'm dying to have a look,' Jack replied. Then to Bess he said, 'I'm going out for a while.'

Another short cab ride brought them to their destination and Jack whistled at sight of the house. 'It's a hell of a size!'

Unlocking the front door, Dolly was surprised. It looked very different now it was empty, she thought, as they wandered from room to room and she listened to Jack's comments about how big it all was.

Eventually she asked, 'What do you think?'

'I think we should move in here!' he said with a laugh. 'Seriously, I think the kids are gonna love this! Who wouldn't?'

Locking up again, they boarded the cab and on the way back Jack asked, 'How are you going to organise it all?'

'I thought to take your advice and gather the runners in order to gauge their number first of all. Then I can see how many we can fit in comfortably. I don't want it to seem like a workhouse, though, with beds crammed in and no space to move.'

'How would you know what it's like in the workhouse?'

'I can guess, Jack, and I want much better for those children.'

Back at the Emporium, they stepped down and the cabbie waited patiently. Jack whistled and an urchin came running.

'Is there any way you can get all the runners together in one place?' Dolly asked.

'Ar, it shouldn't be that hard,' the boy said.

'Good. Tomorrow morning at ten o'clock.'

The boy nodded. 'Where?'

'Do you know the big house on the corner of Corporation Street?'

'Dorchester Manor? Yes.'

'Then I'll meet you all there. You can go through the gates because the place is empty now.'

'What's going on?'

'You'll see tomorrow.' Dolly pulled a half crown from her bag and gave it to the boy, whose eyes almost popped out of his head.

'Half a dollar! Thanks, Dolly!' With that he sped off.

Jack grinned as he helped her back into the cab. 'I'll see you tonight, my love.'

With a kiss through the open door, Jack then closed it before he nodded to the cabbie, who clucked to the horse to walk on.

Back at the Palace, Dolly spent the day with Joseph in the kitchen. She was finding it hard to concentrate on anything, so great was her excitement, and she could barely wait for the following day to arrive.

When Jack saw her that night, he asked, 'Do you want me to come with you tomorrow?'

'Oh yes, please! I was going to ask you.'

'I'd best send an early runner to the Emporium to say I'll be late in, then.'

Dolly laughed and Jack smiled at his beautiful wife. He loved her with all his heart and knew she felt the same about him. He was a very lucky man.

The following day, Jack and Dolly stood at the front door of the massive house. The cabbie parked his vehicle at the side and, as he waited, he lit his pipe and watched as runners began to come pelting through the gateway.

Urchins arrived by themselves, others came in little groups until it seemed they were all in attendance.

'Thank you for coming. Are there any who are missing, does anyone know?' Dolly yelled.

Dirty heads turned as questioning eyes scanned the crowd.

'I think everybody's here, Dolly,' a voice called out.

'Would you please stand in pairs one behind the other so I may count you all.'

Feet shuffled and bodies draped in rags formed an orderly queue. Dolly walked down the line and counted in her head then returned to Jack and whispered, 'One hundred and twenty.'

'Not as many as I thought there'd be,' he said quietly in return.

'I'm going to let you into the house now so you can have a look around. Please be respectful of the place.'

As she unlocked the door, she heard low excited chatter and questions as to why they were here.

Pushing the door open, she watched the children file in and begin to explore. Before long she heard shouts of 'Come and see this!' and 'Look over here!'

'How will we fit them all in?' Jack asked.

'I'll work it out somehow,' Dolly replied, wondering if she would actually be able to.

Suddenly the children spilled out of the door and chased each other around the lawns. Laughter echoed through the outbuildings and, at Dolly's nod, Jack whistled loudly.

The children formed their queue again, without needing to be asked.

'This house belongs to me,' Dolly shouted so they could all hear. 'I bought it with the sole intention of providing a home for all of you. I was able to do this because Aggie left me a lot of money when she passed away, and I think it's what she would have wanted.'

Sad looks passed between the runners then back to Dolly as she went on. 'I must now ask if you would like to live here.'

Cheers, whistles, shouts of hooray assaulted her ears as the children gathered around her.

'I think that's a resounding yes!' Jack yelled above the noise. Then, with another whistle, he brought them to order once more.

'Give me a few days to organise a couple of ladies as house mothers who can live in to look after you, and beds for everyone, and then you will be able to move in.' Another cheer went up and Dolly raised her hand for quiet. 'I would like a teacher to come in every day for those who would like to learn their letters and numbers as well.' A not so loud cheer greeted that statement. 'I'm guessing some, if not all, of you would like to continue to be runners, and that's fine, but now you will have a home to come back to each night. So, leave this with me and I'll be in touch soon.'

The children shouted their thanks and ran off down the drive.

Dolly locked up and she and Jack climbed into the cab to go home.

When they arrived, Dolly made to pay the cabbie but he shook his head, saying, 'That has to be the finest thing I've ever seen! You giving those kids a proper home. Keep your money, madam, buy the kids some suck with it.'

'Thank you, I'm sure the children would love some sweets.'

The following days kept Dolly very busy. Nellie and Nancy joined her along with Sadie and Alice and the women worked out a plan together.

Jack, for his part, visited the Servants' Registry, requesting that potential house mothers visit Dolly for interviews. Once completed, four were chosen and were happy enough to be sharing rooms.

Jack also put in an order for one hundred and twenty-four single beds to be delivered as soon as possible, the invoice to be sent to Dolly at the Palace. Dolly was relieved indeed that Aggie had been such a generous benefactor.

Alice was tasked with ordering bed linen, towels, soap, hairbrushes and toothbrushes and powder. Sadie volunteered to stock the butler's pantry with food as well as equip the kitchen with pots, pans, crockery and cutlery.

Nellie kept a running tally of the estimated expenditure and Nancy sketched a diagram of the rooms as Dolly described them, one of which would become a dining hall. The music room was chosen for this purpose. Two bedrooms were allocated to the house mothers, which left fourteen for the children. Dolly thought four beds to each room would fit nicely. With eight beds each in the sitting room and the parlour, the others would have to go into the outbuildings, which would need a good clean out and whitewashing. At least they were dry and warm.

'The kids will choose where they want to sleep, so no need to worry on that score,' Nancy said.

'Should we separate them? Boys from girls, I mean,' Dolly asked.

'Are they separated now?' Nellie asked.

'I don't know. Oh, I see what you mean.'

'There you go then. Leave them to it, gel, it'll work itself out, don't you fret.'

So she didn't.

56

Jack hired a couple of painters from the breadline to work on the outbuildings as a surprise for Dolly for when she next visited. She was delighted when she saw them all clean and painted. She had gone to open up the following week for the first of the beds being delivered. Nancy and Nellie had gone with her and Dolly left Joseph with his daddy at the Emporium.

Nellie and Nancy roamed around the huge house, marvelling at the size of it.

'Those kids are lucky to have you helping them,' Nancy said.

'It's Aggie who is providing for them, I'm just the one organising it for her.'

'You'll be changing the name I'm guessing.'

'I will. I thought Aggie's Children's Home.'

'It's a bit of a mouthful, ain't it?' Nellie asked. 'Why not just Aggie's Place?'

'Oh yes! Nellie, that's perfect!' Dolly gushed, then stepped quickly out of the way of another bed coming in.

'The factory is working flat out on this order for you, missus,' one of the delivery men said.

'Thank you,' Dolly replied.

'You're gonna need some furniture an' all. Tables and chairs, wardrobes and chests of drawers,' Nellie reminded her.

'Oh, good grief! I'd forgotten that! I'll get them ordered when I get back. Thanks, Nellie.'

'You know I can come over every day to open up for deliveries if you like,' Nellie said. 'It would give me something to do, otherwise I'm likely to get my arse behind the bar again!'

'No you bloody won't!' Nancy snapped.

'Nellie, I would be ever so grateful for your help. To be honest, I'm finding everything a bit much at the moment.'

'I daresay, what with this place, the Palace, the Emporium and the brewery, it's a wonder you ain't on your knees.'

'It's not that so much, it's...'

'What? You ain't ill, are you?' Nancy asked, concern written all over her face.

'No. Ladies, I'm going to have another baby, but Jack doesn't know yet, so...' She got no further as she was smothered with excited hugs from both women.

'That settles it, then, give me those keys. You leave the ordering of the furniture to me an' all,' Nellie said.

'Thanks Nellie. Oh, the bed linen is coming tomorrow, and Sadie and Alice are coming to stock the pantry and kitchen because those deliveries are due also. The house mothers are moving in at the weekend so hopefully the children can too.'

'If the rest of the beds arrive, that is,' Nancy said.

'Fingers crossed,' Dolly replied.

Once the delivery men had gone, Nellie locked up and they climbed into the cab Nellie whistled for at the end of the drive.

'I'm going to tell Jack about the baby when I get back,' Dolly said.

'He'll be over the moon!' Nellie said.

Dolly hoped so.

The cab dropped Dolly off at the Emporium and took Nellie and Nancy home. Bess was cuddling Joseph as she walked in and Dolly led Jack to the quiet dining room.

'What's up?' he asked.

'Jack, I know we have a lot on our plate at the moment, but I hope you're ready for a bit more. We're going to have another baby!'

Jack's face lit up and he hugged her. 'That's the best news I could ever have hoped for.'

'I'm glad you're pleased but, Jack, Joseph is only a few months old. I don't want to spend the rest of my life being pregnant. You do understand that, don't you?'

'I don't bloody blame you! I promise we'll be extra careful, sweetheart,' he said gently.

Dolly smiled and nodded, then they went to share their news with everyone.

'I'm knocking off early today, Bess, so I can carry Joseph home,' Jack said once the congratulations had died down.

'Good idea,' Bess concurred as she gave the baby a little kiss on the forehead.

A cab rolled up as they left the Emporium. 'Need a ride, Jack?'

'Certainly do, George,' Jack replied.

The cab left the Emporium and took them home, where they had decided they would share the news of Dolly's pregnancy.

'Your mum and Nancy know already, but they promised not to tell until you knew. Sorry, I couldn't help but tell them,' Dolly said.

'Everyone will know by now, then,' Jack said with a grin, reminding Dolly fondly of Aggie.

The days passed and by the next weekend all the runners were in their new home, along with the house mothers. Dolly was informed they were awaiting two more beds, but sisters were sharing until they arrived.

Nellie volunteered to take charge of keeping the accounts for Aggie's Place, which now sported a new name plate. She would liaise with Andrew Sharpe when he audited the books. A separate bank account was set up for expenses which Nellie could access, and Dolly was thrilled it had all gone so smoothly. The furniture was delivered and installed and new clothes were bought for the children along with good boots. Dolly was relieved when Mr Blessep told her there was still a good sum of her inheritance left over for the running of the home for years to come.

The runners, of course, continued with their chosen profession and had decided amongst themselves that now they were well fed and cared for, all their tips would go towards the household expenses.

Dolly stayed home more now that her pregnancy was progressing, and so it was that Eli arrived one morning to say that the brewery site was finished. Dolly was delighted and she made a special journey to the bank with Eli so he could be paid immediately.

On her return, John Jeffries was waiting for her. Her new manager showed a relatively short list of things which needed replacing and said, 'We can get going whenever you want.'

'Excellent! Are you able to negotiate with suppliers and buyers?'

'I can do that whilst the lads get set up,' he answered.

'Thank you, John. Carrying another baby is taking it out of me,' she said.

'Congratulations, Dolly, that's good news – about the baby, I mean.'

They laughed together, then Dolly said, 'The increase in

wages will start next week and the bank is aware that you'll be collecting the wages every Friday morning.'

'Thanks, Dolly,' he said before he left.

The following weeks fled past and the brewery became active and thriving once more. John Jeffries was worth his weight in gold, working hard to negotiate good prices for supplies, keeping accurate tallies and organising deliveries to go out on time. The brewers whistled and sang, happy to be in work again and earning a good wage. Dolly had little to do other than keep an eye on the accounts, although she visited Aggie's Place often in the hope of seeing the children. She rarely did for they were usually out running, but she enjoyed tea with the house mothers as often as she could.

The gin palaces were always packed to the rafters and the dining room at the Emporium was full every night, the customers often spilling into the bar to enjoy the music.

Early one morning, as she was relaxing with a cup of tea, Dolly received a letter.

Opening the envelope, she read the contents and smiled. 'It's from Wilton!' she said, passing the letter to Jack. 'Mrs Burton is having another baby!'

'Aww, that's nice,' Alice commented.

'Good news indeed,' Dolly said.

'Let's hope and pray this one survives because the poor bloke and his wife deserve some better luck,' Sadie added.

Dolly nodded and thought herself fortunate to be so happy with Jack.

Her thoughts drifted back over time to when she first met the man who would be her husband. Found lost and alone, Jack's family had taken her in off the streets, and helping behind Nellie's bar had given her a love of the gin palace trade and its patrons. She recalled how she and Nellie had bought the

Daydream between them and how she had gone on to acquire other premises through hard work and determination.

She felt blessed that the staff hired had, over time, become friends and her thoughts lingered on the woman who had made everything possible. Aggie. Dolly sent up a silent prayer of thanks to her benefactor.

She and Jack only had one wish now, which was for Dolly to deliver their child with no risk to either of them.

That wish came true in September when the seasons were changing their colours again. Green leaves turned amber and gold and slowly began to drift to the ground. A chill was felt in the early morning and fires were lit once more all over the town.

It was mid-way in the month and late at night when Dolly felt the first pangs of her labour. She and Jack were delighted when Dolly finally gave birth to a daughter. Both mother and child were safe and well and Aggie Larkin soon let everyone know she had arrived.

REFERENCES

Bostin' Fittle by Pat Purcell

Black Country Dictionary and Phrase Book by Steve Edwards

MORE FROM LINDSEY HUTCHINSON

We hope you enjoyed reading *A Winter Baby For Gin Barrel Lane*. If you did, please leave a review.

If you'd like to gift a copy, this book is also available as an ebook, digital audio download and audiobook CD.

Sign up to Lindsey Hutchinson's mailing list for news, competitions and updates on future books.

http://bit.ly/LindseyHutchinsonMailingList

The Children From Gin Barrel Lane, a gritty Black Country saga from Lindsey Hutchinson, is available now.

ABOUT THE AUTHOR

Lindsey Hutchinson is a bestselling saga author whose novels include *The Workhouse Children*. She was born and raised in Wednesbury, and was always destined to follow in the footsteps of her mother, the multi-million selling Meg Hutchinson.

Follow Lindsey on social media:

facebook.com/Lindsey-Hutchinson-1781901985422852

twitter.com/LHutchAuthor

bookbub.com/authors/lindsey-hutchinson

ABOUT BOLDWOOD BOOKS

Boldwood Books is a fiction publishing company seeking out the best stories from around the world.

Find out more at www.boldwoodbooks.com

Sign up to the Book and Tonic newsletter for news, offers and competitions from Boldwood Books!

http://www.bit.ly/bookandtonic

We'd love to hear from you, follow us on social media:

 facebook.com/BookandTonic

twitter.com/BoldwoodBooks

instagram.com/BookandTonic

CPSIA information can be obtained
at www.ICGtesting.com
Printed in the USA
LVHW031038130921
697709LV00014B/708

9 781838 894016